KENTUCKY WOMAN

A suspense thriller.
MIKE BROGAN

Lighthouse

KENTUCKY
WOMAN

As an infant, Ellie Stuart is adopted by a poor, but loving couple in Harlan, Kentucky. When she's sixteen, they die in an accident, leaving her completely alone in the world. In college, she searches for her biological parents with the help of a law student, Quinn Parker.

But as she gets close to finding them, an assassin tries to kill her.

When they finally discover why - it may be too late - and Ellie and Quinn have to run for their lives.

This books is a work of fiction. Names, characters, businesses, organizations, places, events and incidents either are the product of the author's imagination or are used fictitiously. Any resemblance to actual persons, living or dead, events or locales is entirely coincidental.

Copyright © 2016
By Mike Brogan

ISBN 978-0-9846173-9-5

Library of Congress Control Number: 2015959783

Printed in the United States of America
Published in the United States by Lighthouse Publishing

Cover design: Vong Lee

First Edition

For my Kentucky pals.
Your sun will always shine bright.

Acknowledgments

To all my Kentucky friends, classmates and pals for putting up with this Yankee transplant during my early formative years and teaching me southern hospitality.

To experts Thomas A Lyons III, MD, and Robert Gussin, MD for their medical advice. To genetic specialists at Family Tree DNA and Accurate DNA Testing Laboratories for their genetics guidance. To various Kentucky attorneys for their legal counsel.

To my writing colleagues for keeping me on track. To Rebecca Lyles for her eagle-eyed editorial expertise. To my International Thriller Writers colleagues for their helpful suggestions.

And finally, to my family for their usual generous patience with the novelist in residence.

ONE

LOUISVILLE

403 Brownlee Street

"Wimp . . .!" Elle Steward growled to herself as she rested her forehead on her *Organic Chemistry* textbook.

She was too exhausted to study more.

Eight straight hours of analyzing acid-based formulations had turned her brain to liquid silicone, a.k.a. silly putty. The problem was she had to study more. Tomorrow's exam determined whether she got into the University of Louisville Medical School.

She lifted her bedroom window and the cool breeze swept in, refreshing her a bit. She lay back on her bed to rest her eyes, but her eyelids soon grew heavy and she sensed them falling. Maybe a quick nap. She started counting sheep, but soon was counting ex-boyfriends. Within seconds, she drifted off.

Noise!

Elle bolted awake in her pitch-dark room. She definitely heard a noise.

She listened.

Silence.

Something moved. Her roommate? No, Jenny was in Lexington.

Elle sat up, looked around, saw no one.

The window curtain fluttered. Did the breeze knock over the family picture on the dresser?

She turned toward the noise – as hands gripped her neck from behind, cutting off her scream. She tried to pull his hands away, but couldn't.

Elle knew she was blacking out . . . knew her brain was shutting down . . . knew the last thing she might see in life was the gold metal band around her attacker's ponytail.

TWO

LOUISVILLE

703 Brownlee Street

Ellie Ann Stuart stared at eighty-four-year-old Celeste, who stared at her empty plate. Ellie worried that Celeste stared a lot, and forgot a lot, and lost interest a lot.

"Would you like more toast?" Ellie asked.

"Where is my toast?"

"You ate it, Celeste. Want some more?"

"No, thank you, Annabelle."

Sometimes Celeste called her Annabelle, the bacon slicer at Kroger. And sometimes she called her, Karl, the mailman.

Ellie loved Celeste Barclay, but hated what Alzheimer's was doing to her mind. Each month the disease deleted more of her memory, dialed down the dimmer switch on her brain. There was no cure. All Ellie could do was keep her nourished, and comfort her when she seemed afraid or confused.

Ellie check her watch. Time for school. She looked in the hall mirror. As usual, her sleep hair made her look like the Bride of Frankenstein. She blinked and saw her eyes were bloodshot from studying late again, obscuring the fact that one eye was slightly bluer than the other. Her pale skin suggested too many hours indoors, hunched over textbooks.

The doorbell rang. Sarah Barnes, the next-door neighbor, walked in right on time. Sarah, a Godsend, cared for Celeste when Ellie attended classes at nearby University of Louisville.

"She's just finishing breakfast," Ellie said.

"Good. See you around noon?"

"Right." Ellie turned to leave.

"Ellie . . .?"

"Yeah?"

Sarah looked concerned. "Be *extra* careful today!"

"As always . . ."

"*Extra extra* careful!"

Sarah sounded serious. Ellie waited for her to explain.

Sarah flipped open the *Courier Journal* newspaper and pointed to a headline.

FEMALE U OF L STUDENT ATTACKED IN HOME!

Ellie was shocked to read the attack took place on Ellie's street, just blocks away.

Sarah shocked her even more when she said . . . "The girl's name was *Elle Steward*. Elle . . . not Ellie, like you . . . and also S T E W A R D, not your spelling, S T U A R T."

An icy chill shot through Ellie's body. She was speechless.

"So be extra careful, hon." Sarah patted her arm.

"I will," Ellie said, still stunned by the girl's similar name.

She grabbed her backpack and coffee mug and walked outside. She placed the mug in the handlebar holder of her old beat-up

Schwinn Roadmaster and pedaled her way down the street toward
the U of L campus.

The morning sun was warm and the sweet scent of lilac and
peonies reminded her of back home in Harlan. She couldn't wait to
visit after exams.

Ellie pumped harder as she approached the steep hill she called
Mount Cardiac. Despite her loud huffing, she heard a truck start up.
Then she saw it ahead . . . a dark blue van on the other side of the
street, pulling away from the curb, driving in her direction.

Speeding . . .

Right at her for Chrissakes!

She jumped the bike up over the curb and raced toward the pro-
tection of some trees.

Her front tire hit a root and she flew up over her handlebars,
slammed against the tree, scraped her cheek and landed between the
tree and the sidewalk.

The van screeched to a stop on the other side of the tree. The
driver stared at her. He looked unapologetic, disappointed, like
maybe it wasn't an accident, like maybe he was considering another run at her.

A huge Allied Moving Lines truck turned onto the street.

The van driver saw it too, and sped away.

What the hell just happened? Did the driver loose control – or
was he some macho road-rage psycho jerk trying to scare the hell
out of me? If so, he succeeded.

Or . . . did the guy actually try to *hit* me? That made no sense.

She touched her cheek and came away with tiny splotches of
blood. Getting up, she brushed herself off. Her ancient Schwinn had
a few more dents, but was rideable the last block to campus.

The far more serious crime was her empty coffee mug. Without
coffee, she had no personality. She pedaled down to the corner Starbucks, and even though her budget couldn't absorb such an extrava-
gant expenditure, she bought their cheapest, smallest latte.

Then she got back on the Schwinn and pumped off toward campus.

* * *

Huntoon Harris stuffed a wad of Mail Pouch tobacco behind his lower lip as he sat in his van, watching Ellie Stuart walk out of Starbucks and bike off toward the U of L campus.

She'd reacted much faster than he'd anticipated. He should have attacked her from behind.

So, she'd won this battle.

He'd win the war.

Harris made a phone call, reported in, then hung up.

He checked her class schedule printout on his passenger seat. He knew exactly where she'd be, and when. He shoved a full clip into his Glock 19.

Then he tightened the gold band on his ponytail.

THREE

Ellie parked her wobbly Schwinn at the University of Louisville's Student Center, then wobbled herself toward its entrance. She felt leg pain from hitting the oak tree and knew she looked as bad as she felt.

But at least the campus looked beautiful this spring morning. She smelled the crisp, clean air and saw sunshine glinting gold off the top of Unitas Tower and the nearby Red Barn building. Home Sweet U of L. She loved being here.

Sipping her Starbucks *Café Latte*, she limped toward the door. Beside her, she sensed a tall male student hurrying toward the same door.

He suddenly tripped, went airborne and bumped her elbow, spilling coffee down her jeans, but braced his fall on the steps.

"Oh, crap!" he said, "I'm so sorry."

She looked at her second empty coffee cup of the morning. "It's okay, these jeans are ancient."

"I'm an ass! I wasn't even looking. And my bum knee sorta gave out." His face was beet red.

"It's okay, really."

She recognized the tall, handsome upperclassman with light green eyes. He was the former co-captain of the U of L football team and an all-Big East Conference player. She'd seen photos of him catching touchdown passes in the *Louisville Cardinal* school paper.

"The least I can do is buy you another coffee and pay your dry cleaning bill."

"Dry cleaning would disintegrate these jeans," she said, remembering she paid a dollar-fifty for them at *Sam's Second Hand Shoppe.* "But coffee sounds great."

Inside, he bought two coffees, handed her one and they sat at a corner table.

"Quinn Parker," he said, offering his hand.

She smiled and shook it. "Ellie Stuart."

"Again, Ellie, I'm really sorry."

"It's really okay."

She sipped her coffee fast, before the coffee demons slapped it out of her hand again. It tasted delicious. "So, Quinn, what are you studying?"

"Law. I'm second year here at Brandeis Law." He looked down at her clothes. "Damn, I've committed a felony!"

"What felony?"

"Aggravated assault of a U of L sweatshirt."

She smiled. "You have the right to an attorney! But don't worry about the coffee stains. They'll wash out."

"You sure?"

She nodded.

"So, Ellie, what's your major?"

"English. Pre-law. Do you like Brandeis Law?"

"Love it. The professors are terrific. If you're interested, I could show you around the law school sometime."

"I'd like that."

"Ellie, y'all got a deep southern Kentucky accent!"

"Y'all got right good ears. Quinn." *And right good everything else,* she couldn't help but notice. His broad shoulders, tall muscular build, thick brown hair and nice, easy smile were all a little overwhelming in the Big Man on Campus.

"Where's home, Ellie?"

She hesitated. Once he knew her background, he'd vanish like water on sand. But what the hell, she was who she was. If he had a problem with it, so be it.

"I'm from way down in hill country."

"Where in hill country?"

"Harlan."

He smiled. "I hear the hills are mighty steep down there, Miss Ellie."

"Yep."

"Just how steep are they?"

"Why Mr. Quinn, those hills be so steep you gotta look out the chimney to see the cows coming home."

They both laughed at the ancient joke, then his smile vanished. "Jeez, your face!"

"What?"

"I scraped that too!"

"No. A guy in a van did it. He damned near hit me while I was riding my bike this morning."

Concern flashed in Quinn's eyes. "Was it intentional?"

She paused. "I think so. He drove *at* me like he was trying to frighten me . . . or worse."

"And . . .?"

"He scared the crap out of me!"

Quinn smiled. "A stalker?"

"No. A jerk!"

"You should report it to the police."

"I will after class."

They sipped their coffee.

"So Harlan, huh."

"Yep. I love it."

"You visiting your folks after exams?"

She paused. "No."

She hesitated again, then decided to explain. "Actually, Quinn, I was adopted by the Stuarts as an infant. They were the best parents in the world. But a drunk boater slammed into their rowboat, killing them when I was sixteen." Her chest tightened as she remembered the night at Lake Cumberland when she identified their broken, bruised bodies. Painful images branded onto her memory forever.

"I'm sorry, Ellie."

She nodded and sipped more coffee. "Since then, I've tried to find my birth parents, but haven't had any luck."

He nodded and seemed sympathetic.

"Just two days ago, I phoned the Harlan Courthouse and asked a clerk to check for a record of my adoption. While he was looking, the line went dead. I'll try again after exams."

He nodded. "You might be able to file a petition to get some information. I'll ask my law professor and - "

"How's my Quinny?" a woman said behind them.

Ellie turned and saw a tall stunning blonde walking toward them. The blonde smiled at Quinn, kissed him on the cheek, then stared at Ellie's stained, dirty clothes as though she'd crawled from a sewer.

"I'm fine, except that I spilled coffee all over Ellie Stuart's jeans here. Ellie, meet Jennifer DuBois."

They shook hands.

Jennifer looked down at Ellie's jeans. "Well at least, they're *old!*"

"They're Jurassic Period," Ellie said, smiling, but noticing that Jennifer's designer slacks and silk blouse probably cost as much as Ellie's annual clothing budget.

Jennifer put her arm around Quinn's neck. "Quinny, we have to leave now or we'll be late for my rehearsal."

"Tell me again, why do *I* need to rehearse if *you're* the debutante being introduced into society?"

"So you can learn how to walk."

"I learned when I was one."

"Yes, but you have to walk just right for this."

"I'm a terrific walker! Shuffling, strutting, prancing, knuckle-dragging, you name it!"

Ellie laughed and Jennifer shot her a hard look.

"Come on, Quinny! We'll be late!"

"Okay." He shrugged and stood up. "Ellie, I'll get back to you on that legal question. Do you have a phone number?"

She wrote her cell number on a napkin and handed it to him.

Jennifer looked like she wanted to incinerate the napkin. She pulled Quinn from his seat and they hurried away.

Ellie watched them walk outside. Jennifer was stunning, elegant, poised and obviously came from money. They were a beautiful couple. The kind she'd seen in fashion magazines. A world she'd never experienced . . . and probably never would.

Ellie checked her watch. One minute to class. She hurried out of the Student Center as a red Porsche sped by, Jennifer driving, Quinn in the passenger seat.

Ellie wondered if she'd ever hear from Quinn again. He'd probably lose her phone number.

Or maybe Jennifer would lose it for him.

FOUR

Before class, Quinn Parker sat in his *Estates & Trusts* lecture room reading the *Louisville Courier-Journal.* His knee hurt from tripping on the Student Center steps today. And he could still feel the *crunch* when the three hundred twenty pound defensive tackle accidentally stepped on it, dislodging the patella, severing the quadricep tendon and damaging some lateral ligaments.

The team doctor prescribed Vicodin. Even now, seven months later, he still needed the Vicodin because the pain at times overwhelmed him. But getting his prescription refilled was proving more difficult each time.

He checked the sports section, then flipped to *Business* and noticed a lengthy article about a wealthy Kentuckian named Leland T. Radford. The man, a widower, had passed away recently in Manchester, Kentucky. His only child, a son and U.S. Army Second Lieutenant, was killed in an Iraq roadside explosion.

Radford's huge estate included manufacturing companies, Internet enterprises, stocks and bonds, real estate in London, thoroughbred

---

horse farms, and twelve thousand acres in southeastern Kentucky rumored to hold vast reserves of bituminous coal. His estate would be probated in about a week or so, and with no heirs, the state was already counting the revenue from the sale of the estate properties.

"Interesting case," said a familiar voice.

Quinn looked up and saw his favorite professor, tall, silver-haired, silver-tongued Robert Bossung, scanning the article over Quinn's shoulder.

Quinn smiled. "Yes sir, all that moolah and no heirs."

Bossung nodded. "Maybe *you're* his long lost secret son, Quinn."

"Quite likely, sir."

"Why?"

"He was smart and handsome like me."

"You forget humble!" Professor Bossung smiled as he wiped his horn-rimmed bifocals with a tissue. "Actually, I find this case worthy of closer examination by our Estates class."

"It is intriguing."

"Glad you agree. Because I was thinking it would be terrific if you could go down to Manchester and talk to the executor of the estate, a probate lawyer. Guy named Fletcher Falcone. I met him once. Affable country lawyer. Learn all you can about the Radford estate. Then come back and enlighten your fellow students with your usual succinct and brilliant brief, say by next Wednesday. Of course, Brandeis Law will reimburse your expenses."

Quinn realized Bossung just suckered him into another assignment. But maybe a good one. It would be nice to gaze at green forests instead of yellow legal pads.

"Hang on, Quinn. I'll try to get you an appointment with Falcone."

Professor Bossung took out his cellphone, got Falcone's office number, and dialed. He chatted briefly with Falcone, wrote on a scrap of paper, then hung up and handed Quinn Falcone's Manchester address and phone number.

"Falcone can meet you in his office around this time tomorrow, if you can make it?"

"I can."

"Excellent!"

As Professor Bossung walked toward the front of the lecture room, Quinn Googled *Manchester, Kentucky* on his iPhone. He saw rolling hills and thick forests surrounded the town. He noticed it was not far from Harlan . . . where the girl he'd spilled coffee on was from. Ellie Stuart.

Quinn remembered how excited Ellie was when he offered to help her find out more about her adoption. He also remembered she was smart and had an easygoing sense of humor. But her life had been anything but easygoing. Losing both adoptive parents at sixteen, being left on her own, and supporting herself ever since must have been incredibly painful. But despite all that, she came across as well adjusted and appeared to have handled all her adversity well.

Maybe he could help her find out more about her adoption on his trip to Manchester.

As he folded his newspaper, another article caught his attention:

U OF L FEMALE STUDENT ATTACKED IN HOME!

The young woman had been assaulted in her apartment, robbed and left for dead. Now she was in a coma. Her attack was shocking.

So was her name.

Elle *Steward* - so close to - Ell*ie Stuart.*

Too close maybe.

Like the van that got too close and almost hit Ellie as she rode her bike to school.

What the hell was going on here?

He hurried out into the hall and dialed Ellie's number. It rang several times but did not go into voice mail. He hung up and wondered if she was all right.

As he turned around, his phone vibrated. He saw caller ID and answered.

"Hi, Ellie."

"Hey Quinn. Sorry I didn't reach the phone when you just called. By the way, you're off the hook."

"What?"

"The coffee stains washed right out."

He smiled. "That's great."

"So what's up?"

"My professor asked me to drive down to Manchester to re-search the estate of a guy for our class."

"Manchester's a nice town."

"And not far from Harlan. Anyway, I thought if you'd like to tag along, we could swing by Harlan courthouse, maybe talk to the family court judge. See if we can learn more about your adoption."

No response. "When are you driving down?"

"Tomorrow morning at eight."

"I'd love to go, Quinn. But let me see if my neighbor can stay with Celeste, the elderly woman I take care of. My neighbor's here now. Hang on, I'll ask her."

While she asked, Quinn read that the deceased man, a busi-nessman and philanthropist named Leland. T. Radford, had rebuilt sixty-two New Orleans homes and three grade schools destroyed by Katrina, plus several homes destroyed by tornadoes and floods.

"I can go, Quinn."

"Good. See you at eight."

"I'll be ready."

She gave him her address and they hung up.

Quinn felt good about getting away. It would be interesting to learn more about Leland Radford, a man who'd actually been born in a one-room Kentucky log cabin like old Abe Lincoln who was born in Hardin County, Kentucky.

And now that he thought about it – getting away from Jennifer for a day would be good, too. Over the last few weeks and months, she'd grown increasingly possessive of his time. Very possessive.

In fact, she was probably planning something very possessive of his time right now. He better call and tell her about his trip. He dialed and she answered on the first ring.

"Wow, I was just starting to call you," she said.

"About what?"

"My dress for the Cotillion ball. DuMauriers just got in some new Vera Wangs! I hear they're stunning! Tomorrow morning you have to help me pick one out."

"I'd like to, Jenn, but I've got to drive down to Manchester tomorrow morning."

"Manchester . . .?" She made it sound like North Korea.

"Yeah. My professor asked me to go down and research an important probate case there. I'm leaving at eight to meet the estate executor. What time does DuMauriers open?"

"Eleven, but you *have* to see my dress first."

"I can't wait that late, Jenn, and make my appointment. I'm sorry."

"But I *have* to pick a dress tomorrow so they can start the fittings."

"I understand, but - "

" - Go next week."

"Too late. The probate court date is next week."

He heard a couple of huffs and some harrumphs and feared she might be winding herself up into a hissy fit. But then she seemed to gain some control. "Well . . . okay, but I hate to think of you driving down there all by yourself."

Oh shit! Not telling her about driving Ellie would mean hell to pay if she found out later. Telling her now would mean hell to pay *now! Choose your hell, Quinn!*

"Well, actually, I'm driving someone down there."

"Who?"

"The girl I spilled coffee on."

Silence.

"She's from nearby Harlan and needs legal help in finding out more about her adoption."

Jennifer was silent for so long he thought the line had disconnected.

"Why can't *she* drive herself down?"

"She doesn't have a car."

Silence.

"I can't believe you'd waste time with *her* instead of helping me choose my dress!" He heard anger in her voice.

"Jennifer, you'd look beautiful in burlap. And finding out where she comes from will mean a hell of a lot to her."

"Well my *dress* means a hell of a lot to *me!*"

Quinn took a deep breath. "I understand. But my meeting time is fixed with the estate executor. I have to leave tomorrow morning early."

"Fine! Take Daisy Mae with you! But make sure you do one thing on the way down."

"What's that?"

"Stop at all the bars and trailer parks."

"Why?"

"So she can ask - *Who's my daddy?*"

Jennifer hung up.

Quinn leaned back, let the air drain from his lungs, then shook his head. When they began dating a few months ago, he was blinded by Jennifer's beauty - which blinded him to her flaws.

But then, slowly, her elitist attitude crept into little things she said and did. And then into big things she said and did. And it bothered him a lot. And yesterday, as he drove Jennifer to her Cotillion ball rehearsal, she'd bad-mouthed Ellie Stuart non-stop . . . "Did you notice her cheap dirty clothes and hear her awful hillbilly twang?"

Increasingly, Jennifer showed little interest in anyone from outside her zip code. Which included most of his friends. Her emerging haughtiness, and increasing possessiveness of his time, had been turning him off for weeks. When he tried to talk to her about it, she denied the problem.

He'd have to talk to her again about it. Soon.

A talk he was not looking forward to.

Who enjoys talking to a wall?

FIVE

A light night rain sprinkled onto Huntoon Harris. He hid in the shadows of some evergreens near a small wood frame house. He saw his footprints on the wet ground. No problem. The cops would waste hours searching for shoes that will be at the bottom of the Cumberland River in two hours.

He chewed his Mail Pouch and hoiked a gob out - almost. Tobacco juice dribbled down onto his brand new camouflage shirt.

"SHIT" he whispered, trying to wipe the brown stain off.

He lifted his powerful Special Ops binoculars and focused on the gray-haired woman in the nearby house. Mary Louise Breen, seventy something, sat in her den, reading a newspaper and petting her tabby cat. Television lights flickered across her wrinkly face as she sipped what looked like red wine. She reminded him of his grandmother.

Suddenly Mary Breen sat up fast, staring at something in the paper. Excited, she grabbed her phone and dialed.

Huntoon turned on his headset tapped to her landline.

A woman answered Mary's call. Mary and the woman began talking about something that happened many years ago. Then Breen mentioned *the name*. The *same* name the boss told Huntoon to listen for. A name that could cause the boss big trouble.

The two women hung up.

Huntoon phoned the boss and told him what he'd heard.

The boss cursed for several seconds, then said, ""You know what needs to happen."

Huntoon knew a death sentence when he heard one. "Yeah. But I need my money tomorrow. I'll come by your – "

" - not my office! The cash'll be in your P.O. Box by noon."

"Okay."

Four hours later, Huntoon looked down on Mary Breen sleeping in her bed.

He didn't like this job. Nothing wrong with killing. Greasing Towelheads in Iraq was patriotic, fun even. But greasing an old lady who looked like his grandmother just felt wrong, made him a little jumpy. He didn't know exactly why the boss wanted the old lady dead, but knowing the boss, it probably had to do with his money.

And if I didn't need this money so bad, I mighta turned this job down.

Huntoon wanted to do her fast. Easier for her. A bullet in brain. Maybe potassium chloride.

But the boss said *no*. There could be no trace evidence in her blood. It had to look like she passed away from something common in an older woman. Heart attack, stroke. Above all, no bruises.

That left him with one option. A snuff job. He picked up a large pillow and moved over to her side of the bed. She was breathing softly. Just inches away. He looked down at her and couldn't believe his eyes.

Mary Breen's face began to morph into the face of his grandmother, the only person who'd been kind to him after his parents abandoned him in a Burger King bathroom when he was six months old. But Grannie died three years later, and the state managed to toss him into five foster homes, all abusive in some way, until he finally ran away, enrolled in the army and wound up in Iraq. Good times shooting bad guys, until he was court-martialed on lousy trumped up charges.

He blinked the bad memories away, and looked back down at Mary Breen. He hated this job. But it had to be done. Slowly, he lowered the big pillow toward her face.

Suddenly - her eyes shot open. She stared up at him – saw his face – saw what was coming! He had no choice now.

He jammed the pillow down over her nose and mouth – snuffing out her scream.

She struggled hard . . . but four minutes later, her body was still. He lifted the pillow. He detected no pulse, felt no breath coming from her mouth, saw no life coming from her eyes.

He removed the pillowcase that might contain his DNA, put a fresh pillowcase on, tidied up the sheets and bedspread, and closed her eyelids. Then he combed her hair so it looked like nice, because he heard women want to look good when they die.

He walked back to her and whispered, "I'm right sorry Mary Louise. It's just business. Rest in peace."

SIX

E llie licked her fingers and ran them over a stalk of hair that kept popping up like a Whac-A-Mole. She gave up on it and put on her best jeans and least faded *University of Louisville* sweatshirt, $3.00 and $2.00 respectively from *Sam's Second Hand Shoppe*.

She was grateful that Quinn would try to help her learn something about her adoption in Harlan and maybe about her birth parents. Her earlier attempts had failed. And it would be nice to be back home in Harlan.

She grabbed her backpack and walked into the den where Celeste stared at an *I Love Lucy* rerun. She kissed the elderly woman on her tissue-soft cheek.

"I'm going Celeste, but Sarah is here."

No response. Celeste's eyes were like gray stones. She didn't seem to understand.

Then she turned toward Ellie and smiled. Ellie lived for her smiles . . . comforting reminders that Celeste was still in there somewhere.

Sarah walked over. "Good luck in Harlan, Ellie!"

"Thanks Sarah, and thanks for staying with Celeste."

"Anytime hon."

Ellie walked to the front window and looked outside at another beautiful spring morning. Light blue sky hovered over the distant hills painted gold by the morning sun. Two red cardinals splashed around in the birdbath as a Chevy TrailBlazer turned into Celeste's driveway, Quinn driving. She hurried outside and hopped in.

"Harlan Express at your service, ma'am!"

"Thank you, kind sir."

He backed out and drove off. Quinn looked handsome in his powder blue sweater and khakis. The sun poured through the sun-roof, highlighting his brown hair and some tiny white scars on the backs of his hands, maybe vestiges of football cleat cuts, she imagined.

"You excited to go back home?"

"Very excited, Quinn. And thanks a lot for the ride."

"Happy to."

They drove onto the Watterson Expressway, heading east.

"On the phone you mentioned you take care of a lady named Celeste?"

"A very sweet woman. Eighty-four and battling Alzheimer's."

"My aunt had it," Quinn said. "Devastating."

Ellie nodded. The thought of getting Alzheimer's panicked her. She'd watched it devastate a neighbor lady back in Harlan in just two years. And now she watched it steal a little more of Celeste's memory each day.

And last week came Ellie's personal shocker: she learned there was a chance *she* might contract the disease early.

"If we live long enough," Quinn said, "experts say we might eventually all get it."

"I might get it sooner, experts say."

Quinn seemed to realize she was serious. "Really?"

She nodded. "Last year, the university's BioMed Group paid a bunch of us dirt-poor students a hundred bucks to test us for genetic diseases. I needed the hundred bucks. But not the results."

"Why?"

"Turns out I have the E4 form of the APOE gene."

"Which means?"

"That if both my parents have that APOE gene, I might develop Alzheimer's earlier. Fortunately, there are many other genetic variables that determine early onset and whether I even get it."

Quinn nodded. "Still it's important to identify *both* your biological parents."

"Yes."

"That sounds to me like a compelling *legal* reason to petition the court to release their names."

"You think so?"

"I think it's worth fighting for."

"Me, too," she said as she read the flashing billboard ahead.

"WATCH THE KENTUCKY DERBY – ON NBC! THE MOST EXCITING TWO MINUTES IN SPORTS!"

"Ever been to the Kentucky Derby, Quinn?"

"Often. You?"

"Never. I can't afford Roller Derby."

He laughed. "Dad works at Churchill Downs. He gets extra Derby passes sometimes. If he gets enough, you're welcome to come."

"I'd love to, Quinn." But she wasn't sure Jennifer DuBois would like that.

Quinn slowed to a crawl at some road construction. He reached up and pushed the OnStar button on his rearview mirror.

A woman's voice said. "Is everything okay, Mr. Parker?"

"Yes. I just wondered if there's much more road construction between here and Harlan?"

"No, sir. Just the minor slow-down where you are now. It clears up in a half mile."

"Thank you."

"You're welcome, Mr. Parker," she said, hanging up.

Ellie was impressed. "Is the OnStar lady always so helpful."

"Always. Maybe your adoption agency is too. Do you know which agency placed you with the Stuarts?"

"No. The Stuarts didn't tell me they'd adopted me until I was fifteen. My birth certificate actually lists *them* as my natural parents."

"Wonder where they got that certificate?"

"I have no idea."

They drove in silence for a while.

"So where should we go first?" Ellie asked.

"I think the Harlan County courthouse. They may have copies of county birth records. But if they have nothing, I'll call my friend, Tim. He's in records at the state capital in Frankfort. Maybe he can help us."

He said us! She liked that. It felt wonderful having someone with legal knowledge helping her.

"Many years ago," Quinn said, "informal adoptions were much more common. You know, a birth mother dies, then her sister takes the child."

"My adoptive parents, the Stuarts, had no brothers, sisters, aunts or uncles."

"Any cousins?"

"All deceased."

They drove past a large horse trailer filled with two beautiful thoroughbreds, their coats gleaming in the sunlight, reminding Ellie how much she loved Kentucky horse country.

Ahead, she saw a billboard for Chanel #5, featuring a stunning model that looked a little like his girlfriend, Jennifer Dubois.

"So how was Jennifer's debutante rehearsal yesterday?"

He paused a moment. "Very elegant."

"So is Jennifer, Quinn. She has a beautiful smile."

"True, but well . . . she's not smiling about this trip."

"Why not?"

"She wanted me to go with her this morning to pick out her dress for the ball."

Ellie understood. "She wanted you to tell her she looked fabulous in the dress. It's a girl thing."

"Yeah, I guess so."

"Whichever dress she chooses, Quinn, she'll look gorgeous!"

"That's what I told her, but. . . ." He paused.

"But what?"

"Well . . . she also wasn't happy about this trip for another reason."

"What?"

"You . . ."

"Me . . .?" Ellie paused. "Just because you're driving me to Harlan?"

"Yep. Jennifer's kind of ah . . . possessive."

Ellie thought about that a moment. "That's another girl thing."

"With her it's a major thing."

Ellie said nothing.

"Question for you Ellie."

"Shoot."

"How many of these damn girl things does a guy have to worry about?"

"Honest answer?"

"Yep."

"A shitload."

Quinn laughed, but Ellie wondered how Jennifer possibly could be concerned about someone like her. Jennifer was drop-dead gorgeous, a campus VIP who came from one of Louisville's wealthiest families. Ellie was a country bumpkin and came from a loving, but dirt-poor family in Harlan. Jennifer shopped at Neiman Marcus, Ellie shopped at *Sam's Second Hand Shoppe* when she had a couple of bucks.

———

"Almost to Harlan," Quinn said, pointing at a road sign.

"It's always nice to come home. But lately I wonder if my birth mother still lives around here. Maybe she's someone I actually know, but is afraid to tell me."

Quinn nodded and glanced in the rearview mirror.

"I wonder what she was like. A teenager too young to raise me? Did she simply make a mistake one night and felt overwhelmed with the responsibility of raising a baby? Was I a reminder of someone she wanted to forget? Did she never want me?"

"I'm sure she had a good reason, Ellie.

"I hope so. I also wonder if she ever thinks about me . . . or has ever tried to find me? Is she searching for me right now?"

"I know it must be difficult, Ellie." Another glance in the rearview mirror.

"It is."

"I even wonder about darker possibilities. Were my parents bad people, criminals? Or inmates in an asylum? Or in prison? Was I born in prison?"

She noticed Quinn kept staring in the mirror.

"What's wrong?" she said.

"You said a dark blue van tried to hit you while riding your bike to school."

"It almost *did* hit me! Why?"

"A dark blue van has followed us since Lexington."

She turned around. It looked like the same van.

SEVEN

HARLAN

As Quinn turned onto Harlan's Main Street, Ellie was relieved to see the dark blue van no longer followed them.

Moments later, she recognized two elderly ladies chatting outside the Cumberland Jewelry Store. Last time she was in town, they were chatting in the same exact spot.

That's what she liked about her hometown. Stuff stayed put. Stores remained pretty much where you left them.

Like the old *Bank & Trust* Building Quinn was driving past. It had stood on Central Street since 1872. She'd once proudly deposited two dollars a week from her allowance in the bank. Ellie saw the *Margie Grand Theater* building where she and her best friend, Carrie, had worked as ushers on weekends. The building now held a loan office and day-care center. Many women needed the former to pay for the latter. When the coalmines closed, husbands lost jobs and many wives had to find work.

Ahead, she saw the Harlan County Courthouse where she hoped to find some record of her adoption.

They parked, got out and walked toward the entrance. She noticed the big statue of the World War I Soldier that reminded her of Gary Cooper in *Sergeant York*. Her neighbor lady had said, "Ellie, you look just like Gary Cooper's beautiful co-star, Joan Leslie." Ellie thanked her, but then learned the neighbor was legally blind.

They walked past the Coal Miners' Wall built in the 1920s.

"Why does the wall have two water fountains?" he asked.

"One for *Coloreds*, one for *Whites*."

"Ah yes, the old South. But times change. President Obama may now drink at either fountain."

Inside the courthouse, they walked up to a reception counter. Ellie recognized the sixtyish, gray-haired woman wearing a red plaid dress. Around her neck hung gold-rimmed glasses. Her hazel eyes were locked on her computer screen.

"Hi, Mrs. Browne."

Agnes Browne turned and smiled. "Well, I declare, Ellie Stuart, if you aren't getting prettier by the day!"

Ellie felt herself blush. "Thank you, ma'am. "This is Quinn Parker."

Quinn and Mrs. Browne shook hands.

"How you liking Louisville, Ellie?"

"Just fine, ma'am."

"Good. How can I help you, hon?"

"Well, as you know, I was adopted by Harold and Joyce Stuart."

Agnes nodded. "Joyce told me a few years back."

"I wondered if you keep records here of county adoptions from twenty-one years ago?"

"We used to, Ellie, but since 1962 all adoption records are filed up at the Department for Community Services at the capital in Frankfort."

Just like Quinn said they were.

"But hang on," Agnes said. "We keep some old backup files in the storage room. Your record should be back there."

Ellie's hope rose.

"Y'all have a seat while I look." Agnes gestured toward some wooden chairs, then walked into a room filled with wall-to-wall filing cabinets.

Ellie and Quinn sat and waited. She looked around and recognized three other middle-aged women working at computers, but not the young man with a silver earring who was sorting mail into wall slots.

Is he the same guy I talked to on the phone a couple of days ago when the line mysteriously disconnected?

Agnes Browne walked back toward them, looking puzzled.

"What's wrong?" Ellie asked.

"Well, I found the backup files for the year you were born and adopted. But for some dang reason, your file was missing!"

Ellie slumped against the counter.

"Do you have a copy of your birth certificate, Ellie?"

"Yes, ma'am." Ellie took a file from her satchel, pulled out her certificate and handed it to Agnes.

As Agnes scanned the document, she frowned at something in the corner.

"What's wrong?" Ellie asked.

"This state seal, hon, is . . . too small."

Agnes reached into a drawer and pulled out another birth certificate. "This here's the genuine seal. The state's began using this larger seal about eleven years before you were born."

Ellie saw the genuine state seal was at least fifty percent larger.

"I've seen some of these small-seal certificates over the years. Turned out they were all . . . ah . . . well, not genuine, you know, fakes."

Quinn leaned forward. "So whoever set up Ellie's adoption, gave Joyce and Harold this fake birth certificate."

"Seems to be the case," Agnes said.

"What about the judge who oversaw adoptions back then?" Quinn asked.

"Judge Warren Nesbitt. He handled adoptions in these parts then."

"Where is he now?"

Agnes pointed out the window. "Judge Warren's over at the Sunshine Senior Center on Cumberland Street."

"Can we visit him?" Ellie asked.

"Sure. But . . . well . . . I hear Warren's memory is kinda dotty. You know good days, bad days."

"Maybe he's having a good day," Quinn said.

"Damn sure worth a try," Agnes said. "If y'all go, tell old Warren that Agnes Browne said hi."

"Will do. And thank you, Mrs. Browne."

"You're welcome, hon. And good luck!"

As Ellie and Quinn walked from the courthouse, she hoped Judge Nesbitt was having a good memory day.

But the way her luck was running, he probably couldn't remember what he ate for breakfast.

* * *

As he sorted the courthouse mail, Barrett Sinkhorn watched Ellie Stuart and the big guy named Quinn leave the building. Sinkhorn tugged his silver earring, knowing what he had to do. He'd gone on full alert when he'd heard the name *Ellie Stuart* - the name he'd been paid to listen for over the past six years.

And for six years, he'd heard nothing. Then a few days ago, Ellie Stuart herself phoned him and asked about her adoption records. He'd put her on hold, and seconds later, disconnected the line.

Then today, she shows up *here,* snooping around.

Sinkhorn had to report the news immediately.

"Agnes?"

"Yeah?"

"I'm fixin' to go out for a smoke," he said, heading toward the door.

Agnes frowned, but nodded.

Outside, he walked behind the trash bin area, lit up a cigarette, made sure no one was listening, then took out his cell phone and dialed.

A man answered.

"Ellie Stuart was just here."

Long pause. "And . . .?"

"Well, she was asking about her adoption papers."

Longer pause.

"Agnes went to the storage room to check for Ellie's old backup file."

"But you destroyed that file, right?"

"Yes, sir, I sure did."

"Anything else?"

"Well, Ellie's fixin' to go see Judge Warren. See what he remembers."

"He won't remember jack-shit. His brain's mush!"

"You want me to do anything."

Long pause. "We'll handle her from now on."

EIGHT

Quinn and Ellie drove away from the courthouse and headed toward the Sunshine Senior Center. She hoped Judge Warren Nesbitt's "dotty memory" would remember something about her adoption. If he didn't, she had no idea where to search next.

As Quinn paused at a stop sign, Ellie noticed a frail woman in her eighties inching her way across the street.

"She looks like Celeste, the lady I care for."

"How long you been caring for her?"

"Since freshman year."

"Hers . . .?"

"Ha Ha. Everyone's a comedian."

"Does taking care of Celeste cover your tuition?"

"My scholarship covers my tuition, thank God. But caring for Celeste gives me room and board and a little spending money."

"Good for you, Ellie."

"Why?"

"You're bootstrapping your way through college with no assistance from family."

"What family? I'm a family of one. But hey, Quinn, you're no slouch. Football All-Conference, law school scholarship."

"Dad was a terrific athlete, and mom's smart as a whip. Luck of the gene pool."

Again, Ellie wondered about her gene pool and whether it included additional genes for early onset Alzheimer's. Or maybe the BRCA genes for breast cancer.

Diseases that she could do something about now . . . *if* only she knew about them now?

NINE

"So, Quinn, what kind of law do you plan to practice?" Ellie asked as they drove toward the Sunshine Center.

"Criminal law."

"Sounds interesting."

"Yeah. And I just received a nice offer to join Wagner, Hoffman and Musterman after graduation."

"Wow! They're one of Louisville's best firms. How'd you get the offer before you graduate?"

"Well, the Wagner firm handles legal work for *Kentucky Whiskeys*, Jennifer's father's company. He suggested they might want to interview me. They did and made me an offer."

"You should feel proud!"

"I feel lucky to know the right people." He passed a truck stacked with bales of hay. "So Ellie, tell me what kind of law interests you?"

"Miner's law."

"Minors in trouble?"

"*Miners* in mines. Coal miners with lung diseases. Men who've suffered for years from greedy mining companies and greedy health care providers who won't acknowledge their disease."

He nodded. "Don't forget the greedy life insurance companies who keep rejecting their claims until the miners give up or die."

"Sounds like we're both pissed off!"

"Sounds like we should open a free law clinic."

"Sounds like we call it the, ah . . . POMFLAC."

"The what?"

"The Pissed Off Miners Free Legal Aid Clinic."

He laughed as his cell phone rang. He pushed the speaker button.

"Hi, Quinn," Jennifer said.

"Oh, hi. . . . Did you find a nice dress?"

"Yes. It's fabulous. A white, low-cut full bodice Vera Wang."

"Sounds beautiful."

"It is. So how's the drive?"

"We made good time. Already in Harlan."

Jennifer paused. "And so . . . did you stop at all the bars?"

Quinn reached over and quickly turned off the speaker, then placed the phone to his ear. "Well, no . . . none."

Ellie wondered why Jennifer asked about bars? Did Quinn have a drinking problem? He didn't seem the type, but one never knows. And why did he turn off the speakerphone so fast?

She listened to him chat about the Cotillion debutante party. As they talked, Ellie imagined how beautiful Jennifer would look in her Vera Wang dress and how handsome Quinn would look in his tux. The perfect couple.

Quinn hung up. Ellie noticed he seemed a bit upset by the call.

"What's with 'stop at all the bars?'" Ellie said.

He hesitated. "Oh, that . . . well ah . . . you see, Jennifer's advertising class is ah . . . researching bartenders, asking if they think the new Budweiser commercials are working."

"Oh . . ." Ellie sensed he'd made up the answer and wondered why? Maybe he did have a drinking problem. And what about the pain pill he tossed in his mouth a while ago? He'd said it was for a knee injury he got playing football. But he hadn't played football for several months.

"So, Ellie, what about you?"

"What about me?

"Do you have a significant other?"

She paused. "I had one. Mark was a senior when I was a sophomore. We became serious when he began his masters program." She felt the heaviness hit her again. Would it ever go away?

"Did he complete his masters?"

"No. The National Guard called him to active duty. Weeks later, he was stationed near Kabul."

"How long was his tour?"

She swallowed a dry throat. "Four months. The army brought him home in a flag-draped coffin."

"I'm sorry, Ellie."

She nodded and took a deep breath. "After Mark's death, I kinda buried myself in schoolwork."

They drove in silence for several moments.

"Question for you," he said.

"Shoot."

"Do you know anyone in town in a red Ford pickup with a NAS-CAR sticker on the front bumper?"

"No. Why?"

"The one behind us has taken the same four turns . . . make that five, that we've taken since we left the courthouse."

TEN

Ellie watched the red Ford pickup turn down a side street as Quinn parked at the Sunshine Senior Center. Maybe the pickup wasn't following them. Maybe it was being cautious and waiting them out.

Maybe she was growing paranoid.

The Senior Center looked just like it did when she volunteered here during summer break. The magnolia trees were in full bloom, the wheelchair ramp still needed paint, the gardens were filled with crimson roses that smelled wonderful.

But inside, the roses were overpowered by disinfectants and deodorizers and what Ellie called the *air de decline*, old people knowing that the end was drawing near.

They walked up to the receptionist, a middle aged red-haired woman with large butterfly earrings.

"We're here to see Judge Warren Nesbitt," Ellie said.

The woman glanced at her desk clock. "Warren's watchin' *Judge Judy* in the lounge." She pointed down a hallway.

Walking down the hall, they passed residents creeping along on walkers. In one room, Ellie saw a stoop-shouldered woman staring out her window at the hills, perhaps remembering when she'd climbed them with ease.

Inside the lounge, Ellie saw four elderly ladies playing what sounded like a nasty game of Canasta. Nearby, sat an eighty-something, rail-thin man, with white hair riveted on *Judge Judy*.

"Judge Nesbitt . . .?" Ellie said.

The judge held up a finger. "Just a sec . . ."

Judge Judy banged her gavel and said,

> *"Mr. Jones, you're a Mr. Deadbeat Dad. Pay up in a week, or we'll garnish your wages!"*

"Right on, Judy!" Judge Nesbitt said, banging his fist on the chair like he'd once pounded his gavel. He snapped his red suspenders and turned toward Ellie and Quinn with a smile.

"Judge Nesbitt, my name is Ellie Stuart. Mrs. Browne at the courthouse suggested we talk to you."

"Mrs. Browne . . .?" He seemed confused.

"Agnes Browne, the clerk."

A pause. "Oh yes, Agnes. How is she?"

"She's fine and says hi to you."

The judge nodded. "Fine woman, Agnes. And her husband, Carl, no . . . Clete . . . no *Clyde* maybe?"

Ellie's concern about his memory ticked up as she and Quinn sat down.

"How can I help y'all?"

"Well, twenty-one years ago, I was adopted here by Harold and Joyce Stuart."

"Harold Stillwert out on Kitts Creek Road. Had a brother named Fester?"

"No, sir. STUART."

He blinked, then his eyes lit up. "Oh yes, *that* Harold and Joyce. Nice folks. Died in that terrible boating accident on Lake

Cumberland. What a shame! Drunk boater. Fifth DUI. Judge Young tossed his butt in Frankfort for ten years. Right decision." He snapped his suspenders again.

His memory seems to be working fine, Ellie thought.

"Yes. But I wondered, your honor, do you recall handling my adoption?"

He looked at her for several seconds, closed his eyes, then looked at her again. "Wasn't me, young lady. Sorry. You trying to learn who your birth parents are?"

"Yes, sir."

He ran knobby, arthritic fingers through his white hair. "Everything depends on whether they want to be identified. Most don't, you know."

She nodded.

"Talk to Teddy Nichols in town. Good family court lawyer. Handled lots of adoptions back then."

"I've talked to him. He didn't handle my adoption."

Judge Nesbitt looked out the window. "Were you born in Harlan Hospital?"

"According to my birth certificate I was." She decided not to tell him her certificate was probably fake.

The judge nodded. "Go check the hospital records. Talk to the attending physician at your birth. Or your case might have been an informal adoption. You know, one relative gives a child to another. Or you might have been adopted from another state, or another country. Or even an illegal adoption. That would make identifying your birth parents more problematic."

"I understand, sir."

"Try the state records in Frankfort.'"

"Yes sir."

"And try that Internet thing. I hear they got websites that can help kids find parents and parents find kids."

"I've tried those websites. No luck so far."

Judge Nesbitt nodded. "Well, keep trying, young lady. Don't give up."

"I won't, sir."

"Wish I could tell you more. Maybe something'll pop in my head. My memory's like a bad bulb. Flickers on and off. How can I reach you?"

She gave him a card with her name and cell phone number.

They stood, thanked Judge Nesbitt again and left.

As they drove out onto Main Street, she said, "Any chance Judge Nesbitt *forgot* he handled my adoption?"

"Maybe. But I thought his memory seemed pretty sharp."

"I did too."

"Where's the Harlan Hospital?"

"Not far."

★ ★ ★

From the front seat of his red Ford 350 pickup, Huntoon Harris watched the blue TrailBlazer drive off down Main Street. He flipped open his cell phone and dialed a number.

"Yes . . .?"

"They just visited old Judge Nesbitt."

"Where are they now?"

"Heading down 421 south."

"Here's what you gotta do. . . ."

ELEVEN

"Where exactly is Harlan Hospital?" Quinn asked as he drove away from the Sunset Center.

"Down near Gray's Knob."

"Where's Gray's Knob?"

"Over near Hank's Hump."

Quinn smiled. "Bullshit!"

"Yep."

She laughed and it felt good, especially after learning nothing about her adoption from Judge Nesbitt. Maybe she'd learn something at Harlan Hospital. After all, her birth certificate said she was born there. They should have some kind of record.

They drove past a Chevy El Camino that reminded her of her dad Harold's old El Camino. He loved it. Called it the "Cadillac of Pickups." Harold Stuart would always be her dad, the best dad anyone could hope for. But maybe she would grow to love her biological father too, if she ever was lucky enough to identify him. Who said she couldn't love two dads?

But the first question was – who delivered her to Harold and Joyce Stuart?

"Quinn . . ."

"Yeah?"

"I think my adoption was . . . illegal."

He nodded. "It happened a lot back then. And now. Each year in China and Europe thousands of infants are stolen from their parents and hospitals, and then sold."

Ellie felt sickened by the fact.

"And right here in America some women *sell* their babies, even though it's illegal."

"It's also disgusting."

He nodded. "But not everyone agrees. Even a distinguished U.S. Court of Appeals judge recently wrote that he believes a woman has the *legal* right to sell her baby."

"Like on eBay or in a garage sale?"

He shrugged. "I guess."

"So, if mommy can legally sell her baby at six weeks, can she sell her rebellious teenager at sixteen?"

He smiled. "The learned jurist hasn't waxed eloquent on that issue yet."

Quinn pulled in at Harlan ARH Hospital and parked. She remembered childhood visits to the modern, beige-brick medical center nestled among rolling green hills.

Inside, they were directed to the Records Office, where they saw a sixty-something woman with puffed-up gray hair typing at her computer. Her nametag said *Rena Faye*. She looked up and smiled.

"Can I help y'all?"

"I hope so," Ellie said, handing her birth certificate to the woman. "According to this certificate I was born here twenty-one years ago. I wonder if your birth records here go back that far?"

"Hon, our records go back further than *I* do! Yours should be here."

Ellie smiled and felt hopeful.

Rena Faye looked at the birth certificate, tapped on her computer and waited. She frowned, crinkling smokers' lines around her eyes, then turned to another computer, tapped some more and waited. More frowning, and moments later, she looked at Ellie.

"We have no record that an Ellie *Stuart* was ever born here. We've had nine Ellies, but two died in their eighties, three are in their fifties and four are under ten. I'm real sorry."

Ellie's hope sunk. "Perhaps I could talk to the attending physician at my birth, Dr. Jerome Morton?"

Rena Faye blinked at hearing the name, then looked at the certificate and her eyes widened. "Well now, that's right weird."

"What's weird?"

"Dr. Morton . . ."

"Why?"

"Dr. Jerome Morton died six years before you were born, hon. Massive stroke. Died right down the hall here. I was there."

Ellie's eyes went out of focus and she had to steady herself against the desk. A dead doctor delivered her into this world? What the hell was going on? Once again she found herself falling into the murky abyss of her origins. Where the hell did she come from?

Quinn placed his hand on her shoulder.

"Ellie, we'll sort this out. I promise."

She wasn't so sure, but appreciated his confidence.

They thanked the clerk, left and drove back toward Harlan.

Once again, the door slams shut.

She stared out the window as an old recurring dream flashed in her mind. She's trapped in a glass bottle on turbulent ocean waves, unsure how she got there, or where she's heading. The water tosses her bottle back and forth, then underwater, then against the side of a fishing boat. A man's hand reaches down pulls the bottle out of the water. She's rescued! The man opens the bottle and asks. . .

"Who are you?"

"I don't know?"

"Who are your parents?"

"I don't know."

"If you don't know anything, I can't help you."

He tosses the bottle back in the water and it sways back and forth . . . leaving her drifting, hoping for answers.

Like now. She and Quinn had found no record of her adoption at the courthouse. No recollection by Judge Nesbitt. And now no record of her birth at Harlan Hospital where she was allegedly born and delivered by a doctor who'd died six years before she was born.

"You okay over there?" Quinn asked.

She shrugged. "Just trying to figure all this out."

"Only one answer."

"What?"

"You're an alien baby."

"We prefer extra-terrestrial."

"E. T. okay?"

"That works."

Laughing felt good, she realized. Glancing at her watch, she said, "You should leave now for your law school meeting with that lawyer in Manchester."

"You want to come?"

"Can't. My friend Carrie Ann and I are going to talk to some folks who knew Joyce and Harold. Maybe we'll learn something."

"Worth a try. But we got a problem . . ."

"What?"

"Your old boyfriend in the red Ford pickup is back."

"I don't have an old boyfriend here." *Or a new one anywhere for that matter.*

"Well, the same damn pickup is following us again."

"You're sure?"

"Yep. Let's find out."

Quinn swerved over to the curb and stopped, waiting for the red pickup to go by. It didn't. Instead it slowed down and pulled over to the curb about fifty yards behind them.

A second later, the pickup darted down a side street.

TWELVE

Ellie and her best friend, Carrie Ann Norris, laughed as they stared at their high school photos in their yearbook.

"Why's that lampshade on your head?" Ellie asked.

"That's my hair!"

Ellie said. "Look - there's weird Arlo Roadheever. My god – he must weigh four hundred pounds!"

"Momma says he's big enough to have his own zip code."

They laughed as they sat in Carrie Ann's kitchen. As usual, Carrie Ann looked terrific: Thick auburn hair, large dark-green eyes, freckles on perfect skin, and a *Sports Illustrated Swimsuit* figure to die for – despite holding down two part-time jobs, attending Southeast Community College and caring for her sick mother.

She looked around the familiar kitchen. Same green Formica table, same mahogany spice chest, same ancient Frigidaire chugging away in the corner. Nothing had changed.

Except Carrie Ann's mother, Harriet. Her large brown eyes seemed to have sunk deeper into their sockets … and her body deeper into itself. Chemotherapy taking its toll … like it had on her husband, a coal miner, who died after a ten-year battle with black lung disease, aided and abetted by the mining company's refusal to acknowledge the disease or pay for his medical treatment. Bottom line: a two hundred pound man weighed ninety-seven pounds when he died. After law school, Ellie hoped to sue the mining company.

Harriet Norris shuffled into the kitchen and poured her coffee with a shaky hand.

"Mom . . .?"

"Yes."

"Who might know something about Ellie's birth parents?"

Harriet Norris pursed her cracked lips, which Ellie noticed were dotted with dried blood.

"I'd start with Mavis."

"Mavis Biddle?"

Harriet nodded. "I like Mavis, but that woman sucks up more dirt than my Hoover. Queen of Gossip. Lives over there near Wallin's Creek."

Ellie remembered Mavis Biddle. Her husband, Link Biddle, lost his job in the mines twenty years ago, then ran a string of successful moonshine stills before being shot dead in a poker game when some aces slid from his sleeve.

Before his demise, word was he'd stashed bushels of money in an offshore bank account in St. Kitts from which Mavis still drew money.

* * *

"That's Mavis's house down there behind those evergreens," Carrie Ann said, steering her old Chevy Cavalier down a winding gravel driveway.

Ellie looked down at the 1960s brick ranch home situated in a small valley. In the front yard were two white wagon wheels entwined with red roses. Nearby a small creek flowed through a decorative Dutch windmill, its blades spinning with the flow. They parked next to a big shiny new GMC pickup with large deer antlers mounted on the hood.

They got out and walked toward the house.

Suddenly the door swung open and Mavis, eighty-two, in a large muumuu dress with pink flowers and matching pink Nikes smiled with her few remaining teeth.

"I'll be damned - Thelma and Louise!"

Ellie and Carrie Ann laughed.

"I'm Carrie Ann – "

"Hell, I knowed you, Carrie Ann, and you, Ellie, since y'all was knee high to grasshoppers. Git yer cute butts on in here now!" Her tiny gray eyes sparkled in a sea of pink wrinkles. She seemed hungry for visitors.

They stepped inside a living room of heavy maple furniture crowded with pictures of children, grandkids and kinfolk. Over the fireplace hung a huge oil painting of her late husband, Link, holding his 12-gauge shotgun and a shiner's jug of liquor. Mavis clicked off a Doris Day movie, plopped down in a beige Lay-Z-Boy chair and motioned them onto a nearby sofa.

"We called earlier, ma'am," Ellie said, "but no one answered."

"I was out hittin' the bars, lookin' for Mr. Right."

"SHUT UP MAVIS!" someone shouted.

Ellie turned and saw it was a huge green parrot bobbing his head as though guffawing at his own words.

"That's Spike. My husband taught the little bastard to say that when I'm talkin.' Don't pay Shithead no mind. Y'all want coffee, a little 'shine maybe?"

"No, ma'am."

"Carrie Ann, how's your momma doin'?"

"So so, maybe a little better today, ma'am."

"Good for her! Ellie, how you doin' up in that big wicked Lou'vull?"

"I love it, ma'am."

"Your parents would be right proud."

"Thank you. Actually, we came to talk about my parents."

"They were the best!"

"Yes, ma'am. But I'm wondering about my *birth* parents."

Mavis Biddle's eyes widened. She sat back and took a deep breath. "Couple years ago, Joyce up and told me you was 'dopted. I always figgered you wuz what with you bein' taller and well prettier than Joyce, who wuz right pretty her own self mind you."

"She was. Did she ever tell you who my birth parents were?"

"Joyce didn't know. But she wuz tryin' to find out before she and Harold died in that godawful boating accident."

Ellie nodded, flashing back to the morgue.

"Did she tell you anything about my adoption?"

Mavis rocked in her chair a bit. "Well, I promised Joyce I'd never tell anyone. But now, with her bein' gone and all, I reckon you gotta right to know."

Ellie leaned forward, her heart racing.

"You know how Joyce had that problem . . . eendomeetoastasis or whatever the hell they call that stuff that gunks up a woman's uterus."

"Endometriosis," Ellie said.

"That's it. The lining of the womb ain't right. Wouldn't let her git pregnant. So she and Harold got on a six-year-long adoption list. Two weeks later, out of the blue, this fella up and phoned Joyce. Said he had hisself a healthy baby girl, few months old, who they could adopt lickety-split, no questions asked. Wouldn't cost 'em one red cent. The baby would come with a birth certificate that named them as parents. Slam bang, here's your youngun'"

"A black market adoption," Ellie said.

"Yep. But yours wuz right different."

"How?"

"You come with a bonus."

"What bonus?" Ellie wondered what Mavis meant.

"Ten thousand dollars cash money. A heap of money back then."

Ellie was amazed. "The Stuarts received ten thousand dollars for taking me?"

"Sure did. But the money come with a hitch. Joyce and Harold wuz told that they could never try to learn the identity of your birth parents. If they did, the fella said he'd come and take you back!"

Ellie swallowed a dry throat, trying to absorb what she'd just heard.

"Did she tell you the man's name?"

"No. Joyce didn't know."

"Is that's all she told you?"

"That's all she knowed."

Ellie thought about what she'd just heard. "So maybe my birth mom was an unwed teenager whose parents insisted she give up the baby."

"Right possible," Mavis said.

"Did the man deliver me to the Stuarts?"

Mavis closed her eyes. "No. Joyce said they wuz a nice woman what brung you, plus your birth certificate and the ten thousand cash money to their house."

"Do you remember her name?"

Mavis shook her head. "Only heard it once't. Woman had an odd name. Maybe it'll come to me later."

"If it does, please call me." She handed Mavis her card.

"I'll do that for sure. And y'all be sure to tell old Mavis what y'all find out!"

"SHUT UP MAVIS!" Spike squawked.

"Blow it out yer ass Spike!"

Spike ruffled his feathers as though highly insulted.

Ellie and Carrie Ann smiled, thanked her and left.

Heading back toward Harlan, Ellie saw a red Ford pickup four cars behind them. It looked like it might be the pickup that followed Quinn and her from the courthouse. As the pickup pulled within three cars, Ellie glimpsed the driver, a round-faced man.

Is that Ronnie Sneller? she wondered. Ronnie, a creepy high school classmate, had hounded her for years for a date almost to the stalking level.

Then sunlight lit the driver's face.

Not Ronnie. Older guy. Thirties. Wraparound sunglasses, baseball hat, a phone device on his ear, lips moving.

"That red pickup behind us looks like the pickup that followed Quinn and me earlier today."

Carrie Ann checked the mirror. "I'll drive straight home!"

"Thanks."

Once again, Ellie thought, *I'm escaping to Carrie Ann's home.*

She would never forget her first time, six years ago. Late at night, her foster parent, Hoyt Rickter, drunk as usual, came into her room, dropped his pants and started to fondle her. She fought to get away, but he grabbed her ponytail, threw her down on her bed and tried to rape her. She managed to pull a big blue lava lamp off the table and broke it over his head, sending hot wax onto his crotch. As Hoyt fell to the floor screaming and holding his burning genitals, she ran over to Carrie's home six blocks away. Mrs. Norris immediately phoned Hoyt and told him Ellie would not be returning to his house that night, or ever again, and that if he had a problem with that, she would report him to the Sheriff Lonnie Norris, her brother-in-law, who would then report Hoyt to social services as a pedophile and attempted rapist and make sure he was locked up in the Kentucky State Penitentiary.

Hoyt Rickter was never heard from again.

Ellie would always owe Mrs. Norris for that night and for accepting her into her family. And some day, she would find a way to repay her. She just hoped Mrs. Norris lived long enough.

Ellie checked the red pickup again.

It was only *two* cars behind them and moving up.

She saw the NASCAR sticker.

It was the same pickup.

THIRTEEN

MANCHESTER

Quinn drove toward the small town of Manchester, nestled in rolling hills north of Harlan.

He enjoyed the sweet scent of freshly mown hay as he passed a chestnut mare and her colt grazing in lush grass behind a white picket fence. Kentucky horse country. As a kid, he visited world famous Calumet Farms with its picturesque acres of white fences, green fields, magnificent thoroughbreds, and immaculate barns.

Quinn drove into Manchester and passed a white-steeple church and rows of tiny shops and folks chatting, smiling, and waving at people driving by. Another small town big on neighborliness.

He hoped Fletcher Falcone, the probate attorney executor of Leland Radford's estate, was also friendly ... and gave him a comprehensive overview of the Radford estate and the upcoming probate process.

Quinn parked and walked toward the attractive law office of Falcone & Partners, housed in a large, perfectly preserved Queen Anne style mansion with a steep gabled roof and a large porch that wrapped around three sides. A big bay window jutted out into a garden filled with purple tulips dripping water from the sprinkler.

He entered the lobby. Lots of modern chrome and glass décor that blended nicely with antique chairs and tables.

"May I help you?" asked the young, very blonde, very buxom receptionist smiling at him over the top of *True Confessions.* Her nameplate read, 'Ramada.'

"Yes, I'm Quinn Parker, a law student. Mr. Falcone offered to spend some time with me around now."

Ramada smiled as though *she'd* like to spend some time with Quinn around now.

"Mr. Falcone is expecting you. He's just dedicated a school playground. He'll be here any second."

"Okay."

"Would you like some coffee . . . Quinn?"

"No thanks."

"If you need *anything* just let me know." She fluttered her eyes and raked bejeweled purple fingernails through her thick, blonde hair. Her southern hospitality message was loud and clear.

He sat down in a plush leather chair and noticed the facing wall was covered with the logos of some of Appalachia's largest coal mining companies ... obviously important clients for Falcone & Partners. In southeastern Kentucky, *business* was a four-letter word: *COAL.*

Ramada answered her desk phone.

"Mr. Falcone just got in his office. He'll see you now."

Smiling, Ramada escorted him down a narrow hallway, brushing her southern hospitality against his hip a couple of times.

He entered Fletcher Falcone's office and saw a heavyset man, some might say obese, with thick, salt and pepper hair, sitting behind a massive desk stacked with several legal folders. He was on the phone, smiled at Quinn and waved him into a chair.

The man's bushy brown eyebrows swept upward, reminding Quinn of the late John L. Lewis, the famous United Mine Workers president. Falcone laughed at something, scrunching his eyes into slits. He wore an expensive blue suit. His vest had a gold chain, presumably attached to a pocket watch. On his credenza sat a stack of *Racing Post* newspapers, a bottle of Jack Daniels and an enormous bowl of cashews.

Falcone hung up, then stood up. He was about five-foot-eight, maybe three hundred pounds, but whipped round his desk surprisingly fast on small, black tasseled loafers. Smiling, he shook Quinn's hand.

"Welcome, Quinn. Professor Bossung told me you've been cracking those big fat law books extra hard."

"Yes, sir."

"Briefing all those cases?"

"Day and night."

"Don't forget those outlines!"

"I'd be dead without them, sir."

Falcone chuckled.

"Have a seat, son. Something to drink? Cashews maybe?"

"No, thank you, sir."

Falcone grabbed a fistful of cashews, tossed them in his mouth and munched away, dribbling crumbs onto his vest and pants. "So, you're putting together an overview on Leland Radford's estate for your class, is that correct?"

"Yes, sir. I understand you were named executor."

"That's right. You see, I knew Leland for thirty-one years. Been his personal attorney for the last twenty-nine."

Quinn nodded. "Obviously, Mr. Radford was a very impressive man."

"Yes. And *very* successful. Born in a dirt floor Kentucky log cabin. In high school, Leland found some valuable Civil War antiques in a field. Swords, rifles, guns, hats, coins. Made enough money selling them to open a tiny antique store by his senior year. Saved every dime. Earned a scholarship to the University of Kentucky. Started investing in the stock market. The man just had the knack. Made a bundle. Then he bought troubled companies, turned them around without shipping jobs overseas, raked in huge profits. Poured his profits into the money markets. Made bigger bundles. Kentucky's Warren Buffett. Married his high school sweetheart, Dinah Sue. Wonderful woman! Married thirty-one years until she died. Her passing almost killed him."

"What happened then?"

"Zelda happened. Leland's half-sister. His only living relative. She came to live with him at *The Pines,* his estate. Zelda was a piece of work, I reckon. Spinster lady with no kids or kin, ran *The Pines* staff like a marine drill sergeant for years until she died, believe it or not, just one day before Leland died."

What are the odds of that? Quinn wondered, as he made notes. "What about Leland's children?"

Falcone paused for several moments, looked out the window, and tossed more cashews in his mouth. "That's a right sad story. Just one child. Rick. Nice young man. Second Lieutenant in Iraq. Roadside bomb killed him. Leland was flat out devastated."

Quinn nodded.

"He was never the same after."

"Was his son married?"

"No."

Quinn jotted more notes. "So, did Leland's will leave everything to Zelda?"

"Off the record, it sure did. Except for some very generous bequests to his household staff."

"So no other children?"

Another pause. "No."

"So now, I assume, Zelda's heirs will inherit?"

"Afraid not."

"Why?"

"Zelda had no heirs. Not a damn one. No family. No relatives. Plus Zelda hadn't made her will yet, even though I told that woman a gazillion times to write her will over the years. Stubborn woman. Always said she wanted to think about it more. Well, she waited too damned long!"

"So what happened?"

"Well, the day Zelda died of a massive heart attack in her flower garden, I was in New York. So I phoned the hospital where Leland was hospitalized to see how he wanted to revise his will. But the doctor told me Leland was slipping in and out of consciousness and that I better hustle back here immediately. So I grabbed a flight and got here four hours later to find Leland had just slipped into a coma. Never came out of it. Eleven hours later, he passed away."

"No other relatives, cousins?"

Falcone shook his head. "Not a dang one."

"No other living relatives seems kinda rare."

"It is! But it happens, Quinn. Leland's parents were only children. So was Dinah Sue, his wife. And frankly, Zelda was too damned mean for anyone to marry and have kids with. So bottom line - no kinfolk on either side. Isn't that something?"

Quinn nodded.

"It happens more than people think." Falcone tossed more cashews in his mouth, then glanced at his pocket watch.

"So as executor, I assume, you're responsible for probating the estate, and then selling off the assets, properties, the home, businesses, and paying taxes, and so forth all in accordance with the will and state law."

"That's right, Quinn. And it's a hell of a lot to sell off and liquidate, I'll tell ya. You can get the complete list of all estate assets over at the Clay County court, few blocks over. They're posted there. And call a fella named Heinrich De Groot, Radford's estate and financial manager and tax guy. De Groot and some other estate managers, handle most of the day-to-day management of the estate business and operations."

"Do you have their names and numbers?"

"Sure, do." Falcone took a list from a drawer and gave it to him. "Just tell these guys you talked to me."

Falcone then gave him a quick summary of Radford's major businesses and properties and the respective managers.

"We're talking *big* estate," Quinn said.

"According to De Groot, we're talking over nine hundred fifty million dollars big! Closing in on a billion!"

Quinn was stunned.

"Yep, a billion."

"And with no heirs," Quinn said, "I think I hear the state of Kentucky licking its chops?"

"I hear 'em drooling! The state will get a windfall."

Quinn nodded. "What kind of man was Radford?"

"Hard working, and very generous. Off the record, the will leaves some of his employees at *The Pines* enough to retire."

"Where is *The Pines?*"

"Not far. Just up Highway 80 past Pigeonroost. Can't miss it. Sits up on a big old hill overlooking a lake. Beautiful estate. Shoot, I reckon *The Pines* mansion, its horse stables and barns, the private aircraft landing strip and surrounding nine hundred acres are worth maybe forty million dollars easy."

Amazed, Quinn made more notes.

Falcone glanced at his watch again.

"I know you're busy, Mr. Falcone, but I'd like to get a little better sense of the man. Is there someone at *The Pines* who knew him well? Someone I might chat with?"

Falcone seemed a little taken back by the question, as though he'd just relayed everything worth knowing about Radford. He blinked again, then straightened his red polka dot tie. "Well, I reckon you could chat with old Irene, a housekeeper. She worked for Leland for decades. Knew him as well as anyone. Nice woman. Black as the ace of spades."

Quinn wondered what her color had to do with anything. "Does Irene still live at *The Pines?*"

"Yes. Everyone does until it's sold after probate."

Falcone looked at his watch. "Well, Quinn, I'm scheduled in court. If you have any more questions, just call me."

"That's very kind. And thanks for taking the time, Mr. Falcone. I really appreciate it."

"Glad to help, son.

Quinn left the office, got in his car and wrote more notes. An interesting meeting. The jovial lawyer had been very helpful and forthcoming, but seemed a bit hesitant a couple of times, like when Quinn asked to speak to someone at *The Pines* about Radford. No, he was more than hesitant. Maybe concerned.

Quinn wondered why?

FOURTEEN

LOUISVILLE

In his sprawling office, Mason V. Marweg tied the silk laces of his custom-made, three-thousand-dollar elevator shoes. The alligator wingtips, one of sixteen similar pairs of various shades in his closet, raised his height five full inches, up to four-feet eleven and a half. Quite normal.

What wasn't normal were his three wolverines. He gazed at the beautiful sleeping animals. He'd raised them since birth with the help of his on-staff veterinarian who'd used growth hormone and gene therapy to nearly triple their normal size. The massive carnivores - Shamar, Goba, and Goliath - weighed nearly one hundred sixty pounds each. And although semi-domesticated, they remained vicious flesh-eating predators, trained to obey only his commands. He loved watching them doze in the sun.

He clicked his clicker. Instantly, the three muscular bear-like animals sprang to their feet, snarling and baring their two-inch canines, hoping to sink them into whoever was behind his office door.

Satisfied at their response, Marweg snapped the clicker twice. Immediately, the wolverines sat back in the sun. He opened a small refrigerator and removed three large chunks of raw one-hundred-fifty-dollar-a-pound Kobe beef, and tossed them to the animals. They devoured the meat in seconds.

Shamar, Goba and Goliath were his protectors, 24x7. They even slept with him in his double-king-sized bed, steel-reinforced to support their additional five hundred pounds.

Marweg stood in his penthouse office atop his twenty-story Marweg Industries Building in downtown Louisville. He looked down at the Ohio River and watched the nation's oldest operating steamboat, the *Belle of Louisville,* paddle-wheeling its way up river. Passengers were smiling.

Marweg smiled, too. He'd just added two major properties to his mining empire. At the sale closing, the former mine owners refused to speak to him because he'd forced them into bankruptcy. He couldn't care less. The fools didn't get it. Business is war! A land war in his case.

And his next land acquisition - Leland T. Radford's massive twelve thousand acres chock full of coal - would soon be his.

For years, he'd tried to buy Radford's land, but the tree-hugging fanatic repeatedly refused to sell, babbling on about the ecological balance "of my pristine forests." *Well, my pristine coal haulers will soon roll out of those forests with tons of black gold - coal.*

Because Radford was now dead.

Marweg's phone vibrated in his pocket. He saw Caller ID and answered.

"Yeah...?"

"Something's come up," the caller said.

"Explain."

The more the man explained, the less Marweg liked what he heard. He didn't need this aggravation now.

"Handle it," Marweg said, "or I'll shift my assets elsewhere."

"I will."

Marweg hung up. If the man didn't handle it, Marweg would. Just because he was four feet eleven and a half, certain people thought they could take advantage of him. The corridors of business were now stacked with tall ex-CEO bullies who tried to push him around.

After all, he'd handled every problem since the day his father abandoned him and his cancer-ridden mother, leaving them penniless. Marweg was fifteen. That same day he walked to the nearby Crawford Mine to beg for work. As he neared the office, someone threw a razor-sharp chunk of coal that ripped open his cheek beneath his eye.

The miner who'd thrown the rock, Cletus Buttes, shouted, "We don't hire no fuckin' dwarfs!" Cletus and his four pals howled with laughter and threw more coal at him as he ran home, bleeding.

Marweg swore revenge.

Seventeen years later, he got it. After acquiring huge success in the money markets, Marweg bought a network of coalmines, including the Crawford Mine. That same day, he fired Cletus and his four pals. Marweg waved to them as they walked out the gates. Cletus and his boys had lost their appetite for laughing. They'd also lost their pensions. It was one of the happiest days of Marweg's life.

Today, nearly thirty years later, Mason Marweg sat atop mining empire valued at 5.3 billion dollars.

Most of his wealth came from his coalmines the USA, silver mines in Bolivia and two diamond mines in Botswana. The mines gave him an enormous sense of power.

So would the acquisition of Leland Radford's 12,000 acres of rich bituminous coal.

And he would soon acquire those acres . . . one way or another.

———

FIFTEEN

Driving away from his meeting with Fletcher Falcone, Quinn shifted in his seat and felt pain shoot up from his knee. Only one Vicodin left. He needed more painkillers to study for upcoming law exams. If Dr. Swanson wouldn't write him another prescription, he'd have to go cold turkey ... or start shopping doctors.

But first he had to write a report on Leland Radford.

Quinn phoned the financial investment manager for the Radford estate, a man named Heinrich De Groot.

De Groot's secretary answered, Quinn explained his call and was put through.

"Mr. De Groot, my name's Quinn Parker. Fletcher Falcone suggested I call you." Quinn explained his law school assignment.

"Sure, Quinn. How can I help?"

"Just a couple of questions about the Radford estate."

"Of course . . ."

"I'm told you handle many of the financial assets of the estate."

"Most of them. The purchase and sale of stocks, bonds and financial instruments, some tax work and such. I've handled them for some nineteen years now. Leland Radford was a wise investor. Had a knack. Did his research. But of course we advised him along the way."

"His assets seem well-diversified."

"Oh, yes. He has a strategically integrated portfolio of assets and properties. Lots of blue chip, high tech, U.S. equities, some non-U.S. equities. He bought IBM, Apple and Google very early on. Very profitable. Like his many other assets. You'll find the full list at the courthouse."

"I'll check that. So after probate what happens?"

"The five other Radford business managers, and I, will work with the Executor, Mr. Falcone, in the final disposition and liquidation of all estate assets, according to Radford's will." De Groot explained that process in detail.

"Mr. Falcone told me there are no heirs or relatives."

"That's right."

"Seems uncommon . . ."

"It is. Lots of one-child families these days. Had a client last year died with no heirs. Left her cat four million bucks."

"Lucky kitty!"

"Lucky Kentucky! The state got the remaining twenty-three million dollars."

"Amazing!" Quinn said.

He turned in at the gate to *The Pines,* the Radford estate, for his chat with the housekeeper. "Well, thank you for your time, Mr. De Groot. If I have more questions later, could I phone you?"

"Any time, Quinn."

* * *

Heinrich De Groot stared at his office phone for several moments, then looked out his floor-to-ceiling window at the water fountain in the town square.

De Groot was suspicious. Always had been. But it had served him well over the years.

And he was suspicious of Quinn Parker.

Is Parker really just a student? How much does he already know?

And how much can he find out?

SIXTEEN

HARLAN

As Carrie Ann drove down her street, Ellie saw the red pick-up that had followed them since Mavis Biddle's house had disappeared.

"He's gone for now!" Ellie said, feeling her neck muscles relax.

"Probably just some asshole bubba flexing his V8 virility!"

"But he's also the guy who followed Quinn and me earlier."

They parked, hurried inside Carrie Ann's house and locked the door. Ellie smiled at Mrs. Norris sitting in a chair reading a paperback.

"What'cha reading, Mrs. Norris?"

"Kat Martin's sleazy new bodice-ripper."

"What's it about?"

"The Queen's daughter loves the stable master's teenage son."

"Does the Queen approve?"

"Hell no! She wants the horny kid for *herself.*"

Ellie and Carrie laughed.

"So how were Mavis Biddle and Spike the parrot?"

Ellie smiled. "Spike squawked as Mavis talked. But she told me that a tall woman delivered me as a baby to the Stuarts here in Harlan."

"That's helpful."

"It is," Ellie said, as her phone rang. She saw it was Quinn and answered. "Hi, Quinn. Any luck with the lawyer?"

"A bit." He told her about his talks with Falcone and Irene Whitten, the housekeeper at the Radford estate.

"What about you - did *you* have any luck?"

She told him what Mavis said.

"That's a start."

"It is, but Carrie Ann and I were followed back here."

"Who followed you?"

"The same red pickup that followed us near the courthouse."

Pause. "Did it have a NASCAR sticker on the left front bumper?"

"Yes."

"Where's the truck now?" He sounded concerned.

Ellie stood and looked out the window, then up and down the street. "There's a red pickup way down the street, but I can't tell if it's the same one."

"You're inside now?"

"Yes."

"Stay inside! Lock the door and call the police. That guy's stalking you for some reason. I'll be there soon."

Seven minutes later, Ellie saw Quinn's TrailBlazer pull up at Carrie Ann's house. Ellie hurried out and leaned in the window.

"The red pickup drove off a few minutes ago."

"Did you call the police?"

"Yes. The officer said, they'd keep an eye out for it, but he said ". . . red Ford pickups with NASCAR stickers in these parts . . . are as thick as flies on . . . excrement!"

"He said *excrement?*"

"Actually he said *'shit!*', but I didn't want you to think I'm some crude country chick!"

"Too late," he said, laughing. His phone rang and he answered. He listened to the caller, then hung up.

"That was Irene Whitten, the housekeeper I just talked with at *The Pines.* I sensed she was holding something back. And she was. Now, she wants to tell me, but in person."

"You have to drive back up to Manchester?"

"No. She just drove down here to Harlan. She's down the street at place called the Huddle House."

"It's on Main Street. You can't miss it. While you're there, I'll phone friends of my parents. See what they know."

"You'll stay inside? Doors locked?"

"Sure."

She headed back inside and noticed Quinn watching her until she was safely inside the house. Then he drove off. Ellie checked to make sure no red pickups followed him.

None did. She relaxed.

* * *

Three blocks away, Huntoon Harris sat in his red pickup, focusing his military binoculars on the house Ellie Stuart just entered. He watched the big guy in the TrailBlazer drive off, leaving Miss Ellie unguarded.

He flipped open his cell phone and made a call.

No answer. The boss wouldn't let him leave voice mails, so he hung up. Huntoon wondered what he should do now. The boss was always telling him "be more assertive." Huntoon wasn't sure what assertive meant, but he thought maybe it meant he should just go ahead and do stuff.

In other words, I should just go handle Ellie Stuart now!

SEVENTEEN

Quinn parked near the big red fifty-foot high Huddle House sign on Harlan's Main Street. He stepped inside the crowded restaurant and saw Irene Whitten sipping coffee in the corner. She looked nervous and seemed to study everyone who walked in. He nodded to her, bought a large coffee and sat at her table.

"Quinn, I apologize for not telling you everything at *The Pines*."

"It's okay, Irene. Did you think someone was listening to us?"

She nodded. "It's very possible. You see, Leland's sister, Zelda, usta pay our employees to listen in on each other. Especially on me. Her and me - we didn't git along. I don't like to speak bad on the dead – but on Zelda I'm right happy to. She was one mean woman. I still feel like she might have someone listenin' to my conversations. Zelda didn't like me cuz Mr. Radford and I were real good friends for so many years. And she didn't like me because of something else . . ."

Irene checked a man walking in.

"Because of what?" Quinn wondered if Irene was overly suspicious.

"Because she was scared I'd tell Leland something."

"What's that?"

She sipped more coffee. "The secret."

He waited.

"You see, Zelda *forced* me to keep the secret from Leland for many years. Threatened me real bad. But thirty minutes after Zelda died, I rushed into Leland's hospital room and flat out tol' him! I did!"

Quinn noticed Irene's trembling hands and decided to let her proceed at her own pace.

"You said you're a law student, Quinn."

"Yes."

"So if I tell you the secret . . . is it like what y'all call ah . . . privileged information?"

Quinn thought a moment. "Well, no, Irene, because I'm not an attorney yet. So you and I don't have a client-attorney relationship. But you can trust me to not reveal what you ask me not to reveal, unless it's a felony. In that case you should tell a lawyer. And I could recommend one if you - "

"- ain't no felony. Just a secret."

"Go ahead."

She sipped more coffee, Irene looked Quinn in the eye. "Please don't never tell anyone what I'm fixin' to tell you unless you've gotta do it legal-like."

He nodded, his curiosity heating up.

"As I told you before, Leland was devoted to his wife, Dinah Sue, for twenty-nine years. A wonderful woman. When she died, Leland liked to died his own self. Very sad, depressed. Didn't eat, didn't go out, didn't do diddley squat 'cept work, and drink whiskey and sleep. For years. He was sinkin' bad I'll tell 'ya, and we figured he'd never snap out of it. Then real slow like, he started takin' notice of one of our new housekeepers. A nice young woman named Jacqueline Moreau."

"Jacqueline's family came from a small town in France. Batilly-en-Puisaye, I think. They moved to Martinique where Jacqueline was born. Then when she was around twenty-five, Jacqueline came to Kentucky."

Irene smiled. "Jackie was sweet as sugar pie. I loved her. She was funny and made Leland laugh after mournin' his wife all those years. He asked her to give him French lessons and she did. He come alive when Jackie was around. Before long, he liked her a whole bunch! He did! Well, one thing led to another, you see, and pretty soon Leland and Jacqueline were flat out in love. And that's a fact!"

Quinn nodded but wondered where this was going.

"'Cept it didn't last long."

"Why not?"

"Zelda! His half-sister. She all time harpin' and whompin' on poor Leland about how he was so much older than Jackie, and how he should be damn 'shamed of hisself for carrying on with her and all."

"How did Leland feel?"

"He loved Jackie, but like I say, Zelda kept browbeatin' and slammin' him all the time, and after a while he began to think well, maybe Jackie was jes', you know, infatuated with him. He started to feel that she deserved someone more her own age."

"How did *Jacqueline* feel?"

"Didn't give a hoot about their age difference. Leland was young looking and strong for his age. And she loved him true. But, like I say, Zelda, she jes kept cussin' out Leland, sayin' they're ain't no fool like an old fool, that Jackie was after his money, even though Jackie said she sign one of them pre-wedding papers. But Zelda just kept on harpin'. . . saying Jacqueline was wrong for him, and he was ruining Jackie's life."

"So what happened?" Quinn asked.

Irene Whitten shook her head. "Eventually Zelda wore Leland down. He figured Jackie did deserve a younger man she could start a family with and all."

"How did Jacqueline take that?"

"Real bad. It hurt her. But, after a few days, she figured it'd be easier for everybody if she up and left *The Pines*. So Leland gave her a three-year-salary severance, plus a real good job as a French translator in his magazine publishing company up in Covington."

"So she left *The Pines?*"

"Sure did. Heartbroken and crying like all git out!"

"And Leland felt terrible bad, too. Went back to workin' too hard, and then started drinkin' too much after a while"

"That's too bad."

"Yeah, but Jackie didn't leave alone. . . ."

"Someone went with her?"

"Yep."

"Who?"

"Their baby."

EIGHTEEN

Quinn's jaw dropped open. "She left *The Pines* pregnant?"

Irene nodded. "Jackie didn't know it at the time, and neither did Leland, but she was one month pregnant with his child when she up and left *The Pines*."

Quinn's mind raced with the legal implications. "How did she *know* it was Leland's child?"

"Jackie said it couldn't be nobody else's!"

"So then what happened?"

"Well, when Zelda found out Jackie was carrying his child - Zelda throwed a fit! She said Jacqueline could never tell Radford! Threatened her real bad!"

"With what?"

"Deportation. See, Jacqueline had entered the United States sorta illegal. Zelda threatened to sic Immigration on her and send her back to Martinique."

"So did Jacqueline agree to *never* tell Radford?"

"Yes. She was *scared* to go back to Martinique! See, a man back there swore to kill her for testifying against him. And his brother damned near killed her once or twice! Her folks snuck her into America."

Quinn nodded.

"And the other thing is she wanted her baby borned in America."

"So what happened?"

"Zelda happened. She took over everything. Handled Jackie's pregnancy and birth."

"And Jacqueline had the baby?"

"Oh, yes." Irene smiled bright as a Hawaiian sunrise. "A healthy baby boy."

"So did Jacqueline ever show the boy to Mr. Radford?"

"Oh Lordy no! Zelda never let Jackie or her baby anywheres near *The Pines.* Wouldn't even let Jacqueline phone Leland or me! She changed all the phones, blocked the new numbers. Told Leland that Jacqueline went back to Martinique, got married later. Wasn't no email or cellphones in those days."

"So where are Jacqueline and her son now?"

Irene slumped in her chair, took a deep breath and closed her eyes. When she opened them, Quinn noticed they were wet.

"What's wrong?"

"Three months after she gave birth, Jacqueline died in a car accident out there on 421."

Quinn felt his stomach twist.

"But praise the Lord, her son was not with her!"

"What happened to him?"

"Zelda adopted him out!"

"To whom?"

"I could never find out. Only Zelda knew. There was a rumor it mighta been a couple up in Dayton or Detroit. I asked her several times, but she flat out refused to tell me."

Quinn shook his head in amazement. "Zelda seems like a real warm person, huh?"

"Only time Zelda warmed up was when she died."

Quinn smiled. "Why didn't *you* tell Leland about his son?"

"Zelda threatened me bad too."

"To fire you?"

"Worser!"

She sipped her coffee, bit her lower lip, as though deciding how much to tell him. "See, when I was twenty-two, a man named Dontrell down in West Virginia where I'm from, he tried to rape and stab me dead in our garage. He left this on me!"

She ran her finger along a thick gray eight-inch scar on her forearm.

"Dontrell had done kilt one of his rape victims and got away with it. Man's crazier than a shithouse rat! He run at me, unzippin' his pants and swingin' his Johnson. Well, I swung a crowbar hard into it and Dontrell buckled over and commenced to groaning like he was birthin' a baby! I run off, told the police. Then at trial, I testified against him and sent him to prison for life. Dontrell swore that he'd break out and kill me. Seven years later, he did break out. But he didn't know I was over here in Kentucky. Then he flat-out disappeared. I been scared he'd find me ever since. Still am."

Her eyelids fluttered like a spinning window shade.

Quinn placed his hand on her to calm her.

"Anyways, Zelda somehow found out about Dontrell. Then she hired a private detective who found Dontrell hiding out down in Mexico. Showed me a picture of him wearing a sombrero. Zelda said if I told Leland about his son, she'd sic Dontrell on me. She would too!"

Quinn was stunned. "There's an important legal term for someone like Zelda?"

"What's that?"

"*Bitch!*"

Irene laughed and slapped her thigh. "That's a true fact!"

"So Radford never knew he had another son?"

"No sir! Not until I told him the day before he died. Lord, Leland was so happy when I told him! He cried. I cried. Even the nurse cried. Leland told me he had loved Jacqueline all these years and asked me to try to find his boy so he could meet him. He wanted his son to inherit everything."

Quinn swallowed. "He said that to you?"

"He sure did. Twice."

"Do you remember exactly what he said, Irene?" Quinn's heart began to pound.

"Uh-huh. He said, 'Above all, find my son. I want him to inherit my estate, everything, 'cept what I leave you and the rest of my staff and the charities.' And the nurse lady heard him say it, too."

Quinn scribbled the words in his notebook. He realized the probate case had just been blown wide open.

"What'd Jacqueline name the boy?"

"Been tryin' to remember his name, but cain't. I only heard his name once't through the grapevine. Then a week later, Jackie was dead."

"Any idea where the boy is now?"

Irene shook her head. "Only Zelda knew and the secret died with her. I've been trying to find him, with no luck. That's how's come I'm talking to you."

"Why didn't you ever tell Mr. Radford's attorney, Fletcher Falcone, about the boy?"

"Zelda said if I told Falcone, he'd hafta tell Radford, and then Zelda would know I told Falcone. And then she'd tell Dontrell where I was at."

Fear flashed in her eyes.

"Irene, you're safe now. I'll help you. But we're required to inform Falcone about this. He needs to place a legal notice in the newspaper to try to notify the boy, who's now a young man, to come forward before the probate court date in a few days."

"I understand."

"Falcone will also need to take your sworn affidavit, a legal statement about all this."

"Any time he wants."

Irene seemed to relax from finally unloading the heavy secret she'd been forced to carry for too many years. Quinn could see it had been very painful for her. And he was pleased to now see great relief in her eyes.

One second later, she looked terrified.

Quinn turned and saw why.

Irene was staring at the tall black man who'd just walked into the restaurant.

NINETEEN

Irene Whitten relaxed as she got a better look at the tall black man who walked in the Huddle House.

"Ain't Dontrell!" she said, setting her knife back on the table.

Quinn was relieved to see Irene relax.

Suddenly, she stood up. "Well, Quinn, I got to get back to *The Pines*. Thanks a bunch for listenin' and helpin' me."

"Sure. If you remember the boy's name, let me know."

"I will."

They walked out, said goodbye and drove off.

As Quinn drove back to meet with Ellie Stuart, he thought about the mindboggling implications of what Irene Whitten had told him.

Leland T. Radford had a second son, a son that his estate executor, Fletcher Falcone, knew nothing about.

Quinn had to let Falcone know now.

Quinn dialed his direct line and was relieved when he picked up.

"Falcone."

"Quinn Parker."

"Hey, Quinn, you have a good chat with old Irene?"

"Yes sir, I sure did."

"Betcha five bucks she whomped on Zelda!"

"You'd win five bucks!"

Falcone chuckled. "Oil and water, those two. Like I told you, after Leland's wife died, Zelda moved in and ran *The Pines* like a Parris Island drill sergeant. She was a vile, nasty woman! She despised Leland's staff, nice folks, especially Irene. Treated them like dirt."

"I got that impression."

"So, did you learn what you needed to know about Radford?"

"Yes, sir I did."

"Good."

"I also learned something *you* need to know about Radford."

"What's that?"

"Leland Radford had another son."

The line was silent so long Quinn thought his phone dropped the call.

"What did you –?"

"Radford had a son by a housekeeper at *The Pines,* a woman named Jacqueline Moreau."

Long pause. "Jackie Lynn who . . .?"

"No. Jacqueline M-o-r-e-a-u."

"But Radford would have told me!"

"He didn't know."

"How could he not know his housekeeper was pregnant? He saw her every day."

"She left *The Pines* when she was only a month pregnant. *She* didn't even know she was pregnant."

Long pause. "Well, I will be damned! If this doesn't beat all!"

"When Zelda found out, she blackmailed Jacqueline into not telling Radford she was pregnant with his child."

"Blackmailed her?"

"Threatened to have her deported back to Martinique."

"Jesus! But why the hell didn't Irene just come and tell *me* about all this. I could have sorted things out."

"She *couldn't* tell you. Zelda blackmailed Irene, too."

Falcone sputter himself into a cough. "What a witch!"

"So it seems. But Irene had more to say."

"What?"

"An hour after Zelda died, Irene went to Radford's hospital room and finally told him he had another son. Radford was overwhelmed with joy. Said he always loved Jacqueline. Said the worst mistake he ever made was letting her leave *The Pines*. And he told Irene to please go find his son because he wanted him to inherit his estate."

Falcone's cough sounded like gravel shaking in a tin can. "Radford said *those words?*"

"Basically, yes."

"Will Irene swear to that under oath?"

"She will."

"Good Lord Almighty! We gotta find the son fast! Where is he now?"

"Irene has no idea. Zelda kept everything secret!"

"What? What about the boy's mother, this Jacque . . .?"

"Jacqueline."

"Where's she now?"

Quinn paused. "Sadly, she died in a car accident when the boy was a baby."

"Good Lord!"

"And then, Zelda handled the boy's adoption."

"To whom?"

"Only Zelda knew . . . and the answer died with her."

"Damm! This keeps getting worse, Quinn. What's this boy's name?"

"Irene's trying to remember it."

"Awww shit! No first name. No last name. No name of the adoptive parents. No date of birth. Dead mother. I've got nothing to work with here, Quinn." Falcone coughed hard again.

"I sorry, Mr. Falcone. That's all Irene knew."

"How am I going to find this boy?"

"I don't know, sir."

"If he knew Radford was his father, he probably would have come forward by now, right?"

"Right."

"Boy, Quinn, this changes everything. I'll put out a legal notice immediately in the local media. But I can't even put in his *name,* or the date he was born . . . and I sure as hell can't run a notice in every damn newspaper in the country."

"Try the Internet. Put a notice on those sites that connect children with birth parents and vice versa. And try Facebook and Twitter."

"Good ideas. But I gotta get my ass in gear. Our probate court date is just days away!"

"Good luck, sir!"

"Thanks, Quinn, for informing me. But if you or Irene remember anything else about the boy, let me know fast."

Falcone huffed a few times like he'd just sprinted a hundred-yard dash. Quinn was afraid the three-hundred-pound attorney might keel over any second.

"I will."

They hung up.

Quinn wondered if the son would ever see the notice. And if he did, would he realize he was Radford's son? The boy was only three months old when his mother died.

What if the son lived in another state or another country? Or serving in the military. He was the right age. What if by some incredibly cruel twist of fate the boy died in Iraq like his half-brother, Rick Radford?

But, if by some miracle, the boy was located, he'd have to prove that he was Leland Radford's son. And prove it in the next few days."

Quinn's cell phone rang. It was Irene.

"Quinn, I just remembered."

"What's that?"

"The name of Leland and Jacqueline's son. She named him Alex."

"Alex. That helps, Irene! Thanks."

He immediately phoned the boy's name to Falcone who sounded greatly relieved to at least have a first name to work with.

Moments later, he pulled in to a Phillips gas station and filled up. The station triggered another name. Maude Phillips. They'd dated his senior year, until she transferred to the University of Miami to study dolphins. Only time he lost a girlfriend to a fish. At Maude's farewell party, she introduced him to Jennifer. And when Maude moved to Florida, Jennifer moved to Quinn. She started hanging around his law school, phoning, inviting him to her sorority events, mildly stalking him until they began dating.

Jennifer was stunning, outgoing, and a DuBois, one of Kentucky's oldest and wealthiest families. In the beginning, Quinn was swept away by her lively beauty – and frankly by her family's affluence. He'd never known such wealth. Once, at her parents' home when the chef asked him what he'd like for lunch, he'd jokingly said a peanut butter sandwich. Quinn watched in awe as the chef took fresh cashews, peanut oil, brown sugar, molasses, and put them in fancy blender. One minute later, he ate the best peanut butter sandwich in his life.

Jennifer and he grew closer. But after a few months, he noticed a subtle, but disturbing change in her. She was demanding much more of his time. Time he didn't have because of his law studies, legal clinic hours, and his part-time job at the car dealership. She also kept suggesting he stop hanging with his football player buddies. She dismissed them as "knuckle-draggers" even though some had higher grade point averages than she did. But more than anything, it was Jennifer's need to know where he was, and with whom, at all times.

Clearly, it was time for a heart-to-heart talk, something he'd been putting off for too long.

He needed time apart from her, time to think.

It would be difficult for both of them.

TWENTY

Ellie saw Quinn's TrailBlazer turn into Carrie Ann's driveway. She said good-bye to Carrie Ann and her mother, then hurried out and got in.

"So how was your meeting with the housekeeper, Irene?"

"Incredible. Turns out, Leland Radford had - " Quinn froze, obviously realizing he shouldn't reveal anything more.

"Had what?"

He shook his head. "If I told you, I'd have to kill ya!"

"That's strict!"

He smiled, but wouldn't tell her.

Her cell phone rang and she answered. "Oh, hi, Judge Nesbitt."

She pushed the speaker button so Quinn could hear the Judge whom they'd visited earlier. Quinn leaned closer and she smelled his pleasant, lemon-scented aftershave.

"Ellie, I remembered something," the judge said. "You see, my brain's rustier than a wrench left out all winter. I jumpstart it with crossword puzzles. This morning I needed a seven-letter name for a pipe tobacco that started with a *D*."

Ellie wondered where the good judge was going with this.

"Then bingo, I remembered – *Dunhill*!"

Judge Nesbitt cleared his throat.

"See, there's a tall woman named Dunhill lives over in Barbourville. Drucilla Dunhill. Midwife. Delivers more babies than an obstetrician. Folks call her The Stork."

Ellie's pulse ticked up a notch.

"But Drucilla also is rumored to handle informal adoptions that, you know, circumvent the legal system. No official documents. Drucilla apparently delivers babies of young women who aren't capable of raising the infant due to young age, drugs or whatever. Drucilla finds only good homes for the babies. Never charges one red cent."

"But I was adopted here in *Harlan* County."

"Drucilla has delivered lots of babies to Harlan County and all over Kentucky. Even Tennessee. She worked mostly with the House of Grace, a good home that helps young pregnant girls and women. Mind you, Drucilla's no spring chicken!"

"Where's the House of Grace?"

"Also in Barbourville. Drucilla works with a woman there named ah . . . Mary Louise. If you see 'em, tell 'em I said hi . . . and good luck!"

"I will and thank you, Judge."

They hung up.

"That sounds promising," Quinn said. "And the House of Grace is right on our way back to Louisville."

"Great!" Ellie felt hope. *Just maybe Drucilla delivered me to the Stuarts . . . or knows who did . . . or maybe she even knows my mother!*

Ellie could barely contain her emotions as Quinn drove off. But a hundred yards later they came to an abrupt stop. A thick tree limb blocked most of the narrow country road.

Quinn started to back up and drive around it when they both heard a loud *BANG!*

A second later, something ripped into the car's roof pillar inches from Ellie's head.

"Ellie, get down! Someone's shooting!"

They ducked down to the floor. Ellie's finger hit 911.

★ ★ ★

Huntoon Harris cursed himself for missing the easy shot. He lay hidden in the forest, maybe ninety yards from where he'd dragged the big tree branch across the road.

But instead of driving over the small end of the branch, the Chevy driver backed up fast, screwing up the timing of his shot.

Huntoon flipped open his cell phone and reported in.

The boss was enraged, but gave him new marching orders.

Huntoon put away his Ruger.22 hunting rifle, took out his Glock and shoved in a full 15-round clip.

TWENTY ONE

"An officer's here, Ellie," Quinn said.
They stepped from the TrailBlazer, introduced themselves to the tall Harlan County deputy and explained what happened. The tall, muscular deputy, whose badge read Bill Greenlee, looked quite concerned. He fingered his moustache, then walked them around to the hole in the side roof pillar.

He aimed a pin-light into the hole. "Yep. That's a bullet down in there."

Ellie realized the bullet struck four inches from her head.

Officer Greenlee pulled on a latex glove, took out a skinny tool, pried the bullet out, studied it, then dropped it in a baggie.

".22 Hornet. Small hunting caliber. The angle suggests it came from over yonder. That forest."

Ellie looked over at the thick forest.

Greenlee nodded. "Folks hunt turkeys back in there a quarter mile. Not supposed to aim toward the road! But some idiots forget where this road is. These damn stray-bullets happen now and then. Could have caused a terrible accident!"

"We're not sure it's an accident," Ellie said.

"Why's that ma'am?"

She and Quinn explained about the attack by the van as she rode her bike to school and the red pickup truck that followed them around Harlan.

Officer Greenlee grew serious. "In that case, ma'am, I'm gonna check out who's huntin' with .22 Hornets in that forest today . . . and whether any of them drive red pickups. And if I find the guy, I'll question him. Where can I reach y'all?"

Ellie and Quinn handed him their phone numbers, thanked him and left as Officer Greenlee walked toward the woods.

Quinn drove toward Barbourville. Ellie emotions raced wild partly because a bullet had nearly slammed into her head. But mostly because she'd soon be at the House of Grace where she might meet Drucilla Dunhill and Mary Louise . . . two women who may have known her mother – and may still know her.

Quinn's phone rang. He answered, listened for a minute and hung up.

"That was my pal Tim at the State's Community Based Services. I'm sorry, Ellie, but Tim can't find any record of your adoption in the state files or in Harlan County's. He even checked Indiana and Tennessee databases and came up empty."

Ellie nodded. "Did he search for my birth record?"

Quinn paused. "Tim found nothing, Ellie. Sorry."

Ellie slumped in her seat. The familiar frustration flooded back.

"How can there be no records of my birth or adoption?"

Quinn shook his head. "I wish I knew, Ellie."

"It's natural to want to know your biological parents . . ."

"Of course."

"Not knowing them makes me feel . . . I don't know . . . disconnected from my ancestors, my natural family . . . maybe unwanted . . . like a feather blowing in the wind."

Quinn started to speak, stopped, then placed his hand on hers. It felt comforting.

She remembered the first time she wondered whether Joyce and Harold Stuart were her natural parents. She'd been on an eighth grade school bus trip to Cumberland Falls. Their teacher pointed to a magical mist hovering over the waterfall and told them all to make a wish.

The mist created a stunning white arc in the night sky . . . a Moonbow. Ellie looked at the Moonbow and wished for a college scholarship. Years later, her Moonbow wish came true – she was awarded a full scholastic scholarship to the University of Louisville.

The Cumberland Falls class trip had been great fun until the bus ride home . . . when Lurleen Gatlin, Queen of the Mean Girls, walked up the bus aisle, pointed at Ellie and announced in a loud voice for everyone to hear, "My Momma says you gotta be 'dopted, cuz you ain't lookin' nothin' like what them Stuarts does. Momma says them Stuarts pulled you out of a garbage can."

Ellie's face turned beet red. Lurleen's words had hurt because some people laughed, but also because the words had the sting of truth. Ellie had wondered why she was taller and thinner and lighter skinned than Harold and Joyce.

Now, years later, she checked herself in her visor mirror. She *did* look different than the Stuarts. Her face was thinner, and she had higher cheekbones and blue eyes, not brown like theirs.

As to Mean Lurleen, word was she worked at Popeyes Chicken on the gravy machine and weighed two hundred fifty pounds.

"Hey there," Quinn said, "You're kinda quiet."

"Just thinking . . ."

"About what?"

"Well, what if my mother was not the wonderful mother I've always pictured – the woman who wept and gnashed her teeth as I was ripped from her arms? Maybe she couldn't wait to dump me! Maybe my father was an axe-murderer!"

Quinn looked at her. "Maybe you'd rather visit the House of Grace another day?"

"No. I've waited too long for *this* day."

"Good. Because we're here."

He pointed up at the House of Grace, a massive, three-story Victorian home set high on a hill.

* * *

Huntoon Harris had kept his black Navigator a few vehicles behind the TrailBlazer. He'd been told to follow Ellie and Quinn, and report where they went. He watched them park in front of a rambling three-story house.

Why here? he wondered, sipping vodka from his flask.

Huntoon made a call. The man answered on the first ring.

"They just parked in front of a place called the *House of Grace.*"

The man cursed under his breath for several seconds.

"When they come out, check their faces. Let me know if they seem pleased or happy."

"What do I do if they seem pleased or happy?"

"Then you have an assignment."

"What?"

"The same assignment you just fucked up in Harlan!"

TWENTY TWO

BARBOURVILLE

Ellie stared up at the charming House of Grace, a licensed and highly respected home for unwed mothers according to her Google search. The large three-story 1930s home sported a fresh coat of white paint and a roof that sloped down to eaves with charming blue trim. A bay window jutted out into a garden where pink and blue tulips surrounded by rows of white peonies.

At the front door, she and Quinn paused at a life-sized statue of a young mother holding her infant.

Did my mother hold me like this . . . perhaps right on this spot?

In the lobby, they approached a red-haired teenage receptionist working on an iPad lodged atop her very pregnant stomach.

Ellie explained why they were here.

"Oh, y'all wanna talk to Director Smythe. She's down that hall. Last office."

They thanked her, walked down the hall, passing a pregnant teenager laughing on her cell phone, and stepped into Director Smythe's small, wood-paneled office. Smythe, around fifty, was on the phone and waved them into two pink velvet chairs faded by the sun pouring through the window.

Ellie looked around. Walls filled with numerous professional awards, a Ph.D. in Sociology from the University of Kentucky and photos of smiling young mothers with babies. Smythe was a trim woman with large green eyes framed by salt and pepper hair. Her blue blazer, rimless glasses and immaculate desk suggested a buttoned-up Director.

She hung up, smiled at them, and extended her hand. "Ashley Smythe. Welcome."

Ellie and Quinn shook her hand and introduced themselves.

"How can I help you?"

Ellie leaned forward. "Judge Nesbitt over in Harlan suggested we might talk to a Drucilla Dunhill here. He said Drucilla sometimes delivers babies from here to families in the area, including Harlan."

"That's true. But sadly, Drucilla passed away two years ago."

"Oh . . ." Ellie felt her hope fade.

"Drucilla was a wonderful woman. Handled many of our babies."

"I may be one of them. I was delivered to Harold and Joyce Stuart over in Harlan twenty-one years ago. They've since passed away."

"Oh, I'm sorry, Ellie." Smythe seemed genuinely saddened by the news. "I wasn't here back then, but Drucilla's old file should tell us if she delivered you from here to the Stuarts. Let's take a look."

She unlocked a nearby cabinet and took out a metal box. She unlocked it, flipped through a stack of large index cards and moments later pulled one out.

"Here we are. Drucilla picked up a baby girl here and delivered her to Harold and Joyce Stuart in Harlan."

"That's me!" Ellie's heart pounded. "Does it mention my mother's name?"

Dr. Smythe looked at the back of the card.

"No. It doesn't, Ellie. Sorry."

"Could her mother's name be in your computer files?" Quinn asked.

"It should be. Since you were picked up here. Let me look."

"Thank you."

"But Ellie, as you probably know, whether we can reveal your mother's name depends on whether she gave us permission to."

"I understand."

"Most mothers who give up their babies don't give permission."

"I know, but I've heard some mothers permit the release of non-identifying information, like age, ethnicity, and the general area where they live?"

"That's true, but again the mother decides if we're allowed to release that information."

Dr. Smythe turned her computer screen away from them, then typed on the keyboard. She typed some more and waited. Her face revealed nothing. After several more commands, she faced them.

"That's quite strange."

"What?"

"Even though Drucilla's card indicates you were picked up here, there's no record in our files that your mother, or you, ever stayed at the House of Grace."

Frustration hit Ellie like a screen door.

Quinn leaned forward. "Judge Nesbitt also mentioned another woman who works here. Mary Louise . . ."

Ashley Smythe fell back in her chair and lowered her head.

"What's wrong?" Ellie asked.

Smythe's eyes moistened and she took a deep breath. "Two nights ago . . . Mary Louise was . . . *murdered!* The police say the poor woman was smothered in her bed. Mary was a wonderful person. I loved her . . ."

"I'm very sorry . . ." Ellie said.

No one spoke for a few moments. Ellie felt like steel bands were squeezing her chest.

"But if Drucilla's file said she picked me up here, why would my records be missing from your *computer* files?"

"That makes no sense, Ellie. The state board requires very accurate computer records."

"How many people have access to your confidential computer files?" Quinn asked.

"Only my assistant and I."

Quinn nodded. "But maybe someone hacked in and *deleted* Ellie's records."

Ashley Smythe frowned. "I'm told we have an excellent computer security. But I guess if hackers can break into the Pentagon files and the Director of the CIA's files, they can break into ours and delete records."

"But *why? Why* would anyone *want* to delete *my* records?"

Smythe shrugged. "It sounds like your adoption was illegal, Ellie. In other words, there's no paper trail . . . maybe because someone doesn't want you discovering your birth parents."

No one spoke for several moments.

Ellie handed Smythe her card. "Well, Director, thank you for your time, and if you find anything in your old files, please call me at any time."

"I will, Ellie. And good luck."

"Thank you."

Ellie and Quinn turned to go.

"Ellie . . .?" Smythe said.

"Yes?"

"Remember, your birth mother might be trying to find you . . . as much as you're trying to find her."

"I hope so."

TWENTY THREE

As they walked down the House of Grace hallway, Ellie wondered if she was never meant to know her birth mother. Maybe fate was shielding her from some godawful truth about the woman.

Still, whatever it took, however long it took, Ellie would not stop until she knew her mom.

I was picked up here. My mother had been pregnant with me here, had walked down this same hallway. And Ellie wanted to savor the closeness a few more minutes.

She saw a sign above a hall door. *Café Bébé.*

They looked inside the empty café. It was decorated with pink and blue teddy bear wallpaper, pink and blue tables and chairs, even pink and blue vending machines. Wall charts displayed pre-natal exercises.

"My treat," Ellie said. "Coffee with sugar, right?"

"Right."

She dropped coins in the vending machine, got two coffees and handed one to Quinn, suddenly remembering that it was her *spilled coffee* at the U of L student center that brought this helpful guy into her life.

"I've come to an obvious conclusion," Quinn said as they sat down.

"That someone intentionally deleted all information about my birth parents."

"Yep."

Behind her, pans rattled. She turned and saw a heavyset, sixty-something woman in a blue *House of Grace* uniform arranging pans behind a food counter. Her badge read *LORETTA MAE.*

Loretta Mae smiled at them. "Y'all visitin' one of our girls?"

"No, ma'am. Just visiting."

Loretta Mae's dark hair was tied back in a bright red bow. Smooth ebony skin framed her big warm smile. She took out a large serving dish of meat loaf.

"*You* one of our girls?"

"I think so."

"What's your name, child?"

"Ellie Stuart. Twenty-one years ago, Drucilla Dunhill picked me up here and delivered me to my adoptive parents in Harlan."

"Drucilla was a fine woman. She find only the best parents."

"She did for me!"

Loretta Mae smiled, then scrunched up her chubby face as though studying Ellie. "Betcha you tryin' to find your birth momma."

"Yes, ma'am. Were you here twenty-one years ago?"

"Hon, I was here when Dan'l Boone come through."

Ellie laughed loud – which caused Loretta Mae to put down the meat loaf and stare at her.

"What's wrong?"

"Your *laugh!*"

"What about it?"

"Sounds kinda familiar to me! Laugh agin for me!"

Ellie tried the same high loud laugh, but missed by several decibels.

Loretta Mae studied her face, then blinked as though searching her memory.

"Twenty-one years ago?"

"Yes, ma'am."

"What month wuz you borned in, hon?"

"December . . ." *If the date on my fake birth certificate is right.*

Loretta Mae closed her eyes a few moments, then ran her hand over her face. "December . . . twenty-one years ago."

"Yes, ma'am."

Loretta Mae took out a big dish of jello, then stared at the wall. All of a sudden, she smiled like the Cheshire cat.

"I know'd yo' momma."

Ellie's heart stopped.

"Know'd yo' momma good! She pretty jes' like you. Lord knows you got her big eyes and her mouth. And lots of hair jes' like hers, maybe a little browner. And you got her laugh – that's a true fact!"

"You knew my mother?"

"Sho' did. Sweet young thing."

Ellie stood up, her heart pounding like a jackhammer, her mind spinning. "Did she come from around here?"

"Oh no. She come from far away, she did."

"Another county?"

"No."

"Another state?"

"No, hon, 'nother *country*. One of them foreign ones."

Ellie couldn't speak.

"She had an accent, too!"

"My mother was foreign? What was her name?

"Les see . . . somethin' like . . . Genevieve, or Jeanne . . . or Janine . . . no, been so long, shoot!"

Ellie leaned forward in her chair, waiting.

Loretta Mae closed her eyes and shook her head. "Wait, I 'member now!"

"What?"

"*Jacqueline!*"

Quinn spurted his coffee all over the table.

TWENTY FOUR

*W*hat's with Quinn? Ellie wondered. *Doesn't he realize he's just spewed hot coffee all over his chin and shirt?*

His stared at Loretta Mae as though she'd just levitated.

"*Jacqueline's* my mother's name?"

"That's right, hon!"

"Did she have a French accent?" Quinn asked.

"Sho did! All time say stuff like *'Bonjour'*, and *'oui, oui!'*"

"Do you recall her *last* name?" Quinn asked, leaning forward, as coffee dribbled down his chin.

"Uh-uh. We jes' go by first names 'round here."

"Who brought her here to the House of Grace?" Ellie asked.

Loretta Mae closed her eyes for several moments. "Older woman. Bossy old battle-axe, you ask me. Nasty mean! Look like a catfish. The kind of woman who'd throw a drowndin' man both ends of the rope."

"Her mother?"

"No way! That woman wasn't no kin neither, Jackie told me. But that nasty old woman, she run the show. Bossin' Jackie 'round like a little kid. Jackie didn't like her one dang bit!"

"Do you remember the nasty woman's name?" Quinn asked.

Why is Quinn so obsessed with names? Ellie wondered.

Loretta Mae closed her eyes. "No. The woman only come here once't . . . maybe twice't. I never spent no time wit' her. Thank you Jesus!"

"Was I born here?"

Loretta Mae shook her head. "No, hon. See, 'bout three weeks before you was fixin' to be borned, the mean woman, she come back here and took yo' momma away."

"Took her where?"

"I din't never find out. . . ."

"So maybe I was born in a local hospital."

"Uh-uh. Me and Mary Louise checked all the local hospitals. They din't have no record of your momma, or you being borned there."

Loretta Mae's eyes suddenly filled with tears.

"What's wrong?" Ellie asked.

"Poor Mary Louise, bless her. She was kilt in her own bed the other night. Murdered! She never hurt nobody! Mary was my bes' friend here. She know'd your momma good. She know'd who you daddy was. But she would never tell." Loretta Mae sat down and closed her eyes.

"I'm sorry, Loretta Mae . . ."

Loretta Mae nodded.

Ellie waited for the woman to compose herself. Moments later, she did.

"So, after my mother left here, did you see her again?"

Loretta Mae smiled. "Sho' did. After you wuz born, your momma, she bring you here to show me and Mary Louise a few times. You wuz cute as a bug's ear! Still are."

Ellie felt herself blush.

"Do you remember what my mother named me?"

Loretta Mae closed her eyes. "Les' see . . . your momma, she give you a different kinda name. Lordy, lemme think on it. . . . Cassandra . . . no . . . Annabelle . . . no . . . Antoinette, no! Dadgummit, it ain't comin' to me cuz I'm tryin' too hard. Betcha I wake up wit it tonight."

"If you do, please call me right away." She gave Loretta Mae her phone number.

Loretta Mae nodded, then reached into the sink, grabbed a dirty frying pan, sprinkled some cleanser onto it and started scrubbing.

Then she stopped cold and stared wide-eyed at the can of cleanser for several moments. Then she smiled, turned and faced Ellie.

"I 'member!"

"What?"

"The name what yo' momma give you."

Loretta Mae held up a can of Ajax.

"My mother named me . . . Ajax?

Loretta Mae laughed and slapped her thigh. "No, hon. Your momma named you *Alex!*"

Quinn spurted the rest of his coffee halfway across the cafeteria.

TWENTY FIVE

"*Alex?*" Quinn said, staring at Loretta Mae, coffee dripping from his face.

"That's right!"

"You're absolutely positive?"

"'Course I am!"

"Why are you freaking out over the names?" Ellie asked.

"Because the names are freaking me out!"

"Why . . . ?"

"Because two hours ago, Irene Whitten, Leland Radford's housekeeper, the woman I met in the Huddle House in Harlan, gave me two names."

Ellie waited.

"Jacqueline and Alex, her baby *boy*."

Ellie stared back, amazed that Quinn heard the same two names in two different towns within a couple of hours.

"Irene told me that many years ago, Leland Radford and his housekeeper, a woman named Jacqueline Moreau, had a baby boy, and Jacqueline named it Alex."

"But *that* Alex was a *boy!*" Ellie said.

"Maybe not."

"Why not?"

"Because Irene never saw Jacqueline's baby. Wasn't allowed to. She wasn't even allowed to see or talk to Jacqueline on the phone after she left *The Pines.* So Irene *assumed* Alex was a boy. But in France Alex is also a girl's name."

Speechless, Ellie stared at Quinn.

"Radford never even knew Jacqueline had his baby."

"Why?"

"Because Zelda, Radford's sister, the mean woman Loretta Mae just mentioned, blackmailed Irene to never tell him. He only learned of his baby the day before he died."

Ellie tried to speak, but nothing came out.

"Loretta Mae?" Quinn said. "Are you absolutely positive that Jacqueline here had a baby *girl?*"

"Damn sho' am!"

"And named her *Alex?*"

"That's right."

"But how can you be so positive that Ellie here is Jacqueline's baby Alex?"

"'Cuz she got her momma's face and hair. And she laugh 'jest like her. And listen here . . . old Loretta Mae done changed your diapers a few times, girl!"

She smiled, walked over, bent down and said, "I'll eat live lizards if y'all ain't gotta birthmark shaped like Florida on your left butt, right about chere!" She touched Ellie's upper left butt . . . an inch from her birthmark . . . *shaped like Florida.*

Ellie laughed out loud. "You're right! My name is *Alex!*"

"'Course it is!"

Ellie felt warm tears spill from her eyes.

Quinn walked over and hugged her. So did Loretta Mae.

Ellie whispered, "You knew my mom . . ."

"Knew her right good." Loretta Mae handed Ellie a glass of water. She sipped some, wiped her eyes, then hugged the large woman again. "Thank you so much, Loretta Mae. Thank you so very much . . ."

"You're welcome, chile. Your momma wuz sweet as sugar pie! Smart as a whip, too. And fun? Lord, that girl make me fall down laughin', she truly did."

"Do you have any idea where she lives now?"

Loretta Mae's smile sank like a winter sun. She turned and looked out the window for several moments, then slowly faced Ellie with moist eyes.

"She wit the Lord, hon."

Ellie slumped back in her chair.

"A few months after you wuz born, your momma died in a car accident out on 421. Rainy night, bad curve. Police said a big black tarp blowed off a truck, covered her whole windshield. Couldn't see a lick. She crashed down into a ravine thousand feet below. I cried most a week."

Ellie felt nauseated as fresh tears welled up. She had found . . . and lost her mother in five minutes.

"That confirms it!" Quinn said, wiping coffee from his chin.

"Confirms what?"

"What Irene told me. Jacqueline Moreau died in a car accident when her baby was an infant."

No one spoke.

Loretta Mae placed her hands on Ellie's shoulders. "Listen to old Loretta, chile. Yo' momma loved you more than you can know. She held you all the time, kissed you and nursed you and sing them pretty French songs and you smiled up at her . . . and that's a fact!"

Ellie *felt* her mother's love flowing through Loretta Mae's hands into her, like her mother was actually here again, holding her in her arms. And it felt wonderful.

"Please tell me about her."

And Loretta Mae did. Each story revealed a kind, smart, funny, attractive young woman, the mother Ellie had long prayed for. And best of all, a mother who *wanted* her!

"Thank you, Loretta Mae."

"You're welcome, chile."

"If you remember anything else, please call me." She gave Loretta Mae her phone number.

"Sho' will."

They thanked Loretta Mae again, stepped outside and headed toward Quinn's TrailBlazer. Even the light drizzle couldn't wipe the smiles from their faces.

"What now?" Ellie asked.

"Now we go visit the soon-to-be-shell-shocked Fletcher Falcone, Executor and Attorney at Law, and suggest he seriously amend the Radford will. Fast."

* * *

"They're laughin' and smilin' as they're walking out of the House of Grace," Huntoon Harris said on his phone as he watched Ellie Stuart and Quinn Parker hurry toward the TrailBlazer.

The boss cursed a blue streak.

Huntoon knew when to stay quiet.

"Here's what you do . . ."

TWENTY SIX

As Quinn and Ellie drove away from the House of Grace, she tried to picture the wonderful mother Loretta Mae had just described.

If only I could have known her, talked with her, done things together, learned about our family. What did she look like? Will Irene, the housekeeper at The Pines, have a photo?

"You excited?" Quinn asked.

"Does a wild *ursus defaecare in forestis?*"

"You bet wild bears shit in forests. So do I in a pinch."

She laughed as Quinn passed an orange Allied Van Lines truck.

"Where's your head?" he asked.

"In spin cycle. *Finally*, I may know who my birth mother was."

"And most probably, your birth father."

"*If* Irene is right. Did you learn much about Mr. Radford?"

"Only that he was a successful, well-respected and generous man."

"That's good to know."

"And oh yeah, one other thing."

"What?"

"He was fabulously wealthy. Ellie, you realize you may be the heiress to his massive fortune."

"*If* I'm his daughter."

"You gotta be."

"How can you be so sure?"

"The facts, ma'am."

"What facts?"

"First, Irene the housekeeper swears Jacqueline Moreau and Leland Radford only had eyes for each other and were very much in love."

"Right."

"Second, Irene said Jacqueline was one month pregnant when she left *The Pines.*"

"Right."

"Third, Loretta Mae swears Jacqueline was very pregnant with you at the House of Grace."

"Right."

"Fourth, both Irene Whitten *and* Loretta Mae said Jacqueline gave birth to a baby named Alex nine months after leaving *The Pines.*"

"Right."

"Fifth, both Irene and Loretta Mae said that sadly, Jacqueline died in a car crash a few months after giving birth to Alex."

Ellie nodded and felt a wave of sadness hit her again.

"Sixth, Loretta Mae says Jacqueline's baby, Alex, was a *girl.*"

"Right."

"Seventh, you're a girl!"

"Thanks for noticing."

"Eighth, Jacqueline's baby girl Alex was delivered to the Stuarts in Harlan by a woman named Drucilla Dunhill."

"Right."

"And ninth, and most compelling, Loretta Mae says the baby Alex had a birthmark on her left butt – "

" – leave my butt out of this!"

103

"Your butt's too big to leave out!"

She tried to elbow him, but missed.

"Putting my butt aside for the moment, there's one other strong possibility," she said.

"What?"

"My mother had another . . . lover."

Quinn shook his head. "Not according to Irene. She insists Jacqueline and Leland were completely in love. Your mother brought him out of his depression that lasted many years after his wife died."

She nodded. "Please tell me everything Irene said about him and his family."

Quinn told her.

When he finished, Ellie shook her head and said, "Wow - Mr. Radford's half-sister, Zelda, sounds like an angel."

"Think Lucifer.

Ellie nodded and looked at Quinn. She was suddenly overwhelmed for all he'd done for her. His consideration in driving her to Harlan and the House of Grace, his legal advice, his discovery of Jacqueline Moreau – and then his connecting the dots from Jacqueline back to her. It was a miracle. Far more than she could ever have hoped for. She was indebted to him forever!

She was also, unfortunately, finding herself attracted to him. Which was an absurd, no-win game, since he and stunningly beautiful, obscenely rich, debutante-to-be, Jennifer DuBois, were a serious couple. Jennifer turned men's heads like a red Lamborghini. Ellie turned heads like a rusty Farmall tractor.

"Thank you, Quinn, for everything."

"Hey, we got very lucky, Ellie. But now, I've got to tell Leland Radford's attorney, Fletcher Falcone. The man will go ape-shit when he learns about you."

"You have his number?"

Quinn fished Falcone's business card from his pocket and handed it to her. She dialed and Quinn punched the speaker button.

"Mr. Falcone's office. Ramada speaking."

"Hi, Ramada. This is Quinn Parker."

"Oh, hi, Quinn. Where you at?"

"Heading to your office."

"You wanna have drinks and go square-dancing later?"

Ellie watched Quinn's face turn pink.

"Well, I'm real busy today, Ramada. Sorry. Is Mr. Falcone there?"

"He's over at the airport donating some new radar equipment. He donates stuff to airports. He'll be back here in ten minutes."

"Is he a pilot?"

"No. But many years ago, his wife and twin nine-year-old daughters died when his airplane crashed in a storm down near Paducah."

"That's terrible."

"Yeah. And Mr. Falcone, well, he kinda blamed hisself. So ever since, he's donated radar and stuff to other small airports around the state."

"Good for him. Do you have his cell number, Ramada? It's quite important."

"Sure." She gave it to him.

He dialed and it rang.

"Falcone."

"Quinn Parker."

"Hey, Quinn, what's up?"

"You sitting down."

"I better be! I'm driving. Almost back at the office. Why?"

"Because I think I'm looking at the long-lost child of Leland Radford and his housekeeper, Jacqueline Moreau."

Long pause. "Good Lord, you already found his son, Alex?"

"Not exactly."

"What?"

"I found his *daughter,* Alex!"

A long pause, followed by a coughing fit.

"Hang on - are you saying Alex is a . . . *girl*?"

"Very much so."

"Jesus Christ and Mary on the handlebars!"

"Her mother was Jacqueline Moreau. She had Radford's baby *girl* and named her Alex."

"How in hell did you discover this?"

"At the House of Grace in Barbourville."

"The house of what . . .?" Falcone coughed again.

"I'll explain everything later."

"Where are you now?"

"Almost to your office."

"Good. Who'd you tell so far?"

"Only you."

"Bring her right to my office. We need to establish DNA proof of her relationship to Radford immediately. I'll line up the DNA test."

"We're on the way."

They hung up.

"Falcone has lots of work to get done fast," Quinn said.

"Like what?"

"Like adding a few codicils."

"What?"

"Modifications to the will, supplements. Lots of paperwork I imagine."

"But only *if* I'm Mr. Radford's daughter."

Minutes later, in the side mirror, Ellie saw a large black Navigator racing up behind them. Quinn was changing radio stations as he drove up a steep hill.

Ellie watched the Navigator start to pass – then swing directly in front of them, forcing them off the road.

"Quinn!"

Quinn slammed on the brakes, skidded to a hard stop on the shoulder of the road.

"Asshole!"

Ellie started to get out – but froze. She was staring down into a rocky ravine several hundred feet deep.

TWENTY SEVEN

BAGHDAD

Nafeesa Hakim adjusted her black veil as she strolled down Al-Nidhal Street in Baghdad's Green Zone. The cool night breezes from the Tigris River had swept away the vestiges of the hot steamy day and surrounded her with the sweet scent of roses.

The breeze also ruffled her long, silky black chador, revealing the short red dress beneath. Once inside the *La Sheik Bar*, she would take the veil and chador off. *La Sheik*, a saloon operated by Bech-Tech Construction out of Houston, was actually two double-length Windsor trailers welded together.

She caught a trace of her Chanel No 5 and hoped the nice young American contract worker she met in *La Sheik* last night would too. He obviously wanted the kind of companionship she could provide, and he could afford based on his Rolex.

Nafeesa couldn't believe how the war had brought her to this life. At least it brought Saddam to his well-deserved grave.

She thought back to the good days, back when her family had been middle-class, back when she won a scholarship to the American University of Iraq, back when her life was so full of hope . . .

Back to the night all hope died - when bombs killed her father and brothers, injured her mother, destroyed her family's business and the bank that held their family savings.

Overnight she had to support her mother, two sisters-in-law and their toddlers. She worked in three stores until they closed. Then a wealthy young Iraqi promised her a job and asked her to a dinner-interview. After dinner, he raped her and left her devastated. He also left her a thousand US dollars. Feeling ashamed and shattered, she grabbed the money and ran home. Weeks later, with no hope of jobs, she realized her body was the only way to feed her family. She became a licensed pleasure girl for some of Baghdad's elite young men and some U.S. military personnel.

Now, as she reached *La Sheik*, the door opened and out walked an old friend, Bob Darnell, ex-US Army, now a military advisor helping fight ISIS. She hadn't seen Bob in months. He'd introduced her to First Lieutenant Rick Radford - a man she'd cared deeply for until a roadside explosion took his life.

Bob Darnell saw her and smiled. "Hey, Nafeesa, how's it going?"

"Good, Bob. Where you been?"

"Top secret . . ."

She smiled at his stock answer. Nor did she want him to answer. Many Baghdad prostitutes sold information to Al Qaeda or to American and Mahdi soldiers. She refused to reveal information that might result in anyone's death.

"Actually, I went back to Najafi Street last week," he said.

Her stomach stiffened at *Najafi*. "Why go back? Najafi must be as painful for you as it was for me."

"Yes, but . . . well . . . some of Rick still lies in that field."

She nodded, her mind flashing back to when the enormous roadside IEDs blew Rick Radford and his two fellow soldiers over a seventy-yard area.

"I placed a plaque there in his honor," Bob said.

"Thank you."

He nodded. "By the way, Rick's father passed away a few weeks ago."

"Oh . . . I'm sorry." She paused a moment. "Rick told me he and his father were close."

"They were."

"He said his dad lived in a place called Kentucky on a big . . . how you say, ranch with horses?"

"Yes. His father was quite wealthy."

"Really?"

"Oh, yes."

She'd assumed Rick had come from money when he kindly offered to support her and her family if she stopped working the bars. She'd agreed on the spot, and their life together had been wonderful . . . until his death.

"I know you and Rick were close."

"We were very close," she said, meaning every word.

"Too bad he didn't marry you, Nafeesa. You might have inherited some money."

Rick and she talked of marriage just weeks before his death. Suddenly, a crazy idea flashed in her mind. Should she try it? What did she have to lose?

"Rick didn't tell you?" she asked.

"Tell me what?"

"I can't believe he didn't tell you."

"What?"

"Our secret. Two weeks before he was killed, we were married!"

Bob Darnell's mouth fell open.

"A small ceremony . . . here in Baghdad."

Darnell stared back. "But Rick would have told me."

"He *couldn't* tell you, Bob!"

"Why not?"

"He hadn't told his commander yet. But we married anyway. Spur of the moment. Kept it secret."

"Well, I'll be damned. Did you have witnesses?"

"Of course. Iraqi law requires two."

"Who were they?"

She scrambled for names. "You knew them, I think. Private Bray, the HumVee driver, and Corporal Rectenwald. They were with us when we decided to marry. But as you know, they both died with Rick in the explosion."

Nafeesa felt terrible lying about the two men.

"They were good soldiers. Who married you?"

Her mind searched for a name, then she remembered a recent obituary article in *Stars and Stripes.* "Father Perkins."

"The tall priest from Camp Victory?"

"Yes. A very nice man."

Darnell closed his eyes. "Aww shit!"

She knew why he was upset. "What's wrong, Bob?"

"ISIS terrorists killed him while he was saying Mass two weeks ago."

She closed her eyes and shook her head. "I hate war, Bob. Thousands of good and innocent people are dead. And for what?"

"I agree. But, listen Nafeesa, did you get an official marriage certificate?"

"Of course. From the Iraqi Social Status Court," she lied, wondering how she could get one. "I keep it to remind me of Rick and our brief time together."

She'd never been so thankful as the day Rick offered to support her and her family. Within weeks, their relationship had grown strong. She'd cared deeply for him, probably even loved him. And he seemed to love her, despite her background. Everything was wonderful.

And then he was gone . . .

"Guard the certificate with your life."

"Why?"

He paused. "You might be entitled to Rick's inheritance."

TWENTY EIGHT

After hanging up with Huntoon Harris, the man spun around in his three thousand dollar executive chair and watched the Ohio River flowing along nicely.

Things were not flowing along nicely for him. Ellie Stuart and Quinn Parker were causing problems, snooping around and uncovering information that had to remain buried.

If they didn't stop soon, *they'd* be buried.

After all, he'd *earned* the financial success he'd built over the years. He'd dedicated too much of his life to growing Radford's investments and achieving enormous wealth for the man. And in the process, for himself.

Like my four million dollar home in Indian Hills and membership in the exclusive Meadows Golf Club. A long way from the snake-infested shack on Florida's Lake Kissimmee where he grew up.

His mind flashed back to those days, back to the worst day in his life. He was nine and could still see his father trying to dislodge their outboard motorboat blades from the mangrove roots in the swamp

. . . still see the blades jerk loose and slice into his arm and shoulder and spew blood into the water

. . . still see the six alligators attacking, ripping into his arm and legs, and his father managing somehow with his good arm to push him up into the boat where he cowered, weeping, and watching as the gators ripped and gnawed his father to death.

A police boat rescued him.

But unfortunately, Florida Family Services then placed him with more dangerous reptiles: abusive foster parents. They were so cruel and abusive, he ran away three times before finally escaping. All of which taught him life's big lesson: do what you want, and take what your want.

Like his rightful chunk of the Radford probate revenue.

It was *his*. He'd earned it.

And he wasn't about to relinquish any of it to others.

TWENTY NINE

"Why do I feel like Cinderella?" Ellie said as Quinn parked near a massive, turn-of-the-century home with white and blue gingerbread trim. The sign in front read *Falcone & Partners.*

"Because your DNA slipper is going to fit!"

"How do you know?"

"Because people been shooting at you and trying to drive you and me off the road?"

She nodded.

As they walked toward the entrance, she looked up at the home's charming turrets, balconies, bay windows and lush gardens. She'd always dreamed of strolling through a beautiful Queen Anne style home like this, and now amazingly, maybe she could live in one if she was Mr. Radford's daughter.

They stepped inside the lobby. The blonde receptionist smiled big at Quinn and batted her eyelashes so rapidly Ellie wondered if she had Tourette's.

"Well, hey there, Quinn. How you doin'?"

"Just fine, Ramada . . ."

Ramada fiddled with an Elvis pendant hanging down between her large breasts. Elvis seemed to be singing *"The Hills are Alive."*

"This is Ellie Stuart."

Ramada stared at Ellie like she was trash stuck to Quinn's shoe.

"Mr. Falcone's 'specting y'all."

They followed Ramada down the hall toward Falcone's office. They entered, and saw Falcone on the phone. When he saw them, he smiled and ended his call. He hoisted his considerable girth and scurried around his desk.

Quinn introduced Ellie and they shook hands.

Falcone studied her face for several moments then smiled. "By golly, yes, I do see some resemblance. I swear I do. You've got Leland's blue eyes, and your cheekbones seem kinda similar. And well, you're tall like him. And your brown hair seems close to his brown before it turned gray."

Ellie was relieved to bear some resemblance to the man who might be her father.

"Please sit and tell old Fletcher how y'all figured all this out."

They told him about the House of Grace where Loretta Mae recalled Jacqueline had a baby girl named Alex . . . and how baby Alex was delivered to the Stuarts in Harlan.

Falcone wrote notes.

When they finished, Falcone sat back in his chair, took a deep breath, shook his head and smiled. "Incredible! Flat-out incredible!" He looked back at his notes.

"So, when Irene finally told Leland in the hospital that Jacqueline had their baby, both Irene and Leland figured the baby was a boy?"

"Right. Because Irene remembered the baby had a boy's name. Alex."

Falcone nodded. "And then Radford told Irene that he wanted the boy to be his heir, is that correct?"

"Yes. A nurse also witnessed Leland Radford make that statement."

"A nurse, too?" Falcone seemed surprised and made another note. "The nurse will help. Do you have her name?"

"Irene couldn't remember it."

"No problem," Falcone said. "We'll get the name. The hospital keeps photos of nurses. It's the law."

"Doesn't Kentucky law also require two witnesses to Mr. Radford's statement?" Quinn asked.

"That's correct, Quinn." Falcone stood and paced. "Well by golly, this sure does change everything y'all. And not a moment too soon. Our probate hearing is just days away. Lordy! I don't know about you two, but this old country lawyer needs a libation! Y'all want something?"

Ellie and Quinn declined.

Falcone poured two fingers of bourbon, gulped it down and plopped back down in his chair. He crammed a fistful of cashews into his mouth and munched away. Some crumbs tumbled out and got trapped between his double chins. Ellie thought he looked a little like Jabba the Hutt.

Ramada sashayed into the office. "They're ready for y'all over at the courthouse, Mr. Falcone."

Falcone turned toward Ellie. "Let's mosey over to the courthouse. A nurse from Manchester Hospital is there to take a sample of your DNA."

Two blocks later, Falcone escorted Ellie and Quinn between the gray pillars of the Clay County Justice Center. She felt reassured that a nurse would take her DNA sample in a courthouse.

Falcone led them down a hallway to a small meeting room where she saw a gray-haired woman in a Manchester nurse's uniform. Her hospital nametag said *Nessie Smith.* Beside Nessie sat a short woman with a courthouse ID badge. The two women sat at a conference table, smiling at something on a cell phone. Falcone introduced everyone.

"Y'all ready for us?" Falcone said.

"Yes, indeed," Nessie said, putting on a pair of surgical gloves. From her handbag, she took out a large tan Manchester Hospital envelope and removed four transparent plastic tubes, each containing a long Q-tip.

"Ellie, just rub these Q-tips against the inside of your cheek. Rub them hard so we get good DNA samples to work with."

Ellie swabbed each of the Q-tips against the inside of her cheek and handed them back to the nurse. The nurse placed the Q-tips back into their individual tubes and sealed them. Each tube had a bar code, a number, and *Ellie Stuart* typed on the side. Nessie placed the four tubes back in the hospital envelope and re-sealed it.

Then she stood up. "I'll have these DNA samples driven right over to Southern Genetic Lab in Lexington. It's one of the best in the state."

"How long for results?" Falcone asked.

"Usually five days. But I've asked for two-day turnaround, 'cuz I heard y'all got a probate court date coming up fast."

"That's right!" Falcone said.

Two days! Ellie thought, wondering if she could contain her excitement that long.

"In the meantime," Falcone said, flashing a big smile at Ellie, "I'll prepare contingency documents in the likelihood that you are Leland's daughter, because I'll tell you what - the more I look at you, Ellie, the more your eyes remind me of Leland's. And that's a fact!"

She smiled back.

"Any questions, Ellie?"

"Just a couple, sir."

"Ask away."

"Do you know where Jacqueline Moreau is buried?"

"I'm sorry, Ellie, I don't. In fact, I didn't even know about Jacqueline Moreau until Quinn told me earlier today."

"What about Mr. Radford?"

"Oh yes . . . Leland's buried up at *The Pines*. Private cemetery in the gardens out back. Irene can show y'all."

"Thank you."

Back outside, Ellie turned to Quinn. "Could we go briefly talk to Irene about Jacqueline and visit Mr. Radford's grave?"

"Take all the time you want, Ellie."

★ ★ ★

After trying - but failing - to force Quinn's TrailBlazer into a deep ravine, Huntoon Harris replaced his large black Navigator with a gray Nissan pickup.

Now, he sat in the pickup, reading an ad in *Soldier of Fortune* magazine. The ad for a security guard in the Middle East paid damn good money. Maybe he should consider the job. This Ellie Stuart job would be over after the probate hearing and he was tired of waiting for business to show up.

Be good to get back whacking towelheads again, and especially those ISIS assholes. Tomorrow, he call the ad's 800 number, check it out.

He looked up and saw Ellie and Quinn leave the law office, get in Quinn's TrailBlazer and drive off. He wondered where they were going now.

His phone rang and he answered.

"Call me on the CVS #4 phone in one hour," the caller said, then hung up.

THIRTY

Huntoon Harris kept his gray Nissan pickup six vehicles behind Ellie Stuart and Quinn Parker as they drove toward Leland Radford's estate, *The Pines.*

Harris grabbed his cell phone and called Bubba Leezer and Narvel Felps, his pals since Desert Storm where the Army unfairly and dishonorably discharged them all on the same day.

"Bubba . . .?"

"Yeah?

"You and Narvel got y'allself a job."

"How much?"

"Double yer rate."

"When?"

"Now."

"Talk to me."

Huntoon explained in detail what the boss wanted.

"Gotta be a accident?"

"Yeah."

"Just her?"

"Yeah. But the guy too if'n he gives you any shit!"

Bubba Leezer paused. "Well what if we can't make it look like no accident?"

Huntoon thought about that a bit. "Then do 'em like we done Cooter and his skanky bitch."

* * *

"Spittin' image!" Irene Whitten said, smiling at Ellie. "You got your momma's pretty face and hair, same high cheekbones too. And you're tall and curvy like Jackie. But your eyes, now them's your daddy's blue eyes! And that's a fact!"

Ellie and Quinn sat with Irene in the gazebo of the colorful flower gardens behind *The Pines.* Irene had just shared everything she remembered about Jacqueline Moreau and Ellie'd snatched up each detail like it was a gold nugget. Her mom was a smart, pretty, friendly, funny young woman with an unabashed *joie de vie,* as she might say.

"Your momma and daddy loved each other very much, Ellie."

Ellie smiled. "That means everything, Irene. Could you show us Mr. Radford's grave now?"

"Follow me, hon . . ."

They strolled behind the garden to a small white-fenced cemetery. Irene pointed to a new marble headstone marked *Leland T. Radford.* Ellie walked over and ran her fingers over his etched name and thought, *If you are my father, I'm honored, and hope I can live up to your expectations . . . If you're not my father, thank you for loving my mother.*

She paused, then turned to Irene. "Do you know where my mother is buried?"

Irene wrote out the directions.

Minutes later, in a tiny country cemetery, Ellie placed her hand on the small stained headstone of *Jacqueline Moreau.*

Sorry I'm late getting here, mom. Wish we could have known each other . . . but well . . . I'll learn more about you in the days ahead. And maybe even meet your family. Nothing could make me happier.

She looked at a photo of her mother that Irene gave her and felt her eyes moisten. She and her mother looked similar and seemed about the same height, 5'9". Ellie looked back at the headstone of the woman who brought her into this world . . . and felt a warm sense of calm and peace wash over her.

She walked back over to Quinn and showed him the photo of her mother.

"You *do* have her eyes," Quinn said.

"No way!"

"Why not?"

"Hers eyes are light brown, mine are blue."

"I meant your eyes are attractive and intriguing."

"Oh . . . "

Ellie blushed and wondered if by 'intriguing' he only meant that her right eye was lighter blue than the left one.

She paused, then looked at Quinn. "Thanks for driving me here, Quinn. It means more than you'll ever know. But I'm ready to go now."

As they drove off toward Louisville, she saw black clouds pushing across the evening sky. Wind gusts swayed the trees and a couple of fat raindrops splished onto the windshield.

"Storm ahead," Quinn said.

"Yeah, but nothing can rain on my parade today."

Quinn smiled.

Minutes later, a steady rain began to fall. Thunder rolled across the sky.

"You're tired," he said, glancing at her.

"Can you tell by my attractive and intriguing eyes?"

"Yep. Close those puppies and I'll wake you when we're back in Louisville."

"Okay." She closed her eyes and listened to the swish of the windshield wipers. A minute later, she felt herself growing sleepy, and soon after, drifting off . . .

THIRTY ONE

"*What the hell?*" Quinn shouted.

Ellie jerked wide-awake in her seat, wondering what was happening?

Quinn slammed on his brakes to avoid an old green RAM pickup swerving in front of him.

He tried to go around it, but was blocked in by a dented blue van.

"Quinn, what's hap – ?"

"Bad guys!"

The RAM pickup and van slowed in tandem, blocking Quinn in, forcing him to stop on the road's shoulder inches from a deep gulley. The van blocked him from the back.

"Quinn – the pickup man has a gun!"

Pickup Man, a big bullnecked guy in a faded Black Sabbath T-shirt jumped from the truck, waving his gun.

The van driver, skinny, wearing dirty bib overalls, aimed a sawed-off shotgun at them.

Ellie saw no other vehicles in the rearview mirror, but noticed the mirror's OnStar button and pushed it.

A second later –

"Mr. Parker?" the OnStar woman said, "is everything all right?"

"No!" Ellie whispered. "We've just been forced off the road by two armed men!"

OnStar woman paused and whispered, "I hear you."

Pickup Man whacked his gun barrel on Quinn's window. "Get the fuck out of the car now!"

"Okay," Quinn said.

Ellie saw him slide something from under his seat up into his sleeve.

"*NOW!*" Pickup Man screamed, his neck arteries bulging like computer cables.

"Okay, okay!" Quinn said.

She and Quinn got out slowly.

"Just take our money and leave," Quinn said.

"Shut the fuck up! I talk. You listen. Walk into that field!"

The two men forced her and Quinn through a wet, knee-high grassy field. Wet briars scratched her legs. Mud sucked at their shoes. Fifty yards in, they stopped behind a wall of evergreens.

"Take my wallet and credit cards," Quinn said. "I'll give you the PIN numbers." He tossed his wallet on the ground. "There's eighty dollars in it."

Van Man reached down and snatched the eighty dollars, but left the wallet there.

"Where's *your* wallet?" Pickup Man asked Ellie.

She held it out to him. As he took it, he rubbed his finger slowly along her finger, sending chills through her body. She jerked her hand away and stepped back.

Smiling, Pickup Man opened her wallet and studied her driver's license for several seconds as though making sure who she was. He grabbed her twenty-dollar bill, studied her license again, then tossed her wallet in the weeds.

He's after *me!* Ellie realized, her heart punching against her chest.

"What do you want?" Quinn said.

Pickup Man grinned, revealing stubby yellow teeth. "Well, see . . . life's kinda borin' back in these hills. Fella's gotta find hisself some fun."

"Go have fun with our credit cards," Quinn said, still concealing something up his sleeve. He looked angry and Ellie feared he'd attack despite the guns aimed at him.

Ellie held her breath.

"I'm thinking fun *here* and *now*, if you catch my drift," Pickup Man grinned.

Van Man snickered so loud, mucous shot from his nostril.

"Hey, Ellie," Pickup Man said, "les' you and me go over yonder, behind them bushes, and git nekkid."

"Save some for me," Van Man said, wiping his nose.

Then, she heard it . . . or maybe she thought she'd heard something. A very faint, brief, high-pitched wail beyond the nearby hills. It couldn't be the police. She'd only hit the OnStar button a couple minutes ago.

Ambulance? Fire engine?

The two thugs didn't seem to hear the sound. Nor did Quinn. Maybe she didn't. Maybe it was wishful hearing.

Pickup Man started pushing her toward the bushes.

Quinn stepped toward him.

"Whoa, big boy!" Van Man said, raising his shotgun. "Move another inch and I'll blow your fuckin' head off!"

Quinn looked like he might attack anyway.

Suddenly, a high-pitched wail blared from around the side of the big hill.

A siren!

Pickup Man and Van Man heard it.

As they spun toward the fast approaching siren, Quinn slid a large pipe wrench from his sleeve – and slammed it down on Van

Man's wrist, cracking bone and knocking his shotgun into nearby weeds.

Van Man screamed as though his arm had been amputated. It almost was - a jagged, bloody bone was sticking out.

"COPS!" Pickup Man shouted. "Run, Narvel!"

"But my fuckin' arm is all broke!"

"Run - or I'll break your fuckin' neck!"

Narvel, shrieking in pain, and Pickup Man ran back to their trucks, jumped in and raced off.

Quinn held Ellie in his arms until a Kentucky State Police car skidded to a stop beside Quinn's TrailBlazer. A tall blond police officer hurried toward them.

"Y'all okay?"

"Yes," Ellie said. "Thank you, officer."

"Thank OnStar," he said. "It gave us your exact location. "Can y'all describe your attackers?"

"To a T," Quinn said.

"Good."

"We can also give you some DNA!"

Quinn pointed at the wrench with Van Man's blood.

THIRTY TWO

A fter filing a police report and agreeing to review mug shots via email, Ellie and Quinn continued driving back toward Louisville.

"That pickup guy *studied* my driver's license too long."

"Making sure who you are."

Ellie nodded.

"And when add we this attack to the black Navigator that tried to force you and me into a ravine, and the mysterious 22 bullet from the forest, we know someone's out to cause you great bodily harm."

"And don't forget the van driver who knocked me off my bike riding to school."

"Or the night before," Quinn added.

"The night before?" she asked.

"That U of L student named Elle Steward - spelled *STEWARD* - attacked in her room and left for dead."

Ellie felt sick at the memory. "How's she doing?"

"She's still in a coma."

Ellie said a quick prayer for her.

"Her attack is related to mine."

"I agree." Quinn said, as he passed an Allied Van Lines truck.

"But why harm or kill me?"

"Only one reason."

"They think I'm Leland Radford's heir?"

He nodded.

"But there's no DNA proof."

"Maybe *they* have proof."

"You're saying they *know* my DNA test will prove it."

"Yeah."

"How can they know?"

He shrugged. "I have no idea."

Ellie took a deep breath and looked out the window at the Ohio River. "One thing I do know . . ."

"What?"

"My DNA will be irrelevant – if I'm toast!"

"Not going to happen, Ellie."

Minutes later, he pulled into Celeste Barclay's driveway. Ellie noticed the house lights were off. Celeste was not back yet from her son's home in Elizabethtown.

"You shouldn't stay here tonight."

"I have to. Celeste's son is bringing her here in a few minutes."

"Maybe she could stay with your neighbor."

"Sarah's helped out so much lately, I can't ask her again. I'll be fine, Quinn, really. Besides, this house has an excellent alarm system. And no one followed us here. I've been watching. Don't worry!"

He looked like he'd worry anyway. "Let me check inside."

"Okay," she said, pleased that he would.

After checking every nook and cranny of the house and that the doors and windows were locked, and finding no one lurking, they came back out to his car.

"Call me if anything seems suspicious. *Anything.*"

"I will."

He turned to leave.

Quinn . . .?"

"Yeah . . .?"

"You changed my life today. Because of you, I may know who my birth parents are. I can never thank you enough."

He smiled. "Like I say, we got real lucky, Ellie."

"Damn lucky. I'll phone you as soon as Fletcher Falcone says my lab results are ready."

"Please do. But we should go over some potential probate issues before Falcone calls. Are you on campus tomorrow?"

"I have a 9 a.m. class."

"Can you meet me in the Student Center about five after ten at our table?"

"Sure." She liked that he said *our* table.

"And above all - take a taxi to school tomorrow morning."

"Okay."

"I'd drive you, but I'll be taking a test then."

"I understand."

She walked to the front door, waved as he drove off, then went inside and locked the door. After resetting the alarm, she leaned against the wall, and thought about how profoundly her life had changed since she left here this morning. After years of trying, she'd very likely discovered her birth mother and possibly her father. All because a nice law student spilled coffee on her.

She was pleased she'd see Quinn tomorrow. No, she was excited.

Her life was moving forward fast in a lot of positive ways.

And one of them was named Quinn Parker.

* * *

Huntoon Harris sat in the comfortable leather seat of the Nissan. He'd watched Ellie Stuart walk back into the house down the street. She was one of those chicks who walked sexy without trying.

Huntoon still couldn't believe how Bubba and Narvel had scre-wed up so bad on the country road. Somehow Ellie or Quinn had contacted the cops when the boys pulled them over. Cell phone pro-bably. Then Quinn broke Narvel's arm with a wrench that had an IQ higher than Narvel's.

But now it's payback time! This bitch has caused me far too much trouble.

Huntoon lifted his binoculars and saw no cars in her driveway. Where's her bike? Maybe he'd totaled it a couple of days ago when he bumped her off the street. He looked to the left and saw the bike beside the house. The bike looked rideable.

He flipped open his cell phone and dialed.

"She's back in Louisville."

"How the hell -?"

"Bubba and Narvel fucked up! Ran off when the cops came. She got away."

The man cursed Huntoon for several seconds.

"Where's she now?"

"Just went into the old lady's house."

"You know what to do."

"Oh, yeah."

"Think you can manage that?"

"Piece a cake," Huntoon said.

THIRTY THREE

As dusk eased into night, Huntoon sipped more Jim Beam and focused his binoculars on the home Ellie Stuart entered an hour ago. The house alarm sign was old. Easy system to disarm. Nothing to worry about.

What *did* worry him was the big middle-aged guy that went inside. Six-four, two-forty with weightlifter muscles! He'd helped an elderly woman inside the house like maybe she was his mom, then he stayed. His Suburban was still parked out front.

Huntoon decided to wait until the big guy left. Leaning back in his seat, Huntoon sipped more Beam and slid a movie, *Navy SEALS Deep 6,* into his portable Blue-Ray player. He loved the flick. Watched it maybe twenty times already. And for good reasons. It had the Big Ts – Terrorists, Testosterone and Tits. What more could a movie offer? It should have won an Oscar.

A Domino's delivery car pulled into the drive. The driver took a pizza to the door, the big guy paid and took the pizza inside.

If the big guy didn't leave soon, he'd have to whack him too. In fact, whacking the big guy might be a smart idea. Make it look more like a breaking and entering that went bad. Not just a hit on Ellie Stuart.

Huntoon shoved a full clip into his Glock.

He sipped more Jim Beam and looked back at the film as the *SEALS* greased the Iraqis and escaped with the chicks wearing Band-Aid sized bikinis.

He thought back to when he was whacking Iraqis. His Special Forces days. Great days. Except the day the asshole army unfairly and dishonorably discharged him just because he waxed three towelheads near Baghdad. *Suspicious* towelheads, all puffed up like they were wearing explosive vests and looking nervous. He wasn't waiting to find out. So he sent them all to Allah. War is war. Collateral shit happens. Any fool knows that – except the butt-covering army officer brass who never came within twenty miles of anything more explosive than a firecracker.

His spineless Captain didn't support him either. Nobody ever had his back. Not even his cokehead parents and slutty wife.

Back in the states, he wrote *dishonorable discharge* on sixteen job applications and got back sixteen *Rejected* notes. He grew so angry he planned to blow up an Army recruiting office in Lexington – but two days before, a guy gave him five grand for an easy hit. That job turned into a string of even bigger jobs over the next few years. Like Ellie Stuart.

Huntoon yawned as he looked back at the *Navy SEALS flick*. It had been a long day. He sipped more Beam, yawned again, felt a little sleepy, decided to rest his eyes a bit.

When I hear the big guy's Suburban drive off, I'll go in and take care of business . . .

✳ ✳ ✳

Huntoon's left cheek felt warm . . . then hot. He peeled open an eye to blinding sunshine.

MIKE BROGAN

The dashboard clock said - *8:28 – in the fucking morning!*

He bolted upright in his seat. The big guy's Suburban was gone! Was Ellie's bike gone? He checked. Still there.

But she had a 9 a.m. class.

She took a taxi. Or walked to school.

I fucking missed her!

Then he saw her. Standing at the window, looking out. She wore an easy-to-spot red U of L sweatshirt. She opened the front door and walked toward her bike. Huntoon drained the air from his lungs.

Game over!

This time, she wouldn't dodge him like she did two days ago.

Unless she had eyes in the back of her head.

* * *

Ellie worried about riding her bike to school. Quinn had insisted she take a taxi and she tried to, but the dispatcher said they couldn't pick her up before class. A class she had to make on time. A big chunk of her semester grade was riding on today's test.

She had to leave *now*. She looked out at the cars parked in front. The usual neighborhood cars, except three she never saw before.

Was someone inside one waiting for her? The tinted windows made it impossible to know.

She had to *assume* someone was waiting for her. Which meant she had to mislead them. But how? If she just pedaled off on a different route, they'd simply follow.

But what if they don't see me pedal off?

She had an idea. She stepped outside, walked around the side of the house, bent down beside her bike and jiggled the chain pretending something was wrong with it. Shaking her head, she rolled the bike into the garage, grabbed some tools and fiddled with the chain and sprocket. Then she pulled down the garage door and peeked through its tiny window. Again, she saw no movement inside the three cars.

Quickly, she opened the back door of the garage, rolled her bike out into the narrow alley and pedaled off fast toward campus, taking a completely new route.

She looked back. No one followed her.

* * *

Huntoon Harris wondered why she was taking so long in the garage. Probably couldn't fix the bike. *Good. She'll have to walk. Make my job easier. But she better hurry, or she'll be late for class.*

He was still pissed that he missed her with his hunting rifle from the forest. And now, the boss said it still had to look like a car accident.

What's taking her so damn long? And why'd she close the garage door and shut out the daylight?

Huntoon thought of something. Does her garage have a back door? Is there an alley back there? Quickly, he drove the Nissan pickup around the corner, and cursing, raced down the alley and stopped at her garage.

Back door!

He jumped out, squinted through the door window.

The bitch is gone! FUCK!

He jumped back in the pickup, raced to the end of the alley, looked both ways. No sign of her. He drove ahead, looked down another alley. Nothing. At the next alley, he glimpsed a red sweatshirt about four blocks away. It was her, pedaling hard down an alley to get to the university. He checked his map and saw the street the alley emptied out onto . . . the only street she could take to enter campus.

He'd be waiting for her.

Looking at her *back*.

Minutes later, he parked on the quiet, tree-lined street, knowing she'd be along any minute. His plan was simple: hit her hard from behind, roll over her like a speed bump a few times, break her neck and as many bones as possible. Excessive? Yeah. But excessive meant dead.

She deserved dead.

* * *

The cool morning breeze felt good as Ellie pedaled her slightly damaged, but trusty old Schwinn down the street lined with thick shade trees. Every few seconds, she checked the vehicles.

So far all seemed normal.

She passed rows of small family homes and smiled. She was no longer a family of one. *She* had a family. She knew her natural mother, and very possibly her father. And knowing them gave her a wonderful sense of belonging, of having roots, of feeling a calm inner peace she'd ever known before.

But even if the DNA test proves I'm not Leland Radford's daughter, I'll go back to The Pines and chat with Irene for hours about my mom. Then I'll visit Loretta Mae at the House of Grace and learn even more.

As she pedaled along, Ellie checked behind her. All looked safe. And she was almost to school.

A hundred feet ahead, she saw a garbage can had tipped over onto the street. A Doberman Pinscher yanked something from it and ran off. As she started to steer around the can, she checked her bike's rearview mirror.

A pickup was moving up behind her. Fast . . .

Too fast on this narrow street!

Suddenly, the pickup raced right at her.

No!

She jumped her bike over the curb and sped toward some trees.

But the pickup sped up. It closed fast. She had no chance. It hit her rear tire, knocking her and her bike several feet into the air.

She landed in a tall hedge and felt sharp branches rake her face and arms as she fell down through them.

The pickup backed up – turned and drove at her again!

She crawled behind an oak tree just in time – forcing the big vehicle to skid to a stop a few feet away.

Then, for some reason, she saw water flooding the pickup's windshield. She followed the stream of water back to a hose held by an elderly woman who was shaking her fist at the driver.

"Asshole! What the hell you doin'?" the red-faced woman screamed.

The driver stared at the old woman, then at Ellie, then backed up and sped off. As he drove by, Ellie saw sunshine glint off a gold loop holding his ponytail.

"You okay, hon?" the old woman asked.

"I think so, ma'am. Just couple scratches." Warm blood trickled down her cheek.

"That bastard *tried* to hit you!"

"Yes, ma'am, he did! Did you happen to see his license?"

"No, hon. The hedge blocked my view."

Ellie took a deep breath, flicked leaves and dirt from her sweatshirt and looked down at her Schwinn.

It looked like spaghetti.

THIRTY FOUR

After limping the last block to campus, Ellie had gone to class, taken her test and sensed she'd done well, probably because her adrenalin-juiced memory kept spitting out the right answers.

Now, in the Student Activities Center, she sat reviewing some literature notes and waiting for Quinn at their corner table.

Hearing footsteps, she looked up, and saw him.

She waved and smiled.

When he saw her face, his smile vanished.

"Did we fall down again?"

"We did."

"Did someone help us fall down?"

"Yes."

"Who?"

"A big pickup."

Quinn's face flushed with anger. "Son of a bitch!"

As she explained, he sat down and she saw his jaw muscles harden into knots.

"Did you report it to the police?"

"Not yet."

"You've got to, Ellie. When's your last class over?"

"At 3:00. But I'm watching Celeste from 3:45 on."

"I'll drive you to the police first."

"But you have a class then."

"My professor will understand."

She felt bad causing Quinn to miss class, but her old Schwinn was now roadkill, she was too frightened to walk, and she didn't bring enough money for a taxi.

"Thank you, Quinn."

"Let's meet here at 3:05."

"Okay."

"*There* you are!" a loud female voice.

Ellie turned and saw Jennifer DuBois wearing a stunning black cashmere jersey and leather slacks and looking, as usual, like she'd just stepped from *America's Next Top Model*. Her eyes widened when she saw Ellie.

"Eewwwww! Your *face!* What happened?"

Ellie knew she looked like a Freddy Kruger victim. "I fell off my bike."

"She was *knocked* off by a pickup," Quinn said.

Jennifer's brows climbed higher.

"Just scrapes. No broken bones."

"Thank goodness," Jennifer said, but Ellie thought she heard the faint hint of disappointment.

Jennifer placed her hand on Quinn's shoulder. "Quinny, you promised to review my accounting cases now, before class."

"Oh, right, okay."

"I'm off to class," Ellie said, standing. "See y'all later." She grabbed her books and headed out. As she walked, she glanced back and saw them bending over her accounting textbook. The perfect couple. . . .

Well, maybe not *that* perfect.

———

Ellie sensed Quinn had concerns with Jennifer. Concerns that had troubled him before he spilled coffee on Ellie a few days ago. She'd noticed it when Quinn first talked about Jennifer, then later when he spoke to Jennifer on the phone while driving to Harlan. His tone and facial expressions had grown tense. Were they just in troubled waters? Or a major storm?

She wondered how Quinn felt about her.

She knew how she felt about him. Incredibly grateful and appreciative. He'd led her to her birth mother and possibly her birth father.

Quinn Parker had forever changed her life . . . a life someone was hell bent on ending.

THIRTY FIVE

At *The Pines,* Irene Whitten settled in at her favorite spot, the wildflower gardens in back. She loved how the red clover spread like a crimson carpet over the fields, and how the snowflake flowers hung like tiny white parachutes. She smelled sweet honeysuckle and watched two red cardinals splashing away in the birdbath.

She looked at the house and sighed . . . *my old Kentucky home . . . But not for long.*

Unfortunately in a few days, after the probate hearing, *The Pines* would be sold off to someone, and part of her would go with it. This was her home, her peaceful, friendly, safe refuge for the best thirty-one years of her adult life.

At least she'd leave here knowing she finally told Leland Radford the secret that his half-sister Zelda blackmailed her for twenty years to not tell him . . . that he had a child with Jacqueline Moreau.

And tomorrow I'll give his executor, Mr. Falcone, the written statement that Leland and I signed on his hospital deathbed – saying he wants his child to inherit his estate.

Irene thought Mr. Radford was perhaps the kindest and most generous man she'd ever known. He even hinted she would receive something in his will. Maybe enough to help rent that nice little cottage in town. Imagine that – my own place!

Behind her, a twig snapped.

She smiled, knowing those two frisky young fawns were back again. They came every day at this time to munch on the wildflowers. No problem, since there were acres to munch. She loved to watch them . . .

Another twig cracked right behind her.

Then . . . a shadow crept onto her bench . . . the shadow of a large man.

THIRTY SIX

Ellie felt overwhelmed and underprepared as she stared at her class notes. She had a ton of catch-up studying to do before exams next week . . . and not nearly enough time to get it all done.

She looked over at Celeste who sat nearby smiling at the movie *Benji* that she'd probably seen fifty times already. Maybe Alzheimer's and dementia had one potential benefit: endless enjoyment of the same movie.

Her phone rang: it was *Quinn*. After class, he'd driven her to the police station where she filed a hit-and-run report on the black Toyota pickup that knocked her off her bike.

"What's up?" she said.

"Irene Whitten . . ." He took a deep breath.

"What . . .?"

"She was just attacked at *The Pines*. Stabbed twice."

Ellie slumped over and closed her eyes. "My God, Quinn . . ."

"Doctors stopped her bleeding, but she's critical from the loss of blood, and may slip into a coma."

Ellie tried to speak, but couldn't. She felt tears well up. "She was attacked because of me."

"No, Ellie . . .!"

"Yes, she was! Because she helped me identify my mother."

"No. The police believe her attacker was a man from her past. A guy named Dontrell Miller. Many years ago, Irene's testimony sent him to prison. He swore he'd escape and kill her. He escaped years ago. Police found a note beside Irene today that read, "I finally found you. Like I said I would."

"This is awful."

"Yes . . . but something's not right about her attack," Quinn said.

Ellie sensed what he meant. "The timing . . .?"

"Yeah. Why after twenty years, does Dontrell suddenly find Irene today?"

"The day before she planned to give Mr. Falcone the signed statement from Leland Radford."

Quinn nodded. "Way too convenient."

"I agree. Where is Radford's signed statement?"

"The police can't find it. They've searched Irene's room and every room at *The Pines.*"

"So now there's no *written signed* statement that Radford wanted his child to inherit."

Quinn nodded.

"What about the nurse that Irene said witnessed Radford sign the statement?"

"She's with *Doctors Without Borders* in Borneo, eighty miles from cell phone or Internet service."

Elle shook her head. "So . . . now, there's only *your* word as to what Irene told you about Radford's dying statement."

"That's right."

"Welcome to the club, Quinn?"

"What club?"

"The You-Too-Are-A-Target Club."

He paused. "Good point."

"Be careful, Quinn."

"Yes, ma'am."

Ellie thought she heard something outside and looked out the window for several seconds, seeing nothing but shadows.

"Ellie . . . you there?"

She looked around the yard and whispered, "Yeah . . ."

"You okay?"

She decided to level with him. "I keep flashing back to the attacks."

"Understandable."

She said nothing.

"But you also seem frightened about something else. Something now, maybe."

"I'm hearing things, and overreacting to every sound I hear."

"Like what . . .?"

"Like a sound that someone was moving around outside the house a few minutes ago. And then again, just before you called."

"That's it! I'm coming over now."

"No, Quinn, I'm fine. Really. I've got the house alarm on. All doors and windows are locked."

"I'm on the way."

"Quinn . . ."

He'd already hung up.

She closed her eyes and felt relieved that he was coming over. *Very* relieved. She sensed danger, even more so now that Irene had been attacked. She decided to check the house again.

She walked over and reset the house alarm, then made sure the dining room and bedroom windows were all locked. Then she walked to the kitchen and froze. The back door was wide open! She'd locked it earlier.

Was someone in the house? She listened, heard nothing.

Then she realized Celeste may have unlocked it. Sometimes she went outside to walk around her small garden. Ellie quickly locked it, then went back and tried to study, but she was too nervous to focus.

Moments later, she thought she heard something outside. Or was it inside?

She held her breath . . .

Then a horn honked three times.

Could that be Quinn this soon?

She hurried to the front door, looked out and saw Quinn's SUV careen into the drive. He jumped out, and hurried up to the front door as she stepped outside.

"You okay?"

"Now I am."

"I'll go check things out."

He hurried around the side of the house, checked the garage, then in back. Seconds later, he came back and looked at her.

"Everything seems fine."

She felt bad that she'd made him drive over for nothing.

Sarah Barnes walked over from next door. "I heard someone between our houses thirty minutes ago, then nothing for a while, then someone just now. Everything okay over here?"

"I also heard noises out here."

Sarah looked at her with concern.

"You shouldn't stay here tonight," Quinn said.

"It's okay. The house alarm works fine, and I have Celeste."

"Not anymore you don't," Sarah said. "Celeste will stay with me tonight. You know how she loves staying over. You stay somewhere else tonight."

Ellie knew they both made sense. "I have a friend I can stay with."

"You're looking at him."

"But, Jennifer – "

"She'll have to understand."

Ellie knew Jennifer would not understand.

THIRTY SEVEN

In Old Louisville, Ellie watched Quinn park in front of a large, charming historic home, *The Brandeis House,* named after Louis Brandeis, the famous Supreme Court jurist from Louisville.

"Wow - you live in this huge mansion?"

"Just one apartment," he said.

Ellie loved this old section of town: forty-eight blocks of turn-of-the-century homes near the University of Louisville. Architectural experts said the neighborhood had the largest collection of Victorian homes in the United States.

Most were still in excellent condition, despite a hundred years of Louisville's wet cold winters and long hot summers. The mansions were originally lived in by whiskey and bourbon barons, Ohio River shipping tycoons, and a few scoundrels. Today, some of their descendants lived there, along with business people, professors, families, and one very lucky law student named Quinn Parker.

He led her inside to a foyer of magnificent, polished auburn mahogany. She loved its full, rich scent.

She stepped into Quinn's apartment and felt like she'd stepped into the 1920s. The antique furniture, kitchen table, chairs and end tables were old, polished maple. A gold and red Tiffany lamp sat on a side table. Law books stuffed his shelves. On his desk sat family pictures of Quinn with his parents and a girl who looked like the older sister he'd mentioned.

But no photo of Jennifer DuBois.

Probably in his bedroom.

His rent had to cost a fortune.

"Quinn – such luxury!"

"Yeah."

"Do your parents know you sell drugs?"

"Not yet. Actually, this apartment's only fifty bucks a month."

"And I'm Lady Gaga."

"Fifty bucks! Really. This house belonged to a successful Brandeis Law School grad who bequeathed it to the school with two stipulations. First, that they rent the six apartments to six former U of L football player law students at fifty bucks a month. And second that the law students do ten hours of pro bono work at a free legal clinic each month."

"Such a deal!"

"Yep." He led her into the kitchen and opened the refrigerator.

"We've got RC Cola, Nehi Orange drink, and . . . hillbilly penicillin."

"Huh?"

"Jack Daniels."

"Jack sounds medicinal."

He fixed two whiskeys and they sat in side-by-side wicker chairs facing the window. She plopped down in one chair, he in the other. They clinked their glasses and sipped. The liquid felt like velvet going down.

"So, Miss Ellie, after two vehicle attacks, some thugs driving us off Highway 25, a bullet hitting my TrailBlazer inches from your head, and a bad guy circling your house, how you feeling?"

"Like Harrison Ford in *The Fugitive*."

He smiled, then turned serious.

"Ellie . . .?"

"Yeah."

"You're safe with me."

She knew he meant it. "I always feel safe with you."

He shrugged. "You know what these attacks mean?"

"Someone believes my DNA will match Mr. Radford's DNA."

"Or *knows* it will."

"But how can they even know about my DNA test? Only Fletcher Falcone, the nurse, and Irene Whitten the housekeeper knew. And they *wanted* me to take the test."

"Maybe one of them mentioned it to the wrong person."

"Which one?" she said, sipping her whiskey.

He shrugged. "The Romans had a wise proverb."

"They had a slew of them."

"I'm thinking of *cui bono.* . . ."

"*Who benefits*," she said.

"Yep. And several people benefit from the Radford estate at this time."

"Like . . .?"

"Like the managers for Radford's many corporate divisions. Radford set up six managers. It's reasonable to assume they fear you might sell off the businesses they manage, or maybe replace them. As a result, they would lose managerial income and lucrative fees. Big money means big fees and big motivation to keep them."

"You talked to these managers?"

"A few. Darrel Simmons controls Radford's businesses and manufacturing. Cecil Crawley controls commercial real estate, a printing company, office buildings, shopping malls. Both seemed like stand up guys."

Ellie nodded.

"I also chatted with Radford's investment manager, Heinrich De Groot. He controls Radford's stocks, bonds, and investment portfolios . . . hundreds of millions of dollars' worth. He also manages Radford's 12,000 acres of coal-rich property in southeastern Kentucky."

Ellie nodded.

"On the phone, these managers seemed like solid businessmen. But who knows? If you inherit the estate, you may sell everything and bingo - they lose fat fees."

"Doesn't Fletcher Falcone, as executor, have overall control of the estate assets?"

"He does. But Leland Radford set things up so these six individual managers run their specific areas and report their numbers to Falcone."

"So if there's no heir, what happens?"

"Then the executor, Falcone, sells off the estate assets and distribute the proceeds according to Radford's will and Kentucky probate law. He'll liquidate all assets, investments, businesses, properties, land holdings, and *The Pines* estate itself, everything. He and the managers would get more fat fees for doing that. And on top of that, Falcone and the others would get compensation for all other services they've been providing. Lots of hours billed. Possibly huge commissions on all assets they sell off."

"Like the 12,000 acres?"

"Yep."

Quinn sipped his whiskey. "The question is - how far would any of these managers go to prevent you from inheriting?"

"*Someone's* willing to go all the way." She touched the scab on her cheek.

Quinn nodded. "Your DNA results will resolve everything."

"If I live long enough to see them." She heard her voice crack.

Quinn seemed to hear it too. "Ellie, look at me."

She turned and faced him. He stood up, raised his arms above his head, made enormous bicep muscles. "Tarzan plenty strong. Two-time All-Eight Conference tight end, meaner than a sack of rattlesnakes. I'll beat the shit out of anyone who tries to hurt you."

She laughed. "Thanks, Quinn, but then I'd have to worry about you."

"Me?"

"Sure. I'd worry about your football knee and your two concussions."

"How do you know about all that?"

"I read. The *Louisville Cardinal* and the *Courier Journal.*"

"Ah . . ."

"And earlier, I saw you take the Vicodin. Is that for the knee?"

He nodded. "Damn thing still hurts at times. But the concussions seem fine now."

"How'd they happen?"

"Helmet to helmet hits. In the past, opposing players aimed their helmets at ours. The more dings on your helmet, the more macho you were. I got semi-knocked out twice in the last season. Concussions. Doctor told me it was too dangerous to play. But we needed three more wins for the league championship. I played. We got lucky and won. Doc said if I kept playing I could expect memory problems, maybe a stroke, brain damage."

"Sort of a no brainer, pardon the pun."

"Yeah. So I turned down an offer to play for the Detroit Lions."

"Smart move."

They clicked glasses and sipped more whiskey.

Suddenly, she yawned big. "Sorry . . ."

Quinn seemed to fight off his own yawn.

"So what now?" she said.

"Sleep."

"Sounds good."

He led her down the hallway toward a small bedroom with an attached bathroom.

"The Presidential Suite. Towels, soap, indoor plumbing, all the amenities - except chocolates on your pillow."

She pictured Quinn lying on her pillow. *Stop thinking like that,* she told herself. *He's practically married to Jennifer DuBois.*

"What time's your first class tomorrow?" he asked.

"Eight."

"Wake you at seven?"

"Perfect."

She smiled and locked on his dark green eyes. She owed him so much. "Again, Quinn, thanks for riding in on your white horse tonight and rescuing this damsel."

"Happy to ma'am." He inched closer to her face. He was going to kiss her. She *knew* it. Her heart raced.

He leaned closer and touched her cheek. "Your scab is healing well."

"Oh . . . good." She smelled his aftershave.

"Sleep well, Ellie. And don't worry. Six big tough U of L football players live here."

"That's what worries me.

"Why?"

"Illegal use of the hands!"

He laughed. "Could happen if your backfield's in motion."

Laughing, she turned and walked down to her room, wondering if her backfield was in motion. He headed the other way to his bedroom. She shut the door and closed her eyes. He'd wanted to kiss her. She was sure. But he'd stopped. Why? Only one reason.

Jennifer DuBois . . . the luckiest girl in Kentucky.

Minutes later, Ellie climbed into bed.

Despite her exhaustion, she had trouble falling asleep. Her mind was on Quinn . . . and on whether he cared for her. And if he did – was she ready to risk caring for him . . . maybe even risk loving him?

She had felt the pain of lost love before.

More than once.

THIRTY EIGHT

He mashed his cell phone to his ear and listened to Huntoon Harris's latest pathetic excuse for not handling Ellie Stuart.

"She's hard to git at," Huntoon said.

"An unarmed college girl?"

"She hangs with that big dude, Quinn. All-conference tight end! And them cops is circling her house like flies on shit!"

"Any more excuses?"

"I kin git her!"

"Forget her!" he shouted, his anger boiling over.

"But – "

"Forget her! She's described you to the cops. I have other work for you. I'll call later."

He slammed the phone down and thought about Huntoon. He'd only hired him because a college friend begged him to. The friend obviously didn't realize Huntoon could only handle life's simpler tasks, like applying a baseball bat to a human skull. Thinking was his Achilles heel. If the IRS taxed brains, Huntoon would get a refund.

A few nights ago, the fool nearly murdered the wrong U of L student, a girl named *Elle Steward,* even though he had the correct name, *Ellie Stuart*, spelled out on a piece of paper.

His phone rang: He checked Caller ID. A neighbor lady. Probably calling again about her son's latest DUI. He pushed his *Not In* button so his secretary would handle it. But 'DUI' triggered something – something he should have thought of sooner: a solution to his Ellie Stuart problem.

The solution was Roy Klume.

A couple of years ago he'd represented Klume after the young man got his fourth DUI. The judge planned to give Klume Kentucky's maximum prison time, plus rehab, plus a five-year driving suspension.

But after I persuaded Klume's wealthy father to donate ninety thousand dollars to the judge's reelection campaign, the judge decided that Roy Klume's DUI was just a nasty antihistamine reaction to his chronic sinusitis, and let him walk.

But . . . I still have proof of Klume's two-times-over-the-limit blood-alcohol, proof that could destroy the Klume family reputation . . . proof that will persuade Roy Klume to help us.

And persuading people is one thing Huntoon *can* do.

THIRTY NINE

Huntoon Harris drove down Old Paris Road toward Lexington.
He was still pissed at the boss for yanking him off the Ellie
Stuart job. *I coulda nailed her with just a little more time.*

Tammy Wynette's *Stand by Your Man* blasted out of his radio.

How's come nobody ever stands by me? he wondered. His drug-
gie parents dumped him in a Burger King bathroom when he was
six months old. His bitchy ex-wife dumped him just for banging her
thirteen-year-old sister who jumped his boner while he was sleeping. What's a man to do? And in Iraq, his lying lieutenant court-
martial him by saying that the towelheads Huntoon shot were
innocent! *Bullshit!*

But life taught him the big bad lesson: Nobody stands by you.
You're alone. You cover your own ass. You do what you have to do.
And the sooner you learn it, the better.

But at least the boss gave him this no-brainer job. Huntoon
turned down a shady street with magnolia trees and modern office

buildings. Moments later, he pulled into the parking lot of a contemporary steel and concrete structure with three stories, massive windows the color of old Coke bottles and a red brick wall in front.

Huntoon cruised down rows of parked cars until he found the only new red Ford Fusion. The license number matched the number his buddy at Motor Vehicle Registrations gave him. The Fusion was Roy Klume's.

Minutes later, Huntoon watched a reed-thin nerdy-looking guy with scrawny, dishwater blond hair, horn-rims and a stuffed pocket protector walk out the entrance. The nerd was Roy Klume based on his Facebook photo. Four other geeks walked with him, snickering like they were auditioning for *Revenge of the Nerds.*

Klume walked toward his red Fusion. Huntoon crept ahead and arrived at the Fusion when Klume did.

"Mr. Klume?"

"Yes?" Klume walked over to Huntoon's passenger window.

"Lookie here!" Huntoon showed him the business end of his .45.

"Jesus Christ!"

"Naw, just me, Roy. But Jesus does want you to git in my car right now. If you don't, your brains is gonna paint that pretty red Fusion of yours! Unnerstand?"

Roy Klume stared at the gun, frozen, then slowly got in Huntoon's car.

"Relax, Roy. This ain't no robbery and I ain't no queer or nothing. I jes want show you somethin'. Then I'll drop you back off right here, safe and sound. Unless, of course, you try something stupid. In which case, I'll drop your sorry ass off - *dead!* Unnerstand?"

Klume nodded, looking scared shitless. Huntoon loved scaring people shitless. The army shrink told him it was because he had deep-seated hatred for certain kinds of people. The shrink was wrong. He had a deep-seated hatred for everyone, except Inez, the crippled Bob Evans waitress who gave him extra bacon.

Keeping his gun aimed at Klume, Huntoon drove out of the lot. Minutes later, he stopped in front of a normal, single-level ranch style home with shrubs, red flowers and a large picture window. A very pregnant blonde lumbered past the picture window. Twin girls, about three, toddled along behind her.

"Home sweet home, right Roy?"

Klume paused, then nodded.

"Your wife's damn purty. And them little girls is cute as buttons. And looks like mama's got one cookin' in the oven. Betcha you wanta keep 'em all alive and well, ain't that right?"

Klume's eyelids fluttered like a spinning window shade.

"*Right*, Roy?"

Klume nodded.

"Well, there ain't but one way you can do that."

Klume swallowed. "How?"

"Pay back a favor what you owe."

"Owe who?"

"That's a secret, Roy."

Huntoon explained in detail what he wanted Klume to do.

Klume shook his head. "It won't work."

"Bad answer 'cuz you're gonna make it work!"

"But our sophisticated quality control processes prevent that."

Huntoon smiled. "Now Roy, you're a real smart scientifical guy. You'll find a way."

"But they'll fire me."

"No buts, Roy. I'm thinkin' you got *A's* in yer chemistry tests, right?"

Klume looked confused, but nodded.

"True or false, Roy. Carbolic acid is nasty shit when it gits on yer skin?"

Klume nodded.

"Wonder what that acid would do to your wife's purty face and body? And them little girls' faces? Yuk! Makes me wanna barf!"

Klume's face turned crimson as he stared at his family in the window.

"Roy, did you know them fuckin' Nazi doctors injected carbolic acid right into them prisoners' bodies? Little kids even. You can look it up! The pain was so bad them prisoners up and begged to be kilt."

Roy Klume looked at his family again, then closed his eyes.

"So, Roy, we got us a deal or what?

Klume nodded.

FORTY

Quinn sat in the Brandeis Law Library, hunched over his *Trusts & Estates* casebook, preparing his presentation on the Leland T. Radford probate case. Behind him, loud heel clicks. Angry clicks maybe. Turning, he saw Jennifer, her face scrunched up in her all too familiar pout.

"I can't believe it!" she said.

"Believe what?"

"That you're *not* coming to my sorority's quarterly Gamma Gala tonight?" She sounded like he'd flushed a million dollar lottery winner ticket down the toilet.

"Jenn, like we discussed yesterday, I just can't make it."

"No! You *choose* not to make it, even though everyone who matters will be there." Her face twisted into a major sulk.

Patience, he told himself. "Jenn, early tomorrow morning I'm making my Leland Radford presentation to class. I'll be up all night finishing it *and* trying to catch up on my chapter outlines."

"All because you spent so much time with Daisy Mae or whatever the hell her name is."

"Her name is Ellie Stuart."

"Whatever. . . ."

"And now I *have* to spend time with her."

"*Have* to?"

"Yes."

"That's absurd! Why on earth would - ?"

" - because she's part of the Radford case."

Jennifer stared back like he'd lost his mind. "How the hell can The Turnip Queen be part of the Leland Radford case?"

He held his anger, then said, "Because she might be his daughter and sole heir."

Jennifer's mouth opened wide enough for a root canal. She was obviously having difficulty processing the idea that a girl who bought her clothes at a thrift shop could soon buy out a Neiman Marcus store.

Her face was crimson and she crossed her arms. "Oh, so now that she might inherit lots of money, she's more interesting than me?"

Quinn couldn't stop himself from thinking, *flat broke she is!* but said, "Jenn, please try to understa – "

" - I understand that even though this is my important quarterly sorority party, and even though my debut is coming up, you could care less! It's like I don't exist for you anymore." She was mushrooming toward a major hissy fit.

"Jennifer, that's not true."

"Well, do I exist for you or not? Do you care? I want to know *now!*" Her voice was loud.

Students looked up from their law books.

"Of course I care – "

"But not enough to come tonight?"

"Because tonight I have no time."

"No – because you won't *make* time for me like you do for her."

She had fire in her eyes as she leaned over the table toward him. "I have just one thing to say, Quinn Parker!"

He waited.

"If you don't come tonight, we're done! I mean it! Finished! It's over! Understand?" Without waiting for his response, she turned and stormed out of the library.

He watched her go, saddened by her outburst, and embarrassed his classmates heard it. But the confrontation had been brewing. He should have spoken with her weeks ago. But exams, the Radford presentation, the free clinic hours and part-time job left him with little time. Still, he should have *made* time.

From the beginning, he'd been fascinated by Jennifer's animated personality. Her wealthy parents had accepted his middle-class origins. Her father, owner of Kentucky Whiskeys, had even helped him get a terrific job offer from Wagner, Hoffman and Musterman, one of Louisville's top law firms. With Jennifer, he'd be set for life.

But what kind of life? he'd been asking himself.

Because a different Jennifer had emerged after a few months. A less likeable elitist who needed to control others . . . a trait probably learned from controlling Mother Dubois.

Jennifer was friendly with *her* kind of people, but dismissive of those from the wrong, or lesser zip codes – which included most of his friends. When he'd mentioned this to her, she'd said he was mistaken and just didn't understand her yet.

He understood her well enough now to know he would be deceiving himself, and her, if he believed their relationship would work out long term. It just wouldn't. And the final proof was today's ultimatum - come to tonight's party *or else.*

He chose *or else.*

And he felt lighter, like he'd inhaled helium. Tomorrow, he'd calmly explain to her how he just didn't think things would work out. And why.

But the truth was, he was also at fault. The reason was simple. When he *really* wanted something, he went for it full throttle – sometimes before he got all the facts. When he met Jennifer, her beauty blinded him to any possible flaws and limitations.

And when the team doctor told him he should stop playing football because of his two concussions, his desire to play the last three games blinded him to the serious risks. He played anyway. Macho stupid!

Now, as he looked down at the Radford presentation, he noticed Ellie's name. So different from Jennifer. Ellie treated everyone - from the homeless to the McMansioned - the same. Her attitude didn't change a bit when she learned she might possibly inherit Radford's massive estate. And her thrift-shop clothes somehow enhanced her natural beauty. He found himself attracted to her more each day.

But how did she feel about him? Obviously, she was thankful he'd helped her get close to finding her birth parents. But beyond that, did she feel anything? Was she waiting for him to share his feelings? Did she think Jennifer and he were a committed couple? Probably. He almost talked to Ellie about how he felt last night.

Maybe it was time he did. . . .

But only *after* he sorted things out with Jennifer.

FORTY ONE

*F*inally, *The Big Day!*
  Ellie could barely contain her excitement. In minutes, her DNA would reveal whether she was the biological daughter of Jacqueline Moreau and Leland Radford. She'd thought of nothing else for the last forty-eight hours.

  Quinn and she were in Lexington, driving past the University of Kentucky campus, heading to Southern Genetics Labs, one of the state's most respected DNA testing facilities.

  "Are we anxious?" Quinn asked.

  "We are vibrating like a tuning fork!"

  "Relax. DNA will prove you're the daughter of Jacqueline Moreau and Leland Radford."

  "Why're you so sure?"

  "Like I said before – all indications are with you."

  "I'd rather have facts."

  "You've got facts."

  "I do?"

"Sure."

"What facts?"

"Well, first, did Leland Radford's housekeeper, Irene, swear that Jacqueline and Leland were deeply in love and only had eyes for each other?"

"She did."

"And did Irene say that you are the spitting image of Jacqueline, and you have Mr. Radford's eyes?"

"She did."

"And did Loretta Mae at House of Grace *also* say that you are the spitting image of Jacqueline?"

"She did."

"And did both Loretta Mae and Irene say that Jacqueline named her baby Alex."

"They did."

"And did a lady named Drucilla deliver Jacqueline's baby Alex from the House of Grace over to Harold and Joyce Stuart down in Harlan?"

"She did."

"And did the Stuarts rename her Ellie?"

"They did."

"And finally, there's the most compelling evidence of all!"

"What?"

"Is there, or is there not, as Loretta Mae pointed out, a birthmark shaped like Florida on your left butt?"

She laughed. "There is!"

"As your legal advisor, I'm required too verify this alleged buttmark!"

"Verify that Kroger truck first!"

Quinn swerved around a Kroger semi backing out of an alley.

"As I said before, there's one other possibility," Ellie said.

"What's that?"

"My mother had an affair with someone else at *The Pines*. A chauffeur, a butler, a traveling salesman, a moonshiner."

"Not according to Irene!" Quinn said, as he pulled into Southern Genetics and parked. They stepped out into the warm humid morning air filled with the sweet scent of lilac. She felt anxious and clutched Quinn's arm as they approached the sprawling, glass-and-brick three-story building.

One minute later, they were led down a hall and into a large, wood paneled conference room with light display boxes mounted on the walls. She saw the Estate Executor, Fletcher Falcone, and three other men chatting around a large gleaming wood table.

When Falcone saw her, he hoisted his three hundred pounds onto his small loafers and smiled. "Ellie, Quinn, good to see y'all again." He waved them toward two empty leather chairs at the table.

A thin man with ruddy cheeks, rimless glasses and a toothy smile stood and shook their hands.

"Welcome to Southern Genetics folks. I'm Doctor Lester Atkins, Director, and this is my associate, Doctor Chester Paul, Director of Laboratory Services." He pointed to a small man who smiled up from a motorized wheelchair plastered with NASCAR stickers.

"Folks call us Lester and Chester," Chester said with a grin.

Ellie and Quinn smiled back.

"Would y'all like some coffee, water, soft drink?" Dr. Atkins said.

"No, thanks," Ellie and Quinn said.

Ellie felt tension crackling around her like static electricity. Her knees trembled beneath the table. Perspiration beaded on her lips. She wondered if she'd used enough Arrid Extra Dry? She wondered if she'd used *any?*

Fletcher Falcone smiled and said, "Doctor Atkins here was just explaining about DNA. Lordy, Lordy, all the maternal DNA stuff, and the father's Y-DNA, and Haplogroups and DYS values. And how the mother's DNA gets passed down from mother to daughter to daughter, down through thousands of years without ever changing a lick! Amazing, but way too scientific for this old county lawyer."

The door swung open and a thin man in a white lab coat walked in carrying three large envelopes. Watery blue eyes and scraggy blond hair dominated his face. He handed the envelopes to Dr. Atkins who unsealed them, pulled out a report and some flimsy films. Dr. Atkins placed one film on a light box and flipped the switch, backlighting the film.

"If you walk over here, Ellie, you'll see your very own DNA blueprint."

She walked over and looked at the rows of letters and little smudge-like marks, some darker and larger than others.

"Your DNA is unique to you, Ellie. Everyone's is unique!"

"And here," he said, placing another film beside hers, "is the DNA of Jacqueline Moreau."

Dr. Atkins stared at both films, then leaned close and studied them further, his face revealing nothing. Then, he checked the written report and turned back to Ellie.

"Ellie, without question, these DNA films prove that Jacqueline Moreau gave birth to you. She is your biological mother."

Ellie felt an incredible sense of calm wash over her . . . a sense of finally coming home . . . of being embraced by the woman who gave birth to her . . . Jacqueline Moreau . . . whose ancestors came from France to Martinique. Ellie felt part of a *family*, probably still had family in Martinique, maybe her grandparents were alive. Some day she'd go see them.

"Congratulations, Ellie!" Fletcher Falcone said, smiling.

"Thank you."

"Doctor, how accurate is this test?" Falcone asked.

"99.9% accurate. No question about it. Jacqueline Moreau gave birth to you, Ellie!"

Quinn smiled and placed his hand on hers.

Dr. Atkins unsealed another envelope, pulled out a film and clipped it to the light box. "And this is Leland T. Radford's DNA that I'm placing alongside your DNA."

Ellie's heartbeat pounded in her ears. Dr. Atkins studied Radford's film for several seconds, then Ellie's film, then Radford's again. He paged through the written report, then looked back at Radford's films and hers again. He seemed to study certain long smudges in particular. Then he looked at a series of three-letter combinations for several seconds. His face revealed nothing.

Everyone leaned forward, waiting.

"Well, Doctor?" Falcone said.

Dr. Atkins paused. "Quite clearly, Ellie, these test results show that your DNA and the DNA of Leland T. Radford . . . do *not* match. I'm sorry, but Mr. Radford can not possibly be your biological father."

Ellie felt like she'd been kicked in the stomach.

Looking shocked, Fletcher Falcone stood up, clearly jolted by the news. "But Doctor, just how certain is this result?"

"When proving who the father is, DNA is even more certain. 99.9999 percent accurate."

The room went silent.

"Look, Ellie," Dr. Atkins said, "you can see the differences here and there." He pointed them out and she saw them.

"We use the 16 DNA markers, including the critical 13 CODIS markers."

Fletcher Falcone shook his head and looked at Ellie. "I just can't believe this! Your hair and eyes look like Leland's. I was certain you were his daughter. I even began revising his probate documents to that effect."

Quinn also looked shocked. "Doctor Atkins, is there any chance Mr. Radford's DNA sample was accidentally switched with someone else's?"

Dr. Atkins seemed a bit taken aback. "Fair question, Quinn. But there's virtually no chance. Our ISO and AABB accreditations assure the absolute highest quality in sample-to-name monitoring by our distinguished PhDs . . . at seven checkpoints in our process."

"But, Doctor," Falcone said, "let's be absolutely certain about this. I'd like to request that we run the test again."

"A second test makes sense," Quinn said, looking at Ellie.

Ellie agreed and nodded.

"No problem," Dr. Atkins said, as he turned to the lab assistant who brought the DNA films. "Mr. Klume, do we have sufficient DNA specimen samples for a second test?"

Klume paused, then nodded slowly.

"Good. Then let's do it. And we'll expedite it as well."

"Thank you," Ellie said.

The meeting broke up.

Ellie and Quinn stepped outside and headed toward his TrailBlazer. As they drove away, Ellie noticed Quinn shaking his head.

"What's wrong?" she asked.

"The DNA."

"The DNA says I'm not Radford's daughter."

"*That* DNA test says you're not."

"Are you suggesting the lab - "

" - I'm suggesting lab technicians are people . . . and people make mistakes . . . or sometimes are forced to change the results."

"But Southern Genetics has an excellent reputation."

"Maybe one of their employees doesn't."

They drove in silence for a while.

Then Ellie said, "I think we should do our own independent DNA test."

Quinn nodded. "We're crazy if we don't."

* * *

And crazy if you do, Huntoon Harris thought to himself. He was delighted at how well the tiny listening device in Quinn's car worked.

FORTY TWO

After the disappointing DNA news at Southern Genetics, Ellie had phoned her good friend, Jessica Bishop, and explained what she needed. Jessica, a U of K pre-med student and lab researcher, told her to drive immediately to nearby Gen-Ident. Minutes later, Ellie and Quinn entered Gen-Ident's lobby, and found themselves surrounded by lots of glass and chrome, elevator music, avant-garde artwork. All very modern . . . except for the receptionist's 1960 orange beehive hairdo and puffy bracelets that jingled like Santa's sleigh as she filed her nails.

"Ellie Stuart to see Jessica Bishop."

"Oh . . . yes, Jessie's 'spectin' y'all." She smiled and spoke into her headphone.

"She's fixin' to come right down. Just put these visitor badges on and y'all kin wait over yonder." She jingled her bracelets toward some chairs. They walked over and sat beside a table stacked with science magazines.

Ellie looked up at a wall painting entitled *The Blueprint of Life*. It showed DNA's double helix interwoven like two slinkies twisted together.

"So, how long have you known Jessica?"

"Since clay bunnies in kindergarten. Hers were better."

"What's she like?"

"Nice, attractive and six-three.

"Wow!"

"In eighth grade she was already six-one. Lots of cruel jokes. 'Duck Jessica – there's a satellite!' She laughed it off, but I know it hurt. She smart, earned a pre-med scholarship to U of K."

Ellie heard footsteps. Turning, she saw Jessica in a white lab coat and safety glasses around her neck. Her large dark-green eyes and auburn hair looked good with the band of freckles sprinkled across her face.

Ellie stood and hugged her, then they looked each other over for a second.

"Jessica . . . you look like America's Next Top Model!"

"Marry me!"

"Later," Ellie said. "Meet Quinn Parker."

They shook hands.

"So, Jessie, what's new?"

"Jim is new! Jim is six-feet-seven. Jim is a man I can finally look up to."

Ellie remembered Jessie's prom date was five-six.

"Jessica's pager beeped. She looked at the number, frowned and turned it off. She was obviously busy.

"So, Ellie, on the phone you said you needed an independent paternity test of your DNA."

"Yes."

"Whose DNA do you want us to compare it to?"

"Leland T. Radford."

Jessica blinked as though trying to recall the name, then her eyes shot open. "Wait – the wealthy man who died down in Manchester a few weeks ago?"

Ellie nodded.

"You really know how to pick 'em!"

"DNA will decide that."

"True, but we'll need some of Mr. Radford's DNA."

"Southern Genetic Lab got his DNA from Manchester Memorial Hospital where he passed away a few weeks ago."

"That helps."

"Why?"

"We handle most of Manchester's DNA work here. And I know the right person there. But on the phone you said Southern Genetics determined your DNA did *not* match Mr. Radford's."

"That's right."

"But," Quinn said, "we think that test may have been flawed, or maybe altered."

"Southern Genetics is an excellent facility, and highly respected."

"Yes, but someone there might have been . . . negligent, or maybe even forced to alter the DNA test."

"Forced? Why?"

"Because certain people could lose a lot of revenue if Ellie is Mr. Radford's sole heir."

Jessica paused. "I see . . ."

"The probate court date is in four days," Quinn said. "Any chance we can get the test results in a couple of days?"

"That's quick. Can you ask the court for a postponement?"

"If we do, everyone will know we're running our own independent test."

"So . . .?

"Someone might try to tamper with it here."

Jessica's eyes widened.

"Jessie . . .?" Ellie said.

"Yeah?"

"Please keep this test secret just between us . . ."

"Sure, but why?"

"Someone's tried to kill me."

"More than once," Quinn added.

Jessica's mouth dropped open. "Jesus, Ellie! Why didn't you say so? I'll get your test done within the next thirty-six hours."

The door opened and a lab technician walked in. He swabbed the inside of Ellie's cheeks, placed the swab kit in an envelope, sealed it and left.

"I'll call as soon as I have something."

Ellie and Quinn thanked her and left.

Driving back to Louisville, Quinn said, "I'm concerned they might learn about Jennifer's test and mess with the results?"

"I'm concerned they may mess with Jessica."

FORTY THREE

Ellie was excited, pumped up! She was going on a *date!*
Quinn had called it - 'A date to Celebrate Your Birth Mother.'

But still a boy-girl date!

Tonight, she and Quinn would not spend time with lab technicians swabbing her mouth for DNA.

Tonight, with a little luck, Quinn's mouth might swab hers!

This was maybe her fifth date in two years. And the only one she really wanted to go on since Mark Miller was killed in Afghanistan.

But one thing about tonight's date with Quinn puzzled her -*why me?*

Why ask me out when drop-dead gorgeous, filthy rich, debutante-to-be Jennifer was so clearly in love with him? It made no sense.

Unless . . . Ellie thought, *Jennifer put Quinn up to it, made him ask me out - as a prank - so that Jennifer could then regale her society pals with sidesplitting stories about Quinn's date with the hick chick . . . "poor Ellie had to scrape manure off her clodhoppers before they'd let her in the restaurant."*

Is that what tonight's date is about? A sham? Would Quinn go along with that? She'd only known him a few days. Did she really know him that well? Did she misjudge him?

No – dammit!

The Quinn she knew would never do that to her.

She shook off her hick chick insecurities and checked herself in the mirror. Her slinky black dress, her *only* fancy dress, eleven bucks at *Sam's Seconds Shoppe*, looked pretty good for a second-hand knock-off of a Donna Karan knock-off. She wondered if it was appropriate for the swanky restaurant Quinn said he was taking her to?

The doorbell rang. She walked to the front door and looked through the peephole. Sarah, their neighbor. Ellie opened the door.

"Sorry, wrong house," Sarah said.

Ellie laughed.

"Look at you, Ellie! Quinn hasn't got a chance!"

"Thanks, Sarah."

Sarah stepped inside. "Wow! That dress and those ankle-strap shoes! Promise me you'll have a *great* time."

"I promise."

"And a romantic time."

"Ease up, mom!"

Sarah laughed, but Ellie realized that in many ways Sarah had become her surrogate mom, mentor, confessor, and pinch-hit-caretaker for Celeste. Ellie knew that if by some highly DNA miracle she inherited enough of Radford's wealth, she would offer to pay off the mortgages on Celeste's and Sarah's homes, and arrange for both loving women to live their remaining years like Queens of Sheba.

She heard a car pull into the driveway. Looking outside, she saw Quinn step from his TrailBlazer like a *GQ* model. He wore a blue blazer, light-blue shirt and gray slacks. The evening sun tinted his hair chestnut-brown.

She hurried outside.

"You look wow!" he said, scanning her from head to toe.

"Thanks, and you didn't fall off a turnip wagon."

He smiled. "You up for some great French cuisine?"

"*Oui! Oui, monsieur!*"

"We're dining at *Le Relais*."

"*THE Le Relais?*"

"The very one."

She knew *Le Relais* had long been one of Louisville's best restaurants. Although reasonably priced for a gourmet restaurant, a meal there probably equaled her weekly food budget.

They got in Quinn's car and drove off. As Quinn turned the corner, she saw an unfamiliar gray Saab parked nearby with an unfamiliar bearded man wearing sunglasses behind the wheel. The man watched them as they drove by.

She turned to Quinn. "So, Mr. Parker, how does a struggling law student afford dinner at the very chi-chi *Le Relais*?"

"Dinner's free."

"Really?"

"Yep. Two years ago, a University of Louisville fan won a ton of money when I caught the winning touchdown against Vanderbilt. He gave me three free dinners for two at *Le Relais*. This is my third dinner. I've been saving it for someone really special . . . but no one special came along . . . so I figured what the hell, I'll take you instead."

"Golly whiz, thanks." Ellie laughed, even though she knew the other two dinners were with Jennifer.

Minutes later, they pulled up at the *Le Relais* restaurant located in the old Bowman Field airport terminal. She'd read that Bowman Field was the longest continually operating airport in the United States and that World War One pilots had trained there.

A valet took their car and as they walked under the green neon *Le Relais* sign, she heard a plane take off.

Like her relationship with Quinn maybe.

And just maybe . . . like her relationship with Mark Miller had. As a freshman, she fell hard for Mark, an electrical engineering senior. Mark had a National Guard scholarship, a 3.9 GPA, and *summa cum laude* sense of humor. He was a scary-smart farm boy with strawberry blond hair. They hit it off in part because they'd both been adopted.

She remembered their drive back to his charming home in Shelbyville, Indiana. They visited his foster parents, and his aunts who owned the successful *Three Sisters Books & Gifts* store. Ellie had fallen in love with the people and the town.

Then . . . three weeks into Mark's master's program, the National Guard sent him and his unit to Fort Bragg for basic training and then deployed him to Afghanistan.

Seven months later, he came home. She wept as they carried his flag-draped pine box from the C5 cargo plane. One of twelve KIAs that week.

Mark's death devastated her. Since then, she dated just a few times. Nice guys from school. But no Mr. Magic. To be honest, she wasn't looking for Mr. Magic. She wasn't looking to feel that kind of loss and pain ever again.

But then came Quinn. From the start she was attracted to him. He was considerate without forcing it, intelligent without demonstrating it, a big man on campus without flaunting it, and, oh yeah, *I almost forgot, handsome without strutting it.*

But now, as they walked into *Le Relais,* she saw something had changed in his eyes.

Something was troubling Quinn. And it was serious. As she wondered what it could be, she failed to notice something across the street.

The unfamiliar gray Saab had just parked.

FORTY FOUR

"You're positive?" Mason Marweg asked.

"Yes!" the man said. "She's not his daughter. DNA proves it!" *How many times will this pushy little dwarf ask me the same damn question?*

They sat at a picnic table in a sprawling forest twenty-five miles east of Louisville. They were alone, surrounded by lush evergreens and a crystal blue lake he'd rather be fishing in than listening to the loud-mouthed midget.

He looked at Marweg's three big aggressive wolverines circling the picnic table. He despised the filthy beasts almost as much as he despised Marweg. The man demanded things: *Give me the sole right to buy Radford's twelve thousand acres. Give me two more numbered offshore accounts to stash a few million in. Give me thirty percent off my legal fees. Greedy little bastard!*

On the other hand, the dwarf had paid him fat legal fees over the years.

The wolverines growled, begging permission to attack a squirrel taunting them from a tree.

"How precise is this DNA test?" Marweg demanded.

"99.999% accurate!" he said. "And a second DNA test will be equally accurate in proving she's not Radford's daughter!"

"How can you be so sure?"

"Because I am, Marweg."

"So, when do I get Radford's 12,000 acres?"

"Two months after probate."

"That's too damn long!"

"Two months. Radford stipulated it in his will."

Marweg glowered.

The squirrel jumped to the ground and ran. Marweg snapped his clicker and wolverines raced after it. The squirrel scampered up another tree a split second before the wolverines' jaws snapped shut. The squirrel continued taunting them, thinking they were dogs. Big mistake. The largest wolverine shot up the tree and clawed the surprised squirrel's tail as it leaped to another tree.

Marweg clicked his clicker twice and the bear-like animals came back and sat.

"I want my 12,000 acres!"

"You'll get them!"

He knew Marweg would pay almost any price for Radford's land. As CEO of one of the largest conglomerates of coal companies in Appalachia, Marweg had lusted after Radford's twelve thousand acres for many years. But tree-hugger Radford refused, saying he'd do anything to "protect the forests from strip mines, strip malls and strip clubs!"

"Where's the mining survey that revealed vast coal reserves?" Marweg asked.

"Dead and buried."

"And the surveyor?"

"Dead and buried."

Marweg nodded approval. "And the selling price?"

"Still the same, Marweg. With my fair fee tacked on, of course."

"Of course." The dwarf frowned begrudgingly, then fluffed his wind-blown pompadour up a couple inches.

At thirteen thousand dollars per acre, times twelve thousand acres, the purchase price was nearly one hundred and sixty million dollars. *My sales commission, after everything, is a sweet four million dollar slice of the bituminous pie. Life is good.*

"What if *she* goes outside for an independent DNA test?" Marweg asked.

"I'll know."

"And then what?"

"That test will also prove she's not his daughter."

"And if she goes for another test?"

"Same result. Don't worry, Marweg."

But Marweg would worry of course. His raisin-size eyes zigzagged like a Chinese ping-pong match.

He stood up on his five-inch elevator shoes, clicked his clicker and said, "Car!"

Shamur, Goba and Goliath hurried over and crawled in the back seat of the black Rolls Royce.

The chauffeur then opened the front door. Marweg got in, rolled down the window and asked, "Tell me again why I should not worry?"

"Because dead people don't inherit," said Heinrich De Groot.

FORTY FIVE

Ellie sat in the *Le Relais,* a restaurant she could never afford . . . with a friend she could never thank enough. Quinn had changed her life.

She looked around at the stylish décor. *Le Relais* was the most elegant restaurant she'd ever been in. It was also the *only* elegant restaurant she'd ever been in. She ran her fingers over the starched double linen tablecloths and watched the white-coated waiters glide like skaters between tables covered with damask tableware and green-shaded lamps.

A tall, mustached waiter walked up to their table.

Quinn turned to her. "Ellie, our meal is free . . . so order whatever you'd like."

"Thanks. But my knowledge of French cuisine consists of . . . *le French fry.* Please order for me."

He nodded and ordered, and the waiter soon returned with two large glasses of Bordeaux.

When the waiter left, Quinn stared at her for several moments, his brow furrowing into a very serious look. He started to speak, stopped, then grew even more serious.

What was bothering him?

"There's something I should tell you," he said.

She waited.

"Jennifer and I are. . . ."

Please don't say - engaged!

He paused. "We are ah . . ."

Don't say it -

". . . we're breaking up!"

"Oh . . ."

She leaned back against her chair, stunned, and yes, relieved. And then she saw sadness in his eyes and felt bad for him. Or, was his sadness due to second thoughts about the breakup?

"I'm sorry, Quinn."

He shrugged.

She'd sensed he had issues with Jennifer, but nothing this serious. "It must be difficult for you both."

"Less difficult than continuing, Ellie. The breakup's been coming for months. I spoke with her about it yesterday for a long time."

Ellie nodded. "How is she handling this?"

"Angry at first. But now, she's says I'm just confused and will soon return to my senses – and to her."

"Could she be right?" *Please say no.*

He paused, then shook his head. "No . . ."

She eased air out through her lips.

"But what about the great job offer her father got you at Wagner, Hoffman and Musterman, Louisville's best law firm?"

"It'll probably be withdrawn."

"That's too bad, Quinn."

"*C'est la vie!* as one says in these parts. But hey, I'm senior editor of the Law Review and will graduate with the Order of the Coif. A sleazy ambulance chaser firm might snatch me up."

"A good firm will."

The waiter placed their meals on the table.

Ellie stared at the delicious-looking food. She considered whipping out her phone and taking a picture, but knew she'd look, as the French say, *très gauche.*

They began with *Le Relais'* tasty *Salade Maison,* then a *pâté du chef,* followed with some grilled tomatoes sprinkled with Parmesan cheese, and finally some veal slices sautéed in a light garlic mushroom sauce that made her mouth water. The Bordeaux enriched the taste of everything.

As they finished, she said, "Quinn, everything was fabulous. Incredibly delicious. I've never eaten food this wonderful. But I can't eat another morsel."

"What? Dessert is very special."

"High calorie?"

"No, just *high.*"

"I don't do drugs."

"Follow me, *Mademoiselle . . .*"

They walked through the bar and stepped outside onto a tarmac where she saw a small, old, bright red aircraft with double wings.

"What's Snoopy's airplane doing here?" she asked.

"That's our dessert!"

"What?" She was scared. "Quinn, I've never been on an airplane."

"We'll be *IN* it."

"But there's no roof!"

"It has seat belts . . ."

"But it's old!"

"Yep. World War I biplane - *but* with a modern engine and very sophisticated avionics."

"Like a barf bag?"

"Who's a wuss?"

"Me," she said as he helped her board the open-cockpit aircraft. He strapped her in beside him and nodded to the pilot in the seat behind that they were ready. The small single-engine aircraft raced down the runway at blinding speed, her heart pounding.

She squeezed Quinn's fingers white. In the side mirror her hair reverted to Bride of Frankenstein.

The wheels lifted off and the ground fell away below her. She was *flying – for God's Sake!*

I'M UP IN THE DAMN AIR . . . FLYING . . .

The airplane dipped hard and she knew it was going down. But . . . miraculously it leveled off.

They flew over the Early Times Whiskey distillery and she smelled the scent of fermenting sweet sour mash. And then over the University of Louisville Student Center where Quinn spilled her coffee, and then Celeste's home.

After a smooth landing at Bowman Field, she eased her grip on Quinn's fingers and saw them turn pink again. He drove back to Celeste's home and parked.

Quinn gave her his serious look. "The bad guys know you live here."

"I know."

"You shouldn't stay here tonight."

"I'm not. Celeste is next door at Sarah's. I'm staying over at my friend Lisa's. We're cramming for a big history test."

"Where's Lisa house?"

"Six blocks over. Would you drop me off?"

"Sure . . ."

Minutes later, Quinn pulled up to Lisa's, a small wood, one-story house near campus.

Ellie turned and smiled at him.

"Quinn. . ."

"Yeah?"

"Tonight was incredible. The food, and the airplane . . ."

"The sky's the limit with me."

She laughed, then he got that serious look again and stared at her. "I forgot something."

"What?"

"The other reason I broke up with Jennifer."

"What's that?

"Not what. Who."

She waited.

"A girl I spilled coffee on."

Her heart raced as his lips touched hers.

FORTY SIX

Ellie and Lisa studied to exhaustion. Ellie crawled into bed and closed her eyes, replaying Quinn's goodnight kiss a few thousand times. Finally, she felt herself drifting into dreamland.

And then . . . scraping woke her.

Outside.

She turned and looked at the window. No movement. No more scraping. Only wind gusts.

Then a large shadow swept across the curtain. A tree branch? A passing cloud? A man?

She listened. Only distant thunder. Light rain dotted the window. More gusts swayed tree branches back and forth.

Had she actually heard branches *scraping*? Or someone *prying* open a window?

Or was she dreaming?

Ellie walked to the window and peeked through the curtain. Lightning illuminated a picnic table in the side yard. The wind swept a tree branch beside the window, lashing shadows across the yard. The branch had probably scraped the side of the house. Probably her paranoia was back. Probably she should go back to bed.

But as she turned, she noticed something on the damp ground beneath the window. She squinted and saw *footprints!* A man's! They looked fresh.

Or does the misty rain make them look fresh?

Her heart pounded. Perspiration dotted her lip. She felt another panic attack coming on.

"What's wrong?" Lisa said from her bed in the corner.

Ellie spun around. "Oh, sorry, I didn't mean to wake you. I thought I heard a scraping sound."

"Where?"

"Outside the window. Maybe I dreamed it."

"You look frightened."

"Well, I'm sorta . . . nervous."

"You're *scared!*"

Ellie said nothing.

"You promised to call Quinn if you were."

"I can't call him every time I hear a strange sound."

"You're *terrified*! Call him."

Ellie paused for several seconds, decided Lisa was right, then dialed Quinn's number, feeling guilty about bothering him again.

"Hey Ellie. What's up?"

"You were right."

"About what?"

"I heard something outside. And there's a man's footprint beneath the window."

FORTY SEVEN

Ellie relaxed when Quinn's TrailBlazer and a Louisville Police car pulled up in front of the house at the same time.

She stepped onto the porch as the officer and Quinn rushed up the walk. Quinn hugged her and she felt her tension begin to melt.

"You okay?"

She nodded.

"What happened here, ma'am?" asked the tall, heavyset officer.

"I was awakened by a scraping sound outside that window. I looked out and saw what looked like a man's fresh footprints on the ground."

The officer walked over to the window, bent down and examined the area, then looked up at her.

"You *did* see a man's footprints. And they're *fresh*. Like these fresh scratches on this windowsill. Did you see the guy?"

"No."

The officer looked around. "We have a peeper in this area."

"There's more than peeping going on, officer," Quinn said. He quickly explained about the other attacks. When he finished, the officer stared at Ellie for several moments.

"Ma'am, I'd suggest you stay somewhere else tonight. You gotta place?"

"Yes, she does," Quinn said, looking at Ellie.

She nodded.

"Good." The officer photographed the footprint and windowsill, then called in for a CSI team.

As the policeman circled the house, Quinn turned to Ellie.

"They obviously know about your secret DNA test at Jessica's lab."

"But how? We told no one!"

"They probably followed us to her lab. And they think Jessica's test will prove you're Radford's daughter."

"Or they don't want to risk the chance I am."

He nodded.

"Either way," she said, "only one thing will stop them."

"What?"

"My funeral!"

"Not going to happen, Ellie!"

She prayed he was right.

"From now on I'm your shadow."

She liked the sound of that.

She said goodbye to Lisa, then got in Quinn's car. After making sure no one followed them, they parked a block from *The Brandeis House* and entered its rear entrance. They went up to his apartment, locked the door and left the lights off.

"Red wine?" he said.

She nodded.

He poured two large Merlots and handed her one.

"I cook with Merlot," he said. "Sometimes I even add it to the food."

She laughed, and it helped, but she noticed her fingers trembling. Using both hands, she took a long serious sip. Then she took another long serious sip, and seconds later the wine began to relax her.

Quinn then led her over to a two-seat sofa facing a large window. They plopped down beside each other and sat in silence for a while. She stared across the street into a large Victorian home where students hunched over textbooks, studying, something she should be doing since exams started in a few days.

"Ellie?"

"Yeah?"

"I'm worried they'll try to sabotage your test at Jessica's lab."

"I'll warn her." She dialed Jessica's phone and hit the speaker button. Jessica answered on the third ring.

"Hey, Ellie, I was just going to call you."

"Why?"

"Your new DNA test results will be ready early. Tomorrow afternoon."

"That's great."

"Yeah, but why'd you call?"

"To tell you to, ah . . . be very careful."

"Of what?"

"Of what just happened here."

When Ellie told her, Jessica was silent for a few moments.

"Don't worry, Ellie. Gen-Ident has a very sophisticated alarm system and our computer systems are guarded like Fort Knox. And our night guard is a big, tough ex-Navy SEAL."

"Good. But just to be extra safe, see if you can stay over at your boyfriend's tonight."

"Lemme roll over and ask him."

Ellie laughed.

"He said *yes*."

"Guy's a keeper."

"Oh yeah."

"Promise me you won't go to the lab until regular hours tomorrow."

"Gee mom, you're so strict!"

"Promise me!"

"All right already!"

They hung up.

Ellie sipped more wine and stared out the window. Suddenly, exhaustion hit her like she'd sprinted a mile. She yawned twice and fought off another.

"I'm fading fast," she said, resting her head on Quinn's shoulder. "Can you leave your shoulder here for a few minutes?"

"Only if I can leave the rest of me."

* * *

Quinn listened to her breathing deepen and slow. She was clearly exhausted by the emotional rollercoaster of the last three days. He was amazed how well she handled so many life changing - and life threatening - situations, sidestepping more hard jabs than an Ali-Foreman fight. Yet, she kept her cool. She was a tough, smart, funny, decent person. A rare combination in his experience. And frankly, a combination that had drawn him to her more each day. He kept looking for her flaw . . . but so far he'd only found one. Her sense of inferiority about being, as she called it, "a hick chick from Harlan." As far as he was concerned, the hick chick Ellie was a far better person than most city chicks he knew.

After a couple minutes he turned toward her and whispered, "You feeling safer now?"

No answer.

He saw she was asleep.

He waited a few minutes, eased his shoulder away and lowered her gently on the sofa. From the closet, he took a blanket and covered her.

Then he bent down and kissed her forehead.

He liked kissing her forehead.

He looked forward to kissing it again . . .

FORTY EIGHT

In the shadowy rear parking lot of Gen-Ident Labs, Huntoon Harris stuck his Glock into the skinny neck of his favorite nerd, Roy Klume. At the lab's rear entrance, Huntoon punched in the nine-digit code his pal hacked from the Gen-Ident security system. The door clicked open.

"I don't like doing this," Klume said.

"Tough shit, Roy!"

Huntoon shoved Klume inside, knowing the night security guard would be on his rounds for at least another eighteen minutes. More than enough time.

Huntoon hustled Klume upstairs to a large laboratory and led him over to a computer the hacker had turned on.

"Roy, your job's simple. Destroy Ellie's and Radford's DNA files and their specimen samples."

Klume said nothing.

"Then destroy lotsa other peoples' DNA files and specimens, too. Mess 'em up real bad. Make it look like some employee went fuckin' postal!"

"But these DNA tests might mean life and death to some sick people!"

"Tough shit!"

"But how will they know if they have a terminal disease?"

"They'll know when they die."

Klume hesitated.

"Roy, how's that cute wife and them young girls of yourn?"

Klume sat at the computer.

Huntoon handed over the password his hacker pal gave him. Klume entered the company's private *Intranet*, typed *Ellie Stuart* and then *Leland Radford* and moments later rows of numbers and letters filled the screen. He kept scrolling and hitting *Delete*.

"And destroy them backup systems. And don't fergit that shit up in the Cloud wherever it is. Wipe all that out!"

While Klume worked, Huntoon watched the lab's long window facing the adjoining offices. Even though the lab lights were off, Huntoon worried a night worker would walk by and see them. He also worried the guard might notice the black tape Huntoon stuck on the lab's surveillance camera lens.

"Hurry up!" Huntoon whispered.

"I am hurrying!"

"*Faster!*"

Two minutes later, Klume said, "The files are deleted."

"Now, put Radford's and Ellie's remaining DNA specimens in this leather bag."

Klume walked over to four large, round, stainless steel containers labeled *Cryogenic Storage*. He lifted one container lid and frosty air mushroomed out. Moments later, he took out two icy containers and showed them to Huntoon. One label read *E. Stuart*, the other *L. T. Radford*. Huntoon placed them in the bag.

Klume removed several more frosty tubes, dumped some on the floor and put the rest in the bag, then closed the freezer lid.

Then Huntoon heard something. Beside him.

A key sliding into a side door.

He moved behind the door as a middle-aged cleaning lady stepped in. Before she could turn and see them, Huntoon karate-chopped the side of her neck hard and she fell unconscious. He tied her wrists using her vacuum cleaner cord, then dragged her behind a lab table.

"You've killed her!" Klume said.

"Bullshit! She'll wake up in fifteen minutes."

Huntoon then wiped Klume's fingerprints off everything, threw some file reports onto the floor, then crushed a few DNA frosty tubes with his heel of his boot.

"Roy, look at me!"

Klume looked at him.

"If you screwed with me here and left any of Ellie's and Radford's DNA stuff here, I'll kill your wife and kids and make it look like you done it. And then I'll kill you, Roy. A family-murder-suicide thing. Happens all the time. I seen it on TV. Understand?"

Klume turned sheet-white.

"So tell me – did you leave any of their DNA here?"

"No."

They left the lab and exited the back door.

Huntoon drove off, feeling good. Job done. The boss, Heinrich De Groot, would be mighty impressed.

Minutes later, they pulled up to Roy Klume's home.

"Remember, Roy, if someone asks where you was at tonight, what you gonna say?"

"Commonwealth Stadium."

"For what?"

"Pep rally."

"For what game?"

"Kentucky-Tennessee."

"You're smart as a whip, Roy."

FORTY NINE

Quinn settled in at his usual table at U of L's Brandeis Law School library. He began catching up on reviewing his case summaries when his phone vibrated: Caller ID read: *Jessica Bishop*. He hurried out to the entrance hall where phone calls were allowed.

"Hey, Jessica, what's up?"

"Problem."

"What?"

"Ellie was right!"

He waited.

"Two men broke into our lab last night. Somehow they got our lab's entrance code, came in and hacked into our Intranet system. They destroyed a ton of DNA records and specimens."

Quinn slumped against the wall. "Including Ellie's and Radford's?"

"Yeah."

He felt like punching a hole in the wall.

"Our security video shows the men wore sunglasses, hats and fake beards. Impossible to see their faces."

Quinn slumped in a nearby chair. "Jessica, I'm so sorry. What a disaster!"

"Not completely."

"What?"

"I did a backup test."

"But why didn't they destroy it?"

"It wasn't done here. I did it at our Frankfort lab."

Quinn pumped his fist in the air. "Jessica, you're a genius."

"Tell my boss. Meanwhile, Ellie's Frankfort results should be ready this afternoon."

"Terrific. Who knows about the Frankfort test?"

"Just you, me, and the Frankfort lab technician."

"Do you know the technician well?"

Jessica paused. "No . . . they said he's a substitute.

* * *

Ellie sat in the den as eighty-four-year old Celeste watched her favorite TV show, *Animal Planet*. Celeste giggled. Ellie wondered why? She looked and saw a chimp throw something dark that stuck to the zookeeper's pants, then kinda slid down. *Chimp poop*, Ellie realized. The chimp and Celeste laughed again, and so did Ellie. Anything that made Celeste laugh – even turd-tossing - was good.

Ellie's phone rang: it was Quinn.

A few hours ago, he'd told her that two men destroyed hers and Leland Radford's DNA samples in the lab, but that Jessica had a back-up test done.

"What's up?"

"Your backup test results will be ready in Jessica's Frankfort lab in an hour. Can you leave now?"

"Sure. Sarah's here."

Minutes later, Ellie hurried outside and got into Quinn's Trail-Blazer.

He looked at her and smiled. "So, are you ready to be a Radford?"

"Maybe not . . ."

"Why?"

"It's proving hazardous to my health."

He nodded. "Mine too now that I think about it."

Quinn drove east on I 64. They passed a shiny old red Chevy El Camino and Ellie wondered if it might be Harold and Joyce Stuart's cherished red El Camino . . . the one they had to sell to pay for Harold's miner's lung medications when the mining company and insurance firm refused to pay.

"Ellie, my professor gave me the name of a top probate attorney to represent you. Henri Delacroix."

"I thought Mr. Falcone, the Executor, handled the estate?"

"He does. But he represents the *estate's* interests. Henri Delacroix will represent *your* potential interest."

"*If* I have any. And by the way Quinn, I can't afford a high-priced lawyer."

"Mr. Delacroix is doing this on the cheap as a favor to my professor."

"But I insist on paying him something!"

"He said you could 'pay him whatever and whenever.' I suggest a modest amount if we lose, more if you win."

"Please thank him."

"I will."

Once again, Quinn had come through with the legal advice she could not afford to be without . . . and could not afford to pay for.

Minutes later, as they drove near Frankfort, she noticed Quinn kept checking the rearview mirror.

"Don't tell me," she said.

"What?"

"That the black Navigator or red pickup is following us again?"

"They're not."

"Good!"

"A blue Jeep is."

She spun around and glimpsed the dark blue Jeep behind a vegetable delivery truck, three cars back. Two large men sat in front.

"It's been back there since Louisville. Usually three or four cars back. I slow down, it slows down."

"Right now it's speeding toward us!"

"Hang on!" Quinn hit the gas and raced around a furniture truck.

She checked the mirror. "Forget it. The Jeep just exited."

Ellie exhaled and shook her head, "What's another word for paranoid?"

"*Us* . . ."

She nodded. "But you know what they say about us paranoids?"

"What?"

"We only have to be right once to be right!"

Quinn smiled as he exited I-64 and headed toward the center of Frankfort.

Overhead, Ellie heard the roar of an aircraft. She looked up and saw a twin-engine Cessna descending toward Frankfort's Capitol City Airport. To her right, the huge dome of the Kentucky State Capitol gleamed white against the robin-egg-blue sky. The green Kentucky River, meandering alongside them, headed toward the center of town, like they were.

Quinn turned on Brown's Ferry Road and headed toward the Gen-Ident Lab. They passed a lush emerald golf course, then crossed the river and turned onto East Main Street.

"Quinn . . .!"

"Yeah?"

"Silver Toyota SUV. Three cars back! Made the same four turns you just made."

Quinn made a quick turn onto a narrow street.

Ellie checked. "Make that *five*."

———

Quinn turned onto Mero Street.

She looked back. "Still there!"

Quinn careened onto a wide street and accelerated toward the Capital Plaza area.

The Toyota sped after them.

Quinn shot through a yellow light.

The Toyota *ran* the red light.

"He's gaining!" Ellie said.

Quinn passed some big trucks. "Do you see him now?"

"No. He's blocked behind a car hauler."

Ellie saw the Frankfort Convention Center ahead and pointed at a parking garage.

"Quinn – maybe lose him in the garage!"

He ducked into the garage, grabbed the ticket, shot down to the lower level and said, "Let's take the rear exit."

"*NO!*" she said, pointing. "Look - the exit's backed up! He'll see us in line."

"*Shit!*" Quinn raced to the far end of the garage. "Did he see us enter the garage?"

"I don't think so. But maybe." She pointed to an empty spot beside a yellow Penske truck. Quinn backed in to hide the car's license plate against the wall.

They jumped out and hurried through a side exit door onto Clinton Street where they merged into a mob of noisy conventioneers strolling toward the Frankfort Center.

Ellie looked around and saw no silver Toyotas. They hurried over to a yellow taxi and got in.

"Where y'all goin'?"

"Straight ahead," Quinn said.

The taxi drove off.

Ellie looked back and saw the Toyota pull up near the garage entrance. The driver looked left and right, paused, then drove off in the *opposite* direction.

"Just drive us around town a while," Quinn said to the ear-studded young driver in a blue University of Kentucky sweatshirt. "And tell us if you see a silver Toyota SUV following you."

The driver's eyes shot open.

"Whoa . . . y'all, like, bein' . . . followed?"

"Yeah."

"Awe-some . . .!"

The cabbie gave them the Frankfort mini tour, with non-stop commentary on Daniel Boone's grave, the State Capitol Building, the old governor mansion, the new governor mansion and handed them two 50%-off coupons for Ramsey's Fried Chicken. Minutes later, he stopped back at the Convention Center garage. Ellie saw no sign of the silver Toyota. They returned to Quinn's TrailBlazer and drove out of the garage.

"Next stop, Jessica's lab!" she said.

"Not yet!" Quinn floored the accelerator. Ellie's head snapped back against the seat. In the mirror she saw why.

The silver Toyota bolted from behind a gas station billboard and raced after them.

"Look for Second Street," Quinn said.

"The lab's on *Patterson*!"

"The cops are on Second. The taxi passed it."

Quinn careened onto Main Street, raced ahead two blocks, then turned left and seconds later screeched to a stop in front of the modern, gray-stone Frankfort Police Headquarters.

Behind them, the silver Toyota pulled over to the curb, paused, then shot down a side street.

They hurried inside the station and told a white-haired officer on desk duty about the silver Toyota SUV.

The officer frowned. "Reckon we got us a problem."

"Why?" Ellie asked.

"Ten miles from here is the Georgetown Toyota plant. They build 550,000 vehicles a year. There's thousands of silver Toyota

SUVs in the state, hundreds in this area. We'll put out a BOLO, but finding the *right* one will be like looking for a specific blade of grass at a sod farm."

Ellie felt her frustration surge. "We have another problem, officer."

"What's that?"

"Being followed when we leave here."

"No problem, ma'am. *We'll* be the only one following you! We'll trail y'all for a few miles. Make sure no silver Toyotas or any other vehicle follows you."

"Thanks, Officer," Quinn said.

Ellie and Quinn got in his TrailBlazer and drove off with two police cars tucked right behind them.

Ellie said, "I'm calling Jessica to set up another place to meet."

"Makes sense."

After several seconds, Jessica answered.

"Hey, Ellie, where are you -?"

" – someone was following us, but I don't want them following us to your lab."

"Nor do I."

"Let's meet out of town."

Jessica paused a few seconds. "Okay. McCarthy's Bar on Upper Street in Lexington. Thirty minutes. I'll bring the DNA results. See you there."

If we're lucky . . . Ellie thought.

FIFTY

In the *Rendez Booze Saloon,* a redneck saloon ten miles west of Lexington, Heinrich De Groot sat in a dark corner, squeezing his 24-carat gold Montblanc pen, trying hard not to ram it into the pea-sized brain of Huntoon Harris.

"Explain something!" De Groot said.

"Whut . . .?"

"How can you follow terrorists down an exploding road in Iraq, but can't follow a college kid down I-64?"

"This guy Quinn drives like Dale Earnhardt."

"And you drive like Ray Charles!"

Huntoon's face turned beet red. "I was gainin' on the bastard when he stopped at the police station. Got my ass outta there fast!"

"Only thing you did right!"

Behind him at the bar, De Groot heard someone shout "Fuck you!"

He turned and saw a huge guy taunting a small hunchback about his hump. The hunchback slapped a blackjack against the bully's head so hard the bully's glass eye popped out, skittered across the floor and rolled toward the men's room. As the big guy ran after his eye, the hunchback hightailed it outside and roared off on his Harley.

Trailer-trash! De Groot thought, disgusted he had to meet here to avoid being recognized.

He turned back to Huntoon. "Find out where the hell Ellie Stuart and Quinn went in Frankfort. I'm sure they went to another lab. Find out which one, then tell me immediately!"

"Right!"

De Groot picked up his *Financial Times* and started reading, knowing this was the only time the paper had been in the *Rendez Booze Saloon.*

A minute later, it dawned on Huntoon he'd been dismissed, and he left.

De Groot was concerned about Ellie Stuart. Her follow-up DNA test at Southern Genetics Labs had just confirmed, as he knew it would, that she was *not* Radford's daughter. And last night, Huntoon and Roy Klume had destroyed her and Radford's DNA tests and samples at the Gen-Ident lab.

But De Groot suspected she'd ordered yet another secret DNA test. Why else would she return to Frankfort? It was time to make her DNA irrelevant. It was time for Nicolai Sergei Pushkin.

De Groot took out his untraceable burner phone and dialed. As it rang, he thought about Pushkin. The Russian ex-KGB operative was the most terrifying man De Groot had ever known. And the most reliable.

"Yes . . .?" Pushkin said in a soft whispery voice that reminded him of Peter Lorre, the creepy-voiced old movie star.

"I need some dry cleaning," De Groot said.

"When?"

"Now."

"Short notice."

"Couldn't be helped."

"How important?"

"Very! When can you get to Louisville?" De Groot asked.

Pause. "Plane ready. Two hours."

"Excellent."

"Need all info *now!* Name, address, photo, background, hourly schedule, send all now. Put in email draft folder."

"Will do. The usual fee?" De Groot asked.

"*Nyet!* Express cleaning cost extra."

"How much extra?"

"Twenty thousand!"

De Groot swallowed at the nearly $60,000 price tag, then realized he could withdraw the money from the trust fund of Lucille Puckett, his 87-year-old tobacco heiress client, drooling away with dementia. He'd replace the money from his enormous Radford estate sales commissions.

"Half to Belize account now, half after," Pushkin said.

"Agreed, but this is very important! No screwups."

"Have I ever let you down?"

"No."

Click.

As usual, Pushkin had hung up within sixty seconds. His KGB phone training was too entrenched.

De Groot thought back to the night he'd met the six-foot-five, two-hundred-thirty-pound, blond, muscular Russian – and not a moment too soon. The mob had just given De Groot another pay-up-now threat. De Groot refused, so the mob sent its top three persuaders: Gino Fat Lips, Sam Strunzala and Carlucci Skotzene. They cornered him in an alley and started beating him with a Louisville Slugger.

Then Strunzala pulled out a handgun and aimed it at De Groot's knee. As he started to pull the trigger, the gun flew from his hand - thanks to Nikolai Pushkin who'd appeared from nowhere and rammed Strunzala's head into a brick wall. Strunzala dropped like wet cement.

Gino Fat Lips, enraged and swinging the bat, rushed toward Pushkin. The big Russian didn't move until the last second when he ducked the bat and rammed an ice pick deep into the man's ear. Fat Lips collapsed into a seizure. Carlucci Skotzene was last seen running from the alley.

De Groot had never seen anything like it. He stared down at the two bodies, then at Pushkin. "You saved my life. Why?"

"They have weapons. You have none."

"But I have these," De Groot said, handing Pushkin three crisp one-hundred-dollar bills.

The big Russian seemed surprised, but pocketed the money.

"Are you available for, ah . . . similar assignments?" De Groot asked.

"Always available, if price good."

And he had been available over the years. De Groot helped Pushkin get rid of some major personal immigration problems and Pushkin helped De Groot get rid of some major people problems. The man had never failed him.

Nor would he now.

FIFTY ONE

LEXINGTON

Ellie and Quinn walked inside McCarthy's Irish Bar. She squinted, adjusting to the dim lighting. Customers hunched over small round tables sipping their drinks, a few danced in a back room, some cheered a Kentucky basketball game.

Ellie hoped to cheer her DNA in a few minutes.

Despite just learning that her second DNA test at Southern Genetics reconfirmed she was *not* Leland Radford's daughter, maybe, just maybe she'd have the luck of the Irish here. She'd read that Radford was an Irish name. If she was a Radford – she'd shout, "The drinks are on me!"

She looked around. Lots of blue-collar workers and white-collar businessmen hunched over whiskey, and no-collar students hunched over pitchers of beer. On the jukebox the Clancy Brothers sang about a "Whistlin' Gypsy." On the walls, paintings celebrated the *olde* sod,

---

Ireland, and the new sod, Kentucky, with Derby winners Secretariat, Citation, Whirlaway and others. In Kentucky, the important celebrities have hooves.

She and Quinn sat down to wait for Jessica.

A well-endowed waitress in a red T-shirt strolled toward their table, jiggling her considerable endowments. Ellie noticed Quinn noticing her endowments.

"What can I get y'all?"

Breasts like yours, Ellie wanted to say, but said, "A Guinness, please."

"Same for me," Quinn said.

The waitress checked their IDs, sashayed off and a minute later placed the creamy stout beers in front of them.

Quinn turned to Ellie. "May the wee leprechauns bless your DNA and place a vile curse on your enemies!"

"I'll drink to that!" she said, clicking his glass and sipping some foamy Guinness. She liked its thick malt taste, sort of like an Irish milk shake.

The door opened and Jessica Bishop in her white lab coat, stepped inside. Several customers looked up at the attractive six-foot-three woman.

Ellie waved her over and Jessica zigzagged through the crowd like a broken field runner. She sat down, clutching a large *Gen-Ident* envelope.

"Anyone follow you?" Quinn asked.

"No. I checked."

The waitress appeared and Jessica pointed to the Guinness.

Ellie studied Jessica's envelope. It was secured with red tape and a large wax seal. Jessica gave no indication she'd seen the test results.

Ellie's pulse thumped in her ears.

"This sealed envelope holds your secret back-up DNA test results. It was handed to me just before I left the lab. I have no idea what the results are. I wanted to open it in front of you Ellie, and have you, Quinn, serve as a witness."

"Makes sense," Quinn said, then he frowned. "Wait . . ."

"What?" Jessica asked.

"An *unbiased* witness would be more credible."

Jessica nodded, then turned toward a young student at the next table. "Excuse me. . . ."

The student, a beautiful Asian girl wearing a blue University of Kentucky sweatshirt, looked up from a thick chemistry textbook. "Yes . . .?"

Jessica pointed at the envelope. "Would you please witness me unseal this envelope and take out some documents?"

"That's all?"

"That's all."

"Happy to."

Jessica broke the wax seal, then pulled off the red tape. She reached in and took out a stapled report. She showed the student the report.

"Would you please write your name on the top of the report?"

"Sure." She wrote *Kimberley Han Dolata* and her email address."

"Thank you, Kimberley," Jessica said, then started scanning the test results.

On the jukebox, Tommy Makem sang *Four Green Fields,* a sad ballad about a kindhearted old Irish widow whose property was unfairly taken from her. *Is someone unfairly trying to take Leland Radford's property away from me?*

Jessica flipped through some pages, then rechecked others, her face revealing nothing.

Beneath the table, Ellie's leg jackhammered.

Quinn tapped his beer blotter.

"Well, the results are quite clear." Jessica flipped to the back page again.

"And . . .?" Quinn asked, leaning forward.

"This test proves without question that your DNA and the DNA of Leland T. Radford . . ." She took a deep breath . . . "do *not* match."

Ellie's mind went numb.

"I'm really sorry, Ellie, but Mr. Radford can not possibly be your biological father."

Ellie slumped down, feeling like barbed wire was being pulled through her veins.

FIFTY TWO

BAGHDAD

At the Al Mut'ah Hotel, Nafeesa Hakim stared up at the dim, dangling bulb as Khalid Al-Kareem slid his sweaty, three-hundred-pound, garlic-reeking body off her. For the last twenty minutes, his greasy skin had pinned her to the bed's stained mattress and its protruding spring, which, she noticed, protruded farther than his penis.

She turned her head to escape his fetid breath.

The Al Mut'ah was one of the Baghdad's cheap *Pleasure Marriage* hotels where Iraqi men enjoyed legal sexual encounters with women other than their wives – as opposed to the lavish palaces where Saddam Hussein enjoyed women other than his wife.

Pleasure marriages were cash only. But not tonight. Khalid Al-Kareem did not pay her one single dinar for the pleasure of her sexual delights.

He'd paid her with something far more valuable.

An official Iraqi marriage certificate.

Khalid was a director in Baghdad's Social Status Court, the official government issuer of marriage certificates. Nafeesa's certificate stated that she married First Lieutenant Richard J. Radford in Baghdad on June 4, two weeks before a roadside bomb took his life.

Tomorrow she would show the marriage certificate to her friend, Lieutenant Bob Darnell. Bob would then phone the lawyer in Kentucky, Mr. Fletcher Falcone, and tell him that she and Rick Radford were legally married.

Then, as Rick's widow, she prayed she might receive enough inheritance to support her family and restart her mother's cancer treatments that were stopped for non-payment.

She remembered being introduced to Rick Radford by Bob Darnell. When Rick learned that the war impoverished her family and forced her into prostitution to feed them, he immediately offered to support her - *if* she left her profession. She agreed that second. They became good friends, deeply cared for each other, and even talked of marriage. But before they could work out the details, he was killed.

Today, she regretted using his name to get the marriage certificate. But she was desperate. She wondered if Rick would understand why she was doing this – like he understood her desperate situation when they first met?

Something told her Rick would understand.

FIFTY THREE

As Quinn drove back to Louisville, Ellie noticed he'd been very quiet for a long time. Probably still recovering, like she was from Jessica's disappointing DNA results.

He'd been absolutely convinced she was Leland Radford's daughter.

But DNA is what it is, she realized. *It can't lie. Leland Radford is not my father! End of story! Get over it, Ellie.*

Still, it would have been nice . . .

But one thing still puzzled her. *If I'm not Radford's daughter - why is someone still hell bent on destroying me and all my DNA tests?* It made no sense to her. Nor to Quinn.

She looked over at him. He seemed to be a thousand miles away. Suddenly, she had a gut-wrenching thought. He's not thinking about the DNA test - he's thinking about Jennifer. He's having second thoughts about their breakup . . . he's regretting it . . . planning on patching things up with her now that he knows I'm penniless. Is that what he's thinking?

"You're mighty quiet over there, Quinn Parker."

"Bad news does that to me."

"Bad DNA news?"

"Yeah."

She relaxed a bit.

"I'm just wondering if someone altered your secret DNA test in *Frankfort?*"

"Unlikely. Jessica said there was no break-in. And only the lab technician knew about the secret test."

"But he was a substitute."

"Jessica's friend vouches for him."

"Why?"

"He's a Baptist seminary student."

"Stalin was a seminary student and slaughtered twenty million people."

"Fair point."

Suddenly, he thumped his hand down hard on the steering wheel. "Dammit, Ellie! I was *sure* you were Radford's daughter!"

"Well, fate's' fickle finger says no way!"

He nodded as he passed a large track-trailer belching black diesel smoke.

"So our big question remains – who's my daddy?

"True, but we have an even bigger question."

"What's that?" she said.

"Who's your attacker?"

She nodded. "Because they still think I'm Radford's daughter."

"Yep."

"I phoned Falcone earlier and left a voice message telling him about my new test results. I'll try again."

He nodded. "Once Falcone's financial managers know you're not Radford's daughter, my sense is your life should get safer fast."

She dialed Falcone's number. His phone rang several times and she realized his secretary, Ramada, was probably gone for the day. Ellie left Falcone another message.

"But until he picks up your message you're still -"

" – in the cross hairs."

"Yep. And Celeste's home is not safe."

"Fortunately, Celeste's with her son's family for five days."

"That helps a lot. But whoever's behind this probably knows you stayed at my apartment."

She nodded.

"And my parents have friends staying over for the weekend."

Ellie patted the car seat. "Home Sweet Chevy is comfy?"

"Not as comfy as Uncle's Joe Ryan's home. He and Aunt Rosie are in Florida. He likes me to stay there when they're out of town."

"Sounds good."

Ellie was relieved they weren't going to his parents' home. She wasn't ready to see the disappointment in their eyes . . . the realization that their son had traded in a beautiful, wealthy, debutante for a poor hick chick from Harlan. From their perspective, Jennifer offered Quinn so much more. *From my perspective too, if I'm honest.*

What can I offer him?

What do I know of Quinn's circles? His friends were VIPs, distinguished law professors, star athletes, the upper echelon of campus society. *Everything about me shrieks country girl. And some people have a problem with that. If they do, well, it's their problem!*

But sometimes, she had to admit, it was her problem too.

Like her stupid recurring nightmare. In the dream, she's at the junior prom, dancing with a classmate she liked. Suddenly, people start laughing and pointing at her cheap red dress that has somehow split open halfway up the side. She runs outside, but everyone follows her, laughing, pointing, chasing her. Her high-heel breaks and she falls head first into a swamp. She crawls out, dripping with oily, scummy gunk. Weeds hang from her hair. Her dress has split open even more. Her spaghetti straps have fallen down. She's practically nude and drenched with slime. Everyone howls with laughter.

And then, as always, she wakes up in a cold sweat, afraid the nightmare will never go away. And of course, it hasn't.

"Here's Uncle Joe's shack," Quinn said, steering into the driveway of a massive, stunning Victorian mansion.

She looked up at the three-story home with red brick, dark-stained wood, white gingerbread decor along the roof, pointy turrets, large porches and balconies, expensive landscaping, even a gurgling waterfall.

"Wow! It's magnificent, Quinn!""

"Lincoln thought so."

"*Lincoln* stayed here -?"

"*Jose* Lincoln. He stocks shelves at CVS."

She tried to elbow him but he ducked away.

They drove into the underground garage, got out and entered the large, paneled library. Quinn walked over to the mahogany bar. "Fancy a libation?"

"How fancy?"

He lifted up a half-empty bottle of Shiraz.

"That works."

As he poured two glasses, she pointed to a family picture sitting on a table. "Is that little ankle-biter you?"

"Yep. Age four. Family trip to Disney World."

"I've always wanted to go."

"Everyone your age has gone. It's a kid's rite of passage."

"My family couldn't afford the passage."

"I'll take you when this semester is over."

"Really?"

"Promise."

Ellie felt giddy as a six-grader.

He handed her the glass of wine. They touched glasses and sipped. The alcohol rushed to her head as she realized lunch was her huge Guinness at McCarthy's Bar. They plopped down on a sofa near each other and sipped more wine.

"Feeling safe?" he asked.

"Like Fort Knox."

He put his arm around her and she inched closer. She felt completely attracted to the man beside her, and even more so because
now that she thought about it, his attitude toward her hadn't changed
when he learned her DNA proved she would not inherit fabulous
wealth. If anything, he seemed more sympathetic.

But was it only sympathy? Did he feel anything more?

Moments later she got her answer. They looked into each other's
eyes and suddenly, she didn't care whether she wasn't right for him,
she didn't care that she came from Harlan, didn't care whether Jennifer was a better match, didn't care whether his parents preferred
Jennifer . . .

She only cared about Quinn, cared deeply, and wanted to be with
him now.

He leaned forward and kissed her and in that moment all her
fears and insecurities drifted away . . . and so did their clothes as
they hurried toward the nearest bedroom.

FIFTY FOUR

LEXINGTON

Fletcher Falcone smiled and threw his fist in the air.

He'd just won big money at 12 to 1 odds on Old Tom who'd galloped across the finish line first. Thanks in part to the jockey, Pepe Santos, who was rumored to juice his thoroughbreds with Aminorex, a non-detectable stimulant.

Fletcher drained his whiskey and handed the winning ticket to his waiter.

"Reuben, cash this quick!" he said, fearing the horse might fail the drug test.

"Yessuh, Mr. Falcone."

"And bring me another whiskey."

"Comin' right up, suh."

Falcone took a deep breath and sat back. He loved horseracing. The Sport of Kings was so much more rewarding than flushing money down those state lottery toilets for the brain-dead. He also loved this exclusive clubhouse at Keeneland Race Track, the most respected racecourse in Kentucky. No riffraff in this private club. Right in this room, he'd met movie stars, Saudi princes, even some crowned heads of Europe.

The crowd roared. He saw the Finish Board flash – *OFFICIAL.* The race winnings were his!

He savored the thrill – then felt it vanish as he locked eyes with the big thug that walked in. One of Big Tony Broutafachi's goons. Here to remind Falcone to pay his overdue horseracing IOUs. Big Tony had already reminded him twice, and Falcone explained twice that the Radford case would soon bring millions into Falcone's firm and that he'd pay back the three hundred nine thousand dollars *then.*

But no - Big Tony wanted his money *now!* And to make sure Falcone got the message, sent him photos of a non-payer with his penis stuffed in his mouth.

The muscular thug opened his wallet and gestured for Falcone to put some money in it.

Falcone whispered, "No!"

The thug shook his head, flipped open his cell phone and called someone, probably Big Tony.

Falcone could easily pay the money back now, but hated being bullied by Broutafachi or anyone. *I'll pay him in a few weeks. And I'll be damned if I'll pay before my Radford windfall. No way Big Tony'll kill me without first collecting his money.*

The noisy race crowd suddenly went graveyard quiet.

Falcone turned and saw why: a jockey had fallen from his horse and was getting up slowly.

Rueben pointed at the jockey and said, "Accidents happen!"

The two words hit Falcone hard. They always had since years ago when a National Traffic Safety investigator and Falcone slogged through a snake-infested swamp near Paducah.

"Accidents happen," the investigator had said and pointed at the crashed Cessna.

Falcone's Cessna.

He stared at the smoke billowing from the hot chunks of fuselage. He identified his wife's wedding ring on her severed arm. And he identified his twin seven-year-old daughters, still strapped in their seats, their bodies charred like blocks of ebony.

All dead because of me, Falcone reminded himself. *Dead because I threatened to fire the pilot if he didn't fly back immediately - even after he warned me the weather was too treacherous.*

A minute after liftoff, hurricane-strength windshears slammed the small aircraft down into the swamp.

Their deaths shattered Falcone. He tried to escape through booze and painkillers and food, but the guilt kept eating away at him.

Only one thing helped: Burying himself in his law practice. And the long hours paid off. He won important cases for a major mining company against phony health claims. Those successes brought in new clients and prosperous growth for his firm. When people asked for the secret of his success, he said, "knowing the law."

Actually, his secret was knowing the jurors.

Or more accurately, what they wanted.

All jurors wanted something.

Some wanted to keep secrets, some wanted money or help. Falcone fulfilled their needs. And, in turn, the jurors helped Falcone win critical verdicts for his clients.

Today, Falcone & Partners was a successful law firm, with offices in Louisville, Lexington, Manchester and Cincinnati, had a highly regarded reputation in the coal mining industries. The firm's revenue provided him with a very luxurious lifestyle. It also allowed him to fund *Falcone Charities* that donated enhanced radar and weather systems to small airports. His wealth even allowed him to enjoy his nasty little vices like horseracing . . . and a few others. Vices he'd earned.

And he'd do anything to preserve them. *Anything.*

FIFTY FIVE

Nikolai Pushkin sat in his rental Mercedes watching the *Brandeis Law House*. He focused his powerful Vortex binoculars on Quinn Parker's darkened second-floor apartment. He'd seen no movement for over twenty minutes, or heard any sound from his laser listening device. Ellie Stuart and Quinn Parker were sleeping, screwing, or not there. And Parker's phone number was unlisted.

In a downstairs window, Pushkin saw an old white-haired guy watching television. Probably the house manager.

Pushkin Googled the *Brandeis House* phone number, then dialed it. The old guy picked up.

"Brandeis House."

"Hi, I'm John Harris, a friend of Quinn Parker's. I was coming over to see Quinn, but lost his phone number."

"Oh, Quinn's not here tonight. Stayin' over at his Uncle Joe Ryan's house."

"Is that the house over on, ah . . .?"

"Over on Magnolia," the old guy said. "Big old red brick house. Can't miss it."

"Yeah, I remember it."

"You still want Quinn's phone number?"

"Yes, please."

The old man gave it to him.

"Thanks."

Pushkin hung up. Back on *Google*, he found Joe Ryan's address on Magnolia Street and programmed it into his car's GPS system. A map popped on the screen. The house was nearby and he drove ahead.

"Turn right on Devonshire Street," the GPS woman demanded. "Turn *NOW!*"

Pushkin hated the GPS woman! He hated any woman ordering him around. They reminded him of his mother. He tried to turn GPS woman off and turn down her volume, but couldn't figure out how to do either.

"Turn left at this corner, then turn right in one hundred feet. Turn *NOW!*" she barked.

"Fuck off!" he shouted back.

Moments later . . .

"You've arrived at your destination!"

"No shit, Einstein!"

He turned the car off, looked at the magnificent old Victorian red brick mansion and took a deep breath. It reminded him of another red brick mansion five thousand miles away . . . in Moscow . . . where his heroin-addicted mother and he lived in the mansion's garden shack when Pushkin was six.

He remembered the cramped, filthy shed, the icy gusts of winter blasting through cracked windows, and crying because he was hungry, and sleeping in the lawnmower's grass bag, and foraging in alley garbage cans, and eating moldy, maggot-laced chicken and black rotting potatoes and his mother's "fried chicken" that was really rat. He remembered the Lubyanka subway station where she dumped him at age ten, saying he was better off without her. Only time in her life she was right. He slept in the men's room with vomiting drunks and loved it every minute of it because it had heat.

And years later, he remembered finally escaping the Khitrovka slum thanks to saving a gay KGB agent from being beaten to death by street thugs. The thankful agent got Pushkin into a KGB apprenticeship where Pushkin's physical prowess, street smarts, and the assassination of two important Chechen terrorists quickly promoted him to the KGB's prestigious Second Directorate. But Pushkin's success threatened his boss. So the bastard quickly fabricated evidence that Pushkin sold secrets to the CIA. But the night before he was to be arrested, Pushkin found out and boarded a fishing trawler to Helsinki. From there he moved to the states, where he soon gained a reputation as a specialist in what the Americans called "wet work."

Pushkin preferred to be known as a man who made problems disappear. Wet or dry.

Problems like Ellie Stuart, he thought, as he stared up at the mansion's second floor where she and Quinn Parker had just turned out the light.

FIFTY SIX

Nicolai Pushkin looked through the Mercedes windshield at Joe Ryan's darkened Victorian mansion. He listened to owls hoot to each other in the darkness. *So the omen is true. Owls hoot when death is near.*

The dashboard clock said 2:46 a.m., and although his KGB trainer said 4 a.m. was optimum attack time, he'd go now. After all, he wasn't attacking Navy SEALS. Just college kids.

His syringes held lethal dozes of heroin. His two-shot Taser was fully charged. And his suppressed Beretta had a full clip. Wearing amber-tinted glasses, a fake beard, and a baseball cap, he stepped out into the humid night air. He strolled down the sidewalk toward the sprawling mansion and eased into the tall hedge alongside the property.

He focused his binoculars on the front door lock. Basic, easy to open. He looked at the home security sign. He knew the system and could disarm it within sixty seconds. If not, his Beretta would persuade Quinn Parker to. He saw no cameras.

The owls hooted again.

A breeze kicked up, bringing him the sweet scent of lilac. He loved lilac and could stand here for hours, breathing its gentle fragrance. But not now.

His assignment was Ellie Stuart. Quinn Parker was simply in the wrong place at the wrong time.

Pushkin flicked the Beretta's safety lever off, squeezed through a gap in the hedge and walked onto the lawn. Rich people grass. Cushy as shag carpet. It felt wonderful. He stepped toward the front door.

* * *

Ellie bolted awake.

A shriek – a shrill, penetrating *alarm* - pierced her eardrums as lights streaked across the bedroom window. Beside her, Quinn sat up.

"The yard alarm! Someone triggered it. Quick, follow me!"

Realizing she was nude, she grabbed a robe and ran with him down the hall. They entered a room and Quinn shut the steel door with a thud. He punched a code on a wall panel and a deadbolt clunked into the doorframe.

"What *is* this room?"

"Uncle Joe's Fort Knox. He built it after a break-in last year."

Quinn opened a wall cabinet, grabbed a cell phone and dialed 911. In the cabinet, Ellie saw a mini-fridge, cases of tuna, soup, chili, and Evian water. In the corner alcove sat a mini-sink and mini-toilet. They could survive here for weeks.

He gave the 911 Operator the address, kept the line open and took Ellie into his arms.

"The police will be here in minutes, Ellie. You're safe."

She nodded, and buried her face in his chest.

* * *

Nicolai Pushkin still couldn't believe it. Three feet from the front door, floodlights swept across him like he was an escapee in a prison movie . . . followed by an earsplitting alarm that could wake the dead.

Very impressive system.

Pushkin jumped in the Mercedes and minutes later, drove onto the Louisville Bridge that spanned the Ohio River and deposited him in Jeffersonville, Indiana. He always preferred to stay in a bordering state when possible for jurisdictional distance.

Minutes later, in his Sheraton suite, he looked down at Ellie Stuart's class schedule for tomorrow. He knew where she'd be and when. But the more he thought about it, the less comfortable he felt about the Stuart assignment. He didn't like terminating a person who appeared innocent. Pushkin's past assignments from Heinrich De Groot involved people who'd crossed him: the Mafia goon who threatened De Groot, a prosecutor who accused him of jury-tampering, a competitor who'd won a big piece of business that De Groot wanted, a plumbing contractor who overcharged him. Bad guys.

But Ellie Stuart? A poor college kid on scholarship? What did she do to De Groot? Only one thing made sense. She'd threatened his money somehow. Money was his lifeblood. And if someone threatened it, he'd spill *their* blood.

But Pushkin had agreed to do the hit, so he'd deliver! After all, De Groot had delivered for him. Years ago, De Groot kept him from being deported back to Russia where the KGB would have terminated him. But somehow, De Groot had learned that Pushkin's U.S. Immigration Officer had a nasty predilection for sleeping with eleven-year-old Thai girls. When De Groot threatened to show police the career-ending photographs of the pedophile's felonious activities, the Immigration Officer quickly expunged Pushkin's KGB history from his files and reclassified him as a persecuted Russian dissident.

Since then, Pushkin had lived the good life in America, growing wealthy from various assignments, successful real estate investments . . . and the occasional, lucrative whack job.

He owed De Groot.

Pushkin looked back down at Ellie's photo on his desk and shrugged.

Sorry comrade, my beautiful young krasivaya devushka . . . life isn't always fair.

See you in class!

FIFTY SEVEN

Ellie sat with Quinn in the his uncle's kitchen surrounded by so much stainless steel - refrigerator, freezer, ovens, countertops, cabinets – she felt like she was in an autopsy room, something she almost wound up in last night.

After the attempted home invasion, the police searched all thirty-two rooms and found no evidence of an intruder. A hidden security video showed a large bearded man wearing glasses and a cap walk onto the grass, trigger the alarm, then hurry away.

The police interviewed Quinn and her at length, then promised to drive by every thirty minutes. After the interview, Ellie and Quinn settled in at the kitchen table. Now, after four cups of high-octane coffee, Ellie vibrated.

"It doesn't make sense," she said.

"What?"

"Why they're *still* after me? I left Falcone a second message yesterday saying our independent Frankfort DNA backup test also proved I'm *not* Radford's daughter. By now, Falcone certainly would have told all his Radford managers . . . those with financial interest in my tests."

"And possible *motive* to harm you."

Ellie nodded. "Yet, hours after I left the messages for Falcone, I heard noises and saw male footsteps outside Lisa's house. And hours later a big guy tried to break in here. What's going on?"

"Maybe Falcone hasn't picked up your message yet."

"Or maybe," she said, "we've had it all wrong."

"How so?"

"Maybe a Radford estate manager *isn't* behind the attacks."

"But who else has motivation?"

"Maybe someone we don't know about yet. Maybe Radford had a secret wife, son or daughter who'll pop out of the woodwork."

"No one's popped into probate court with a petition."

Ellie shrugged. "Maybe they will this morning."

Quinn nodded. "Let's find out. It's 8:07. Try Falcone or his secretary again."

She dialed Falcone's direct line. No answer, so she left a another message saying her DNA proved she was not Radford's daughter. She left the same message for his secretary, Ramada.

"So now what?" she said.

"So now they're still after you."

"I know!"

"So you should remain here today."

"I can't, Quinn."

He frowned. "Why not?"

"In one hour, I have a major history exam worth one-third of my grade – and I have to nail it!"

"But someone's trying to nail *you*!"

"I noticed, but - "

An idea flashed in her mind. "I'll be right back."

She headed upstairs, and minutes later walked toward him and got the laugh she expected.

She was wearing his Uncle Jack's baggy jeans with turned-up cuffs, large sweatshirt, Harley Davidson jacket, boots and reflective sunglasses. A *Louisville Bats* baseball hat hid her hair and a mascara moustache adorned her upper lip.

Quinn smiled. "You trying for Hilary Swank in *Boys Don't Cry?*"

"No. Brando in *The Wild One!*" she said.

"Not even close. But your disguise might actually work!"

"Good. But I just realized something that won't work."

"What?"

"Your Chevy. They'll follow it."

"Maybe not." He gestured for her to follow. They grabbed their books and backpacks, headed into the garage where Quinn lifted the tailgate of his uncle's big black Cadillac Escalade and pointed her toward the cargo floor.

"Jump Spike jump!"

Smiling, she crawled onto the floor and lay down, feeling like a golden lab.

Minutes later, Quinn parked in a campus garage. He popped the tailgate. Climbing out, Ellie saw her reflection in the Escalade's window and froze. "I can't!" she said.

"Can't what?"

"Go to class looking like a cross-dressing, mascara-mustached, baggy-pants, gang-banger chick!"

"So go to the restroom, wipe off your mustache, lose the hat and glasses, then go to class."

She didn't have a better solution, so she took off walking down the pathway toward the Humanities Building. A hundred yards later, they entered the lobby, unscathed.

"When you're finished," Quinn said, "text me. We'll meet here."

She nodded, then hurried into a nearby restroom. She rubbed her eye-marker moustache hard, but wound up looking like she'd smeared licorice on her lips. She had no time to fix it.

KENTUCKY WOMAN

She hurried into her lecture hall, sat down and watched eyebrows climb as students noticed her makeover. The girl beside her whispered, "Hey, biker babe, what's with the puffy dark lips?"

Ellie started to say licorice, but said, "Bruised from passionate kissing."

"Good for you . . ."

"You have no idea *how* good!"

It all flooded back. Last night's passionate, magical lovemaking with Quinn. She had wanted it to happen, and so had he. So it happened. Her strong attraction to him, his helping her find her birth mother, his protecting her against the attackers, his physical closeness to her, his leaving Jennifer, everything had converged to create the perfect, overpowering storm of desire between them. Within minutes of the first kiss they were making love, hot intense passionate love, followed by slow intense passionate love, followed by more of both.

After, as they lay there in the afterglow, he whispered, 'Ellie . . .?"

"Yeah?"

"I love you, but - "

" - but what?"

He smiled. "I would have preferred you filthy rich."

She nailed him with her pillow.

FIFTY EIGHT

As Professor Summers walked into the large lecture room, Ellie looked around and noticed some new faces: an older silver haired gentleman, a middle-aged brunette, a large muscular man in a suit and tie. Class auditors maybe. The muscular man looked Slavic and wore thick Kissinger glasses beneath a blond crew cut. He glanced at her like many others did when she walked in, probably wondering about who the macho-chick with the too-big leather jacket and mascara-smudged mustache was.

Professor Summers lectured a minute, then handed out the tests. She looked at the first question and knew the answer. Usually a good sign.

Forty minutes later, she handed the test in, thinking she'd done pretty well. She walked out into the empty hallway and texted Quinn that she was done. He texted back, 'See you in ten minutes.' Down the hall, the elevator opened and a large janitor with a mop and bucket stepped out, glanced at her, then walked into a room.

Three students wandered out complaining about a tough essay question. The guy wearing Kissinger glasses walked out, stared at her and headed down the hall to the bulletin board.

Ellie chatted with the students, getting compliments, and frowns, for her new look. The students walked toward the elevator and entered, leaving her alone.

Alone with Kissinger Glasses, who was still reading the bulletin board. Slowly, he turned and looked in her direction. Something about him didn't seem right. Not a student. Not a professor. Maybe an athletic coach. But even that didn't seem right. The large man made her uneasy.

He glanced at her again and she felt her muscles tighten. She knew she was hyperventilating herself into paranoid mode. More students strolled out and she merged with them as they walked toward the elevators. She'd go down to the lobby and hang out there until Quinn arrived.

The elevator doors opened and the students crammed in ahead of her, jamming the already packed elevator. She tried to squeeze on, but the overload buzzer blared and the doors shut fast, leaving her alone . . .

. . . with Kissenger Glasses.

Who was now walking toward her.

No, he was *hurrying!*

Why hurry if the elevator left?

The second elevator opened and her instincts told her to get on even though it was going up.

She boarded and jammed the *Close Door* button. It didn't close. She jammed it again.

Still didn't close.

She heard the man running now.

A second later, his fingertips scraped the corner of the door as it was shutting - but it slammed shut anyway . . . and the elevator rose.

She drained air from her lungs, got off on the top floor, hurried down the rear staircase to the ground floor lobby and mingled with students, her heart still racing.

Kissinger Glasses was nowhere in sight.

Nor was Quinn. She looked for a campus security guard. No such luck. A group of football players chatted nearby so she walked over and hid behind them.

An elevator pinged open. Out walked two professors, the janitor and a student.

And then Kissinger Glasses.

He scanned the lobby, but didn't see her.

She turned around to talk to the football players – but saw they'd just stepped outside, leaving her exposed.

Kissinger Glasses saw her and hurried toward her.

As she started to run outside, he touched her arm.

"Please wait – I don't mean to frighten you."

Slowly, she turned toward the man, ready to scream her head off. The lobby was empty.

"I just wanted to ask about your leather jacket. It looks fabulous. Who makes it?"

He seemed genuinely interested. She opened the coat and showed him the *Tommy Hilfiger* label.

"Hilfiger! I could have sworn it was a *Lauren*. Well it looks fabulous! A tad large for you, maybe. Again, I'm sorry if I frightened you. Thanks." He got back on the elevator and headed up.

She leaned against the wall, relieved and embarrassed that she'd misread the guy. She told herself to stop suspecting everyone who looked at her. She swallowed a dry throat and saw a water fountain down the hall next to her. She walked down to the fountain, bent over and started drinking.

She heard noise behind her and saw the big janitor holding his mop and pail enter a maintenance closet. He smiled at her and she nodded and went back to drinking water.

Someone grabbed her from behind. Turning, she saw it was the janitor. He yanked her toward the closet.

As he fumbled with the doorknob, she shoved his mop handle deep into his groin hard. He moaned. She shoved even harder.

He moaned louder, buckled over. She kneed him and he released her arm.

She ran outside, caught up with the football players and walked with them, catching her breath. A few steps later, she saw Quinn walking toward her.

When he saw her expression, he jogged up to her.

"What the hell's wrong?"

"A big janitor in a dark green shirt back there just grabbed me."

Quinn looked back toward the building entrance. "I don't see him."

She turned around and didn't see him either. Quinn ran into the lobby, searching for the guy, and came back moments later.

"He's gone! He might be armed. Let's get the hell out of here."

They hurried back to his uncle's Escalade and got in and drove off. Quinn dialed Fletcher Falcone, the Executor, and hit the speaker button. His secretary, Ramada, picked up.

"Is Mr. Falcone there?"

"No," Ramada said. "I haven't heard a word from him since yesterday afternoon."

"Where'd he go?"

"I got no idea! I'm right worried."

FIFTY NINE

Jessica Bishop sat in the Gen-Ident Lab lounge beside her very tall significant other, Jim Williams. A few months earlier, while running the Lexington Fun Run, she fell over his very long leg. That night at the Fun Run Party she fell for the rest of him.

At six-foot-seven, Jim was the first boyfriend she'd ever looked up to. Reason enough to love the guy. But he also happened to be a smart, funny, easygoing, second-year student at the University of Kentucky Med School. They both worked part-time at Gen-Ident doing genetic research on diabetes and Alzheimer's.

During lunch breaks, like now, they watched *CSI*, checking for forensic errors.

And today's *CSI* episode was driving Jessica crazy. It involved a defendant who'd been positively identified by three rape victims, but found not guilty in each trial. For good reason: his DNA did not match the semen DNA recovered from the victims. The defendant swaggered out of court each case, laughing at the frustrated prosecutor.

Two weeks later, the same defendant was arrested for rape. And
again, the victim and her roommate positively identified him. So did
a neighbor who saw him climb from the victim's bedroom window.
But amazingly, the defendant's DNA once again did not match the
semen DNA recovered from the victim. The baffled prosecutor re-
peated the DNA test twice, but got the same results. He was preparing to drop the charges when a lab technician ran into his office and
said, "I know how he gets away with it!"

"So do I!" Jessica said, almost dropping her tuna sandwich.

"Let me guess," Jim said. "His identical twin brother with slightly different DNA took the test for him?"

"He doesn't have an identical twin brother."

"One more guess."

"Go for it!"

"He got a blood transfusion in his arm just before they took his
DNA sample from the same arm. So his test showed the *donor's*
DNA, not his!"

Jessica shook her head. "Nope. He was in jail for forty-eight
hours before the DNA test. And a new study says that's *highly* unlikely to work. Blood circulates too fast. No . . . I was thinking of
something else."

"What?"

"A very special DNA test."

Jim looked confused. "DNA is DNA!"

"Yes, but I should run the test for Ellie."

"Why?"

"Her eyes."

"What about them?"

"A rare possibility I've heard about. I need to read up on it first.
Then I'll explain what I'm wondering about."

Jim shrugged. "Go for it."

Jessica dialed Ellie's phone number. Ellie picked up on the first ring.

"Hey, Jessie."

"Get your cute self back to my lab fast!"

SIXTY

Fletcher Falcone smiled as he drove away from *BoDeene's Feed & Fertilizer,* his secret little side business that brought him massive revenue. Delicious *tax-free* revenue.

In fact, *BoDeene's Feed & Fertilizer* gave him a much heftier profit margin than his law firm, *Falcone &* Partners, thanks mostly to the creativity and cunning of his weird cousin, BoDeene R. Dukes, a chemistry major dropout.

Six years ago, BoDeene begged Falcone for two hundred thousand dollars to produce an "exciting new product" at BoDeene's fertilizer store. BoDeene guaranteed him twenty times his investment within three years. Falcone laughed and turned him down. But when BoDeene showed him the product's marketing plan, Falcone quickly loaned him the money. *Best investment I ever made, by far.*

Who knew cooking crystal meth beneath the fertilizer store would rake in millions annually . . . *pure profit* millions now earning bushels of interest in some numbered accounts in Belize and Nevis.

His phone rang.

"Falcone."

"Hey, fat man," Tony Broutafachi said, "my friend Tito tells me you won a shitload of money on the ponies at the Keeneland track yesterday."

Awww fuck . . . ! I don't need this jerk now! Falcone thought as he slumped back in the driver's seat.

"I'm real disappointed, Falcone, 'cuz you didn't even offer me one red cent of the three hundred grand what you owe me. My feelins' is like, you know, hurt."

"I can expl – "

"No - *I'll* do the 'splainin', Falcone! You got twenty-four hours to cough up the first hunnert grand. Twenty-four hours! Unnerstand?"

"Yeah, yeah."

"And next Monday you're gonna pay me the final two hunnert grand. *Capisi?*"

"Yeah, yeah!" He didn't have the strength to argue with the pushy wop bastard. But he also didn't like being pushed into paying.

"So tomorrow, Falcone, in your office at five sharp, you're gonna hand Tito one hunnert large."

Falcone paused. "Or *what*?"

"Or buy yourself a fat man's coffin!" Broutafachi slammed the phone down.

Falcone was angry. He had more than enough money to pay Broutafachi the measly three hundred grand. But it was easier to pay him out of the Radford estate windfall in a couple of weeks . . . rather than wire-transferring money from his numbered Belize account . . . a transfer that might raise a red flag with US banking watchdogs.

And Falcone hated being bullied. As a kid, he'd been bullied, and even beaten severely because he was fat. But he'd learned how to handle bullies.

He'd learned from the master, Milo Falcone, Daddy Dearest, who'd handled problems by arm-twisting, brow-beating, and knee-busting his way through life. He collected debts and paid off cops and politicians for the Cincinnati mob. But Milo spent all his money on horses and hookers. Which left Fletcher and his mother flat broke most of the time.

He remembered at nine, going to their corner store and asking Mr. Thompson to "Please put this milk on our tab."

"Cash only for the Falcones!" Mr. Thompson shouted. "No more credit!" Fletcher felt his face flush red. Everyone in the store stared at him, even the girl he liked from school. Embarrassed, he ran home.

When Falcone was thirteen, his father left a note saying he was going on an important mission to L.A. The mission it turned out was screwing a topless dancer named Twin Peaks. He never saw his father again. Best thing that ever happened.

He and his mother went on welfare. Humiliated, Falcone swore he would become wealthy whatever it took. At seventeen, he began running numbers for the Cincy mob. But he wanted much more in life. He earned a scholarship to the University of Kentucky, and another to law school. After passing the Bar, he soon discovered his greatest legal talent: knowing when to cross the line between legal and illegal . . .

Crossing it, he learned, proved much more lucrative.

His phone rang. Broutafachi again?

No. His office.

"Oh, Mr. Falcone!" Ramada said. "I've been calling everywheres for you! Your home, your club, your car, then your home agin, and then I called your – "

" - yes, yes, Ramada, I'm coming in now! Any messages."

"Yes. An *urgent* one from Ellie Stuart."

"Urgent?"

"Uh-huh . . ."

"Well . . .?"

"Well what? Oh . . . you want me to play it for you?"

"*Yes! Ramada!*" The woman had cement between her ears.
Falcone listened to the message and blinked a few times.
"Play it again, Ramada!"
She did.
He couldn't believe what Ellie Stuart said.

SIXTY ONE

A security guard escorted Ellie and Quinn, wearing Visitors Badges, into a large, state of the art laboratory at Gen-Ident Labs. She saw technicians working at large-screen computers and sophisticated equipment. More technicians worked in self-contained mini-labs situated around the perimeter of the huge room.

In one mini-lab, Ellie saw Jessica working beside a very tall young man with reddish-blond hair and freckles. Both were jack-knifed over large microscopes.

Jessica looked up and waved them over. "Ellie, Quinn, come meet Jim Williams." Jessica's wink suggested Jim was her Knight in Shining Armor."

They shook hands with the six-foot-seven inch guy, then Jessica led them to the far corner of the lab, away from the other technicians.

"So what's this all about?" Ellie asked.

"Your eyes."

"What about them?"

"Remember how we used to laugh about how your one eye is bluer than the other?"

"Yeah. . . ."

"Well a *CSI* show reminded me of your eyes."

"So . . .?"

"So your different eye colors may be related to your DNA."

"If not mine, whose?" Ellie wondered what on earth Jessica was getting at.

"It's rather complicated, but the bottom line is that I need more samples of your DNA."

"No way you're scraping my eyeballs for DNA!"

"No! I don't need to," Jessica said, laughing.

Ellie didn't get it. "So what's wrong with my mouth swab DNA?"

"Nothing. But I need more DNA samples from other parts of your cute little body. Follow me, Ellie. Girls only, guys. Sorry."

Ellie wondered what the hell was going on. She shrugged at Quinn, then followed Jessica down the hall where they entered the women's restroom. Jessica shut the door.

"Let's start with your hair. This may tingle a smidgeon."

Jessica reached over and yanked out a couple of Ellie's hairs.

"*YEOW!*"

"Sorry, Ellie, but the hair roots have the juiciest DNA goop." She placed the hairs in a plastic tube. Ellie saw her name and a barcode on the side of the tube.

Jessica swabbed the inside of Ellie's cheek again and placed the swab in another plastic tube. Next, she withdrew blood from Ellie's finger.

"Just one last sample." Jessica handed her an extra long Q-tip.

"What's this for?"

Jessica pointed at a toilet stall.

Ellie stared at the long Q-tip, and then at Jessica. "Sorry Jess, but Mr. Poop has left the building."

"How about Ms. Vagina?"

"Still in residence."

"Goodie. Now go in there and swab up some of her wonderful epidermal cells for me."

Ellie shook her head in bewilderment, but went into a stall and moments later emerged with her swab sample in the plastic tube.

They walked back to Quinn and Jim who were talking Kentucky basketball.

"So, what's this weird new test all about?" Ellie asked.

"A DNA condition that's rarely, if ever, tested for."

"Are you saying my previous independent DNA test results were inaccurate?"

"No, they were probably accurate . . . but maybe . . . incomplete."

Ellie still wondered what she meant. "When will you know about the new results?"

"If I super-rush it and call in some favors, maybe late tomorrow. But there's a problem."

"What?"

"We have to rush this test to be ready for the probate hearing. And because there are four separate rush tests it will cost more."

"How much more?" Ellie couldn't afford a huge bill now. She couldn't afford a small bill.

Jessica shrugged. "Even if the lab gives me a deal, the four separate rush DNA tests will cost around a thousand bucks."

Ellie's throat went bone dry. She had one hundred eighteen dollars in the bank.

"Don't worry about the money," Quinn said.

"Quinn, you can't – "

"I have the money. It's okay! You can pay me back at your leisure. The probate hearing is in two days. Time is critical."

Ellie saw he wouldn't change his mind. "I insist on paying you back."

"Okay, but only when you can."

"Thanks, Quinn." She looked at Jessica. "Be honest, what are the realistic chances this new test might alter my previous DNA results?"

Jessica looked out the window. "Well, it's a. . . ."

"A long shot, right?"

"Yeah. A long shot."

"How long?"

"Think lottery winner."

SIXTY TWO

Heinrich De Groot sat in his Cincinnati office, staring down at the statue of The Lady in Fountain Square. Water flowed into her outstretched hands . . . like money would soon flow into his outstretched hands . . . thanks to the Leland Radford probate.

He grabbed his phone and called Fletcher Falcone's office to confirm details for the probate court hearing.

"Mr. Falcone's office," Ramada said.

"Is Fletcher there?"

"No, but he's fixin' to come in right now."

"Still the same time for the probate court hearing?"

"Uh-huh."

"Anything new on the probate?"

Ramada snapped her gum a few times. "Naw, just that girl, Ellie, she up and called. That's all."

"Why'd she call?"

"To leave me and Mr. Falcone a message."

"And . . .?"

"Just that message."

"What did Ellie say, Ramada?"

"Oh . . . I didn't actually talk to her."

De Groot closed his eyes. Ramada had the IQ of a peppermint.

"What did Ellie say in the *message,* Ramada! What did her *message* say?"

"Oh . . . that. Not much, just that her new DNA test from Frankfort proved she isn't Mr. Radford's daughter. That's all."

De Groot bolted out of his chair. *"She said those exact words?"*

"Uh-huh."

"Well fuck me!"

"But I thought you wuz married?"

"What? Yeah!" He slammed the phone down and shot a fist in the air. *Incredible!* Her Frankfort DNA test, an honest test, the only test he didn't know about and couldn't fix, also proved Ellie's *not* Radford's daughter.

So all these years, he didn't need to worry about Ellie's DNA. And Radford's crazy sister Zelda didn't need to worry about Jacqueline Moreau carrying *Radford's* baby. Ellie Stuart was *not* Leland Radford's daughter. Period! End of story!

Amazing!

So, he wondered, *who was banging beautiful Jacqueline twenty-one years ago?* He'd remembered taking a run at the sexy French girl one day. She was waiting for a bus to go back to *The Pines.* He pulled over and offered to drive her back. She knew him from his meetings with Leland Radford, so she got in his car. He suggested they stop for lunch, but she explained lunch would make her late for work.

Two miles later, he drove into a forest, stopped and said, "Jackie, I can increase your income by two hundred dollars a week. Every week. Starting today."

"How?"

"By you and I having, you know, a little fun." He placed two hundred dollars and his hand on her knees.

She tossed his hand and the money back, and bolted from the car.

He caught up and tossed the two hundred out the window to her. "The money's yours, Jackie. But if you tell anyone about this, U.S. Immigration will learn you are an illegal alien and deport you!"

She never told.

And best of all - she did not give birth to Radford's daughter.

Suddenly, reality hit him like a screen door.

Nikolai Pushkin is trying to eliminate Ellie.

Maybe he already has.

* * *

After Ellie gave Jessica four samples of her DNA, Ellie and Quinn drove back to Louisville. Turning onto Southern Parkway, she noticed more traffic than usual and that the gray clouds had given way to a sunny spring sky.

Quinn said, "It's time for something new and exciting."

"What the hell was my vaginal swab?"

"Fun, I bet. But I was thinking of something else."

"Like what?"

"Like meeting my folks."

Ellie swallowed air. She wasn't ready to meet them. Maybe she never would be. And maybe, no make that probably, they weren't all that eager to meet her. On the other hand, how long could she put off meeting them?

"When?"

"Now. . ."

"*NOW?*"

"Yeah, they're expecting us, Ellie."

She couldn't possibly meet his parents dressed like she was. His mother's jaw would hit the floor when she compared Ellie's frayed jeans and faded sweatshirt to Jennifer's designer clothes, stunning beauty and debutante status.

"Quinn, I look like I rolled down a hill."

"You look great!"

"Not for visiting your parent's home!"

"We're not going there."

"Where? To another fancy restaurant?"

"Nope. What's today?"

"Satur – The first Saturday in May! Oh no . . .!"

"Oh yes!"

"We're going to the Kentucky Derby?"

"Yep."

Ellie stopped breathing. In her preoccupation with things like staying alive, she'd completely forgotten today was the first Saturday in May - Derby Day – Kentucky's Biggest Day of The Year. She loved the Derby, but could never afford a ticket.

She also loved how the Derby transformed friendly Louisville into an even friendlier, magical city for a couple of weeks of good-natured fun. People partied at more than seventy official events, like steamboat races, fireworks, parades, charity balls, fancy clothes parties, no-clothes parties, marathons, shindigs, and good old, down-home shitfacings. Everyone celebrated with everybody – regular folks with Kentucky Colonels, billionaires, hillbillies, movie stars and even foreign royalty.

"Like I mentioned, Dad's an exec at Churchill Downs."

"He has tickets?"

"No. A luxury suite. A wealthy Saudi prince cancelled his trip and gave his suite to dad."

Ellie panicked, imagining the women in thousand dollar Chloé dresses, expensive jewelry, Jimmy Choo high heels, and wide-brimmed Derby hats. Perspiration sprouted on her forehead.

She looked down at her clothes. "Quinn, I can't go looking like this. They'll think I muck out stables."

"You look fine."

"No I don't. You've *gotta* give me a few minutes to put something better on. It's a girl thing for God's sake!"

He glanced at his watch. "Okay . . . you've got maybe four minutes, or we'll miss the Derby!"

They raced to Celeste's home, where Ellie ran inside, brushed
her teeth, combed her hair, spritzed on J. Lo Glow perfume, and
realized her only fancy dress, the black dress she wore to *Le Relais*
restaurant, was at the cleaners. Frantic, she selected her only other
nice dress, a black knee-length skirt, and a long sleeve white blouse.

She looked in the mirror and hoped people would say she was
wearing sort of *understated chic* . . .

But they wouldn't say that.

She knew exactly what they'd say . . .

"Waitress, could you take our drink orders!"

SIXTY THREE

In the distant, Ellie saw historic Churchill Downs, its twin spires jutting hundreds of feet into the Kentucky sky like a Cathedral, which it sort of was when you considered everyone prayed their butts off for their horse to win.

In just minutes, America's most prestigious horse race, the Kentucky Derby, the Super Bowl of thoroughbred racing, would be run. Experts called it, "the most exciting two minutes in sports."

One hundred sixty thousand people crammed into the racetrack. Twenty million more sat glued to their televisions, thanks to cameras everywhere – including the Goodyear blimp hovering overhead in the robin-egg blue sky.

Quinn parked in a VIP section thanks to his father's pass. They jumped out and hurried toward the grandstand. Ellie was very excited about seeing the Derby, but very nervous about meeting Quinn's parents.

"The Derby's next, we gotta hustle!" Holding her hand, he led interference for her like the tight end he once was. They wove through thick crowds watching huge flat-screen televisions replaying the last race. He hurried her through a side door of the grandstand and down a long hallway. The crowd noise rolled like thunder.

"And now, ladies and gentlemen, it's time for the biggest event in the Sport of Kings . . . the Big Race . . . the one you've been waiting for . . . the Run for the Roses . . . this year's running of The Kentucky Derby!"

One hundred sixty thousand fans roared at the top of their lungs. The reverberation hurt her eardrums. Quinn led her down a hall, squeezing past men in classic blazers and women in spectacular designer dresses, glittering jewelry and big wide-brimmed Derby hats. She felt like she'd crashed a society event.

"Quinn, I'm nervous."

"Why?"

"I just am." But she knew why. Quinn had said his mother was concerned when Quinn broke up with Jennifer. How concerned? How disappointed? Was his mom devastated by it?

"Have you told your folks anything about my background? You know, my DNA or Leland Radford?"

"No. All I've said is that I spilled coffee on you, and that you plan to attend law school, and that we're working on a probate case together. That's all they know!"

"Do they know you're bringing me?"

"They insisted I bring you."

"*Insisted?*"

"Yep."

Why insist? she wondered.

Then she understood. They wanted to compare her to Jennifer – they wanted to see why on earth their crazy son traded in a Mercedes for a tractor.

And if she was honest with herself, she sometimes wondered the same thing.

Quinn opened the door for Ellie as they entered a large, luxury suite with massive windows overlooking the track's finish line.

Ellie saw about forty well-dressed people mingling around a serving table where a bartender prepared drinks. Another table had silver plates stacked with lobster, shrimp, steak, a variety of cheeses and a chef preparing individual omelets. The food smelled rich. So did the people.

Most sipped from tall frosted glasses with mint sprigs perched on the rim. *Mint juleps.* The official Derby Drink – and Ellie's official downfall. Literally. Two years ago, she drank three M-Js at a Derby party and passed out on a sofa, jabbering like a parakeet.

"Guess who was in this suite one day," Quinn said.

"Who?"

"Queen Elizabeth."

"Really?"

"Yep."

"*Queen For A Day*," a man behind her said. "An old TV show back before you two guys were born!"

Ellie turned and saw a tall handsome man and woman in their early fifties smiling at her.

"Mom, Dad . . . meet Ellie Stuart."

Quinn's mother was an attractive woman with thick brown hair that framed soft brown eyes, a butter-smooth complexion and a warm, relaxed smile. Her beige dress showcased her trim figure. His father had a tall athletic build, like Quinn, and looked distinguished in a blue blazer, tan slacks and blue shirt.

"Nice to meet you, Ellie," he said. "This is Hannah and I'm Jack Parker."

Ellie shook hands, but her knees kept on shaking.

"It's good to meet you, Ellie," Jack Parker said.

"It's real nice to meet youall."

"I hear Quinn spilled coffee on you," Mrs. Parker said.

"Yes, ma'am, he sure did."

Jack Parker smiled. "He also said you earned a full scholarship to U of L, and plan to attend law school."

"Yes, sir."

"Well, good for you, Ellie!"

A little man with red suspenders tugged Mr. Parker's sleeve, then pointed at the TV monitor.

"Jack, look at these new odds on #6, Auntie Billy!"

Jack Parker looked and seemed surprised.

"Come on, Ellie," Mrs. Parker said, "how's about we girl-talk a little before the Derby."

"I'd love that, ma'am." *I think. . . .*

Hannah Parker led Ellie over to the corner where they sat in beige leather chairs facing each other. Ellie was nervous, and prepared herself for a serious inquisition from Mrs. Parker.

But suddenly, an Angel of the Lord appeared with a tray of mint juleps. Mrs. Parker took one and sipped. Ellie took one and sucked like an Oreck until the bourbon calmed her a bit.

"Ellie, you a Kentucky girl?"

"Yes, ma'am."

"Where from?"

Ellie paused. "I'm from ah . . . *go ahead and say it* . . . I'm from way down in itty bitty Harlan." There - she exposed the big bad secret. Got it out of the way. She watched for some hint of disapproval or condescension in Mrs. Parker's eyes, but saw only a warm smile.

"Well, I'll swan, Ellie. . . ."

"What?"

"We're neighbors."

"Ma'am?"

"I'm from ittier-bittier Flat Lick."

My God, Ellie thought, *she's from an even smaller town than I am!*

"Your folks still live down there, Ellie?"

"Well, no, ma'am." She paused. "Actually, I was adopted as an infant by the Stuarts. They were wonderful parents."

"Were . . . ?"

Ellie felt the old pain, took a breath. "They died in a boating accident when I was sixteen."

"Oh my . . ." Hannah Parker's eyes dimmed and she placed her hand on Ellie's. "My momma died when I was seventeen. Cancer. So hard to lose a parent when you're young."

Ellie nodded.

"Did you ever try to find your birth parents?"

Ellie paused. "Well actually, Quinn's been helping me with that. We discovered who my mother was, but learned she died in a car accident when I was three months old. The Stuarts adopted me then."

"Good Lord, how awful." Mrs. Parker shook her head. "Any luck finding your daddy?"

"Not yet, ma'am. But Quinn's helping with that, too."

"Well, good luck, hon."

Her concern was genuine. Clearly, she knew nothing about the extremely remote possibility of her relationship to Leland Radford. And she seemed to accept her as she was, and not comparing her to Jennifer. Ellie felt an unexpected, sense of calm wash over her, and it wasn't just the mint julep.

Suddenly - the bugle blared over the loudspeakers.

"LADIES AND GENTLEMEN . . . THE HORSES ARE ENTERING THE TRACK. . . ."

"Come on, Ellie, it's show time!" Mrs. Parker took Ellie's hand and led her through the guests to the big window with a bird's-eye view of the finish line below, clearly one of the best views in Churchill Downs. Ellie read that one Derby seat in a private suite like this cost four thousand dollars or more.

Quinn walked over to her.

She whispered in his ear. "It's good to know a Saudi prince."

"True. Nice chat with mom?"

"The best!"

"Everyone thinks you're beautiful!"

"Everyone's drunk."

They watched the sixteen magnificent thoroughbreds prance along the manicured dirt track. Even the horses seemed to sense this race was special.

Then she heard it, Stephen Foster's hypnotic melody.

OH . . . THE . . . SUN SHINES BRIGHT . . . ON MY OLD KENTUCKY HOME . . .

And one hundred sixty thousand people began to sing along . . . and within seconds, thousands of eyes, including hers, began to moisten.

As she sang, her throat tightened and she dabbed a tear. She was caught up in everything: the enchanting melody, her love of the Derby, the beautiful horses glistening in the sun, the joy of learning about her birth mother, and, of course, the happiness of being with Quinn. She was slowly and cautiously, but most certainly, falling in love with him . . . something that filled her with joy, but in some perverse way, terrified her. And she knew why. Everyone she'd ever loved, was no longer alive . . . and by drawing closer to him each day, she feared she might somehow be increasing the likelihood of something bad happening to him.

An absurd fear, of course.

Or was it?

The starter's gun popped and echoed across the track.

SIXTY FOUR

"And they're off!"

The powerful three-year-old thoroughbreds bolted from the gates and sprinted down the track.

People screamed at their favorites as though the horses were listening to them. Again, the loud crowd roar dinged her eardrums.

She marveled at how the muscular animals galloped at nearly forty miles per hour without tangling their hooves, and how the jockeys melted into the horses' backs.

> *"And heading into the first turn, Scottish Mist, the favorite, leads by half a length . . . followed by Bluegrass Lady and Big Bad Tom. . . ."*

"Are we having fun yet?" Quinn whispered in her ear.

"Yes, thanks to you."

He held her hand as they watched the horses finish the first half-mile. A mile and a quarter to go. Scottish Mist led by a length and a half, followed closely by five other horses. Mr. Parker's horse, Auntie Billy, was near the back of the pack. Some jockeys started using the whip. The leaders were pulling ahead.

"*. . . they're at the top of the stretch. . . .*"

Thirty seconds later, on the far outside track, she saw a large chestnut horse, Auntie Billy, breeze past two horses near the middle of the pack. He started gaining on the leaders who didn't see him coming.

> *. . . "They're turning for the home stretch . . . and here they come, Scottish Mist in the lead . . . Bluegrass Lady close behind, followed by Big Bad Tom, and on the far outside, staying away from the pack, is Auntie Billy moving up smartly . . . and now . . . hang on to your hats folks . . . Auntie Billy is turning on the jets, blazing past Big Bad Tom and Bluegrass Lady and closing fast on the leader, Scottish Mist as they race toward the finish line thirty yards away! . . .*

The crowd roared even louder.

> *And here's the finish – they're neck and neck, stride for stride and . . .*
> *. . . Auntie Billy wins by a nose!"*

"*Hot damn!*" Jack Parker shouted, waving his Auntie Billy ticket. "I just won eight hundred fifty bucks! Free drinks on me!"
"The drinks are already free, dad."

"Then make 'em doubles!"

Ellie was so excited she almost didn't feel her phone vibrating in her pocket. She pulled it out and saw *Jessica Bishop* on Caller ID. She showed Quinn. He led her into the suite restroom and closed the door so she could hear. She punched the speakerphone button.

"Hey, Jessie. What's up?"

"The lab director just called. He did me a gimongous favor."

"What?"

"Rescheduled all his work so he could finish your four DNA tests *today!*"

"How'd you get him to - ?"

"- promised him my sexual favors."

"That's all it took?"

"Hurry back here smart ass! I'll have your results in an hour."

"To your lab?"

"No. To the Fayette County District Court here. A clerk I know is there today. She'll witness the results."

Ellie looked at Quinn who nodded.

"We're on the way!"

They hung up, stepped back into the suite and explained to his parents why they were leaving. Mrs. Parker smiled and took Ellie's hand in hers.

"Ellie, can you join us for dinner next Sunday?"

Ellie swallowed a lump. "Yes, ma'am, I'd like that very much."

"Let's go," Quinn said. "Mom, Dad, thanks for everything."

He opened the door and froze.

Jennifer DuBois stood there.

She looked drop dead stunning in a cobalt blue dress and matching blue Derby Party hat. Her white pearl necklace cost a year's tuition. She smiled at Quinn.

"Quinny, I heard you were in here, so I had to come by and say hi." Jennifer stepped in and kissed his cheek.

"Hi, Jenn," he said, looking uncomfortable. "You remember Ellie."

"Sure . . ." Jennifer's expression suggested she'd rather see Ellie down on the track being trampled.

"Actually, Jenn," he said, "we're just rushing back to Lexington to pick up some important legal documents. Sorry we can't stay and chat."

Jennifer's face scrunched up in a pout. "Okay, but call me tomorrow. I've been rethinking things . . ."

"Oh . . .?"

"Yeah. Promise to call?"

"Ah . . . okay," Quinn said, rushing Ellie out the door and down the hall.

"Jennifer's folks have permanent seats in *Millionaire's Row* just down the hall. And Jennifer loves horses."

"Quinn . . ."

"Yeah?"

"That's not all she loves."

SIXTY FIVE

After breaking the Louisville-to-Lexington land speed record, Quinn parked on Limestone Street next to the Fayette County District Court.

Ellie looked up at the modern, massive, four-story building. "Very impressive."

"Impressive workload handled here," Quinn said. "All county legal activity, including circuit court, criminal and civil, probate, records - and just maybe some lucky DNA test results!"

"Lucky? According to Jessica, we should think lottery winner!"

"But still worth the try, right?"

"Right," Ellie said, even though she knew there was a miniscule chance, most would say ridiculously impossible chance, that this test would contradict the four other DNA tests that proved scientifically she was not Leland Radford's daughter. DNA doesn't lie. The guys on death row are proof.

But for some reason, Jessica had insisted they try this very rare, very-slim-chance test with a very fat price: one thousand dollars! *I'll be paying Quinn back for the rest of my life.*

But if I hadn't tried the test, I'd wonder about the results the rest of my life.

They walked into the courthouse lobby and Ellie saw Jessica chatting with a short middle-aged woman. Jessica's face revealed nothing as she waved them over.

"Hey guys, meet Nancy Baines," Jessica said. "Nancy works here at the court. She'll witness the test results."

Ellie and Quinn shook hands with the smiling brunette with large glasses and an American flag pin on her flowery dress. Her rosy cheeks reminded Ellie of the lady who baked apple pies in her grade school cafeteria.

"Y'all ready?" Nancy asked.

Everyone nodded.

"Just follow me." Nancy led the group down to a small meeting room where they settled around an oak conference table. Wall paintings depicted two Derby winners, Whirlaway and Citation in large, beautiful gold frames. Below them were two judges in cheap wood frames. Horses get top billing in Kentucky.

Ellie's throat was chalk-dry as Jessica unfolded a portable three-foot-long light box. She placed it on a wall ledge, plugged it in and the screen lit up. From her handbag, she took a large sealed envelope.

"This envelope left the lab thirty minutes ago. It has not been opened. I have no idea what the contents reveal."

She showed the envelope to Nancy Baines, who nodded. Jessica then snapped the wax seal, pulled off the red tape, lifted the flap and took out some file folders.

"As you know, Ellie, these four tests represent the DNA samples I took from your hair, your blood, your saliva, and your woo-woo."

"Her *whuut*?" Nancy asked.

Ellie and Jessica laughed. "As kids, Ellie and I referred to our vaginas as our woo-woos."

"Oh . . ." Nancy blushed.

Jessica set the test results on the table and began to study the films of smudges and pages of indecipherable letters – like AGU, CAG, GUA. Ellie couldn't understand how a human being could be reduced to alphabet letters. What did the letters mean? Were As better than Gs? She looked at the smudges, and numbers, and charts with red and blue spikes. Ellie thought the smudges looked identical to the smudges on her earlier DNA films . . . and why wouldn't they be identical?

My DNA is my DNA for God sakes!

Jessica studied one chart, then another, then looked at the other two charts. She flipped back through the pages, rechecking some. Her brow furrowed, but her eyes were locked in concentration as she scanned each line of data.

The longer Jessica took, the harder Ellie's heart thumped into her throat, and the faster her leg shook. Quinn's fingers tapped Morse Code on the oak table. Nancy fiddled with her iPad.

What's taking so long?

Jessica walked to the light box and placed two films next to each other . . . then placed the other two films beside them.

She stared at the graphs, then started shaking her head slowly as though something was wrong, or puzzling, or disappointing . . . or . . . Ellie thought, *she's working up the courage to tell me the bad news?*

"Well, I'll be!" Jessica said.

"You'll be what?" Ellie asked.

"Hog-tied and scallywagged! Look at that, Ellie!"

"Look at what?"

"Ellie . . . you're a twin!"

"I have a twin?"

"No, *you . . . yourself . . . are twins!*"

"Huh . . .?"

"You are your *own* twin!"

Ellie was completely confused.

"Ellie, you're a . . . *chimera!*"

"What's a khi – ?"

"- a chimera is a person who has *two* genetically distinct sets of DNA in their body. Two completely *different* DNAs!"

Ellie was still confused. "But how can – ?"

" – it began in your mother's womb. Two separately fertilized eggs, each with its own DNA, came together and fused into *one* human being – *you!* You continued to grow in the womb, but with your two different DNAs located in different parts of your body. Your mouth swab and hair gave us one of those DNAs, but your blood and vagina gave us your new *second* DNA."

"Are you saying I'm one person with two completely and distinctly different DNAs?"

"That's exactly what I'm saying."

"*How* different are these DNAs?"

"As different as the DNAs of me and . . . Lady GaGa."

"But I feel like *one* person."

"Because you are *one* person."

Ellie still had difficulty processing the mind-boggling science. "Are there many of us . . . chi . . . meras?"

"Chimeras are rare, we think. But there might be more than we realize."

"Why?"

"Because they look pretty much like other people. But they may have some physical characteristics."

"Like?"

"Like the one that made me think about testing you."

"My eyes?"

"Right. Your right eye is bluer than your left. Different eye colors sometimes signify a chimera. But not always."

"Any other characteristics?"

"Some chimeras have splotchy or different-colored skin, or different shades of hair, or hitchhiker's thumb, a thumb that bends way back. And there are other characteristics. But you have none of those. Nor did you have a bone marrow transplant that can turn a patient into a chimera."

Quinn leaned over the conference table.

"Jessica, are you saying Ellie has a second, completely different set of DNA that has not yet been compared to Leland Radford's DNA?"

"Yes I am!"

"When can we compare her new DNA to his?"

"Here and now."

Jessica gestured everyone over to the light box. She took a folder from her briefcase. The folder label said *Leland Radford*. From the folder, she took out Radford's DNA film and clipped it to the light box.

Then she took Ellie's two new DNA films from her blood and vagina – and clipped them beside Radford's DNA film.

Jessica studied Radford's film, then Ellie's new DNA films. She checked them again.

Then slowly, she turned and stared at Ellie for several moments.

"Ellie. . . ."

"Yeah?"

"Your biological father is Leland T. Radford."

SIXTY SIX

Nancy Baines entered her courthouse cubicle, still amazed by the only chimera DNA test she'd ever witnessed.

She tried to settle quietly into her desk chair, but as usual it squeaked, alerting her nosey assistant, Harley Don Sidebottom. He scurried over to her cubical like Pavlov's dog ready to lap up the latest gossip. Did Lurleen get breast implants? Are Judge Snead and his slutty secretary doing the nasty in chambers? Harley Don lived for gossip. So much so, the flabby, forty-seven-year-old bachelor with silver ear studs and lethal flatulence had to work weekends to catch up.

"Where ya been?" he asked, his beady eyes peering over her cubicle wall, begging for news, the sleazier the better.

"I was over witnessing a DNA test result at Gen-Ident."

"On Saturday? Musta been dang important!"

Nancy said nothing.

"Was it one of them Who-Da-Daddy DNA tests?"

She nodded.

"Did the daddy 'fess up?'"

"No."

"So he agreed?"

"No."

"Then he *musta* denied!"

"No."

"Why not?"

"He's dead."

"Oh. . . ."

She flipped through some pink phone slips, praying Harley Don would go back to his cubicle. When he didn't, she decided to throw him a bone that might send him off to do research.

"But this test was different, Harley Don."

"Different how?"

"It was a multi-specimen DNA test. They took DNA specimens from four different parts of her body. Turns out she's a *chimera.*"

"A whuuut?"

"A Ki-meer-uh. A person with two different sets of DNA."

"But that ain't possible!"

"It is, but rare."

"Did she have like two heads and look weird?"

"One head and she's beautiful."

"Oh. So, did one of them DNAs match the daddy?"

"Harley, you know that's confidential."

"Betcha the daddy's from these parts."

"Maybe. Maybe not."

Harley Don snickered. "Bet it'll be in the newspaper, fancy test like that. Right?"

She said nothing, but felt Harley Don reading her eyes.

"The newspaper means it's high profile."

Nancy realized she'd already told him too much.

Harley Don scratched his head. "Let's see now . . . a Gen-Ident DNA daddy test. An expensive Saturday test. For a girl. Daddy's dead. Newspaper interest. Hmmmm." He tugged his ear stud, then his eyes lit up.

"Betcha she's the one what old Lenny at Gen-Ident told me about. Said they was fixin' to retest this college girl agin yesterday. Girl from down in Harlan. Might be related to the rich old feller over near Manchester who up and died with no kin. Had hisself more money than Fort Knox! What's that old boy's name? Let's see, Rastibert, no Rackyfern, somethin' like that? Betcha I'm right!"

She shooed Harley Don away, amazed and angry that he put it all together so fast. She picked up some papers and turned around to sort them.

"She's related to that old rich fella! I know it!" Harley Don grinned and clapped his hands.

Nancy felt her cheeks redden. "Harley Don, I've got calls to make. And you got stacks of filin' to catch up on. So git going." She turned away, grabbed her phone and pretended to call someone.

Harley Don paused a moment, then chuckled all the way back to his desk.

And then he picked up his phone.

* * *

Heinrich De Groot sat at his office desk in Cincinnati's prestigious Scripps Center, gazing down at the crowds meandering through Fountain Square.

He drew hard on his Cohiba cigar, savoring its rich aroma, and his rich windfall coming from the Radford probate ruling . . . a ruling that would shovel millions into his coffers.

De Groot's private cell phone rang and he picked up.

"Mr. De Groot?"

"Yes . . ."

"This here's Harley Don over to the Fayette County courthouse and – "

"Harley Don, I'm rather busy right now."

"But you wanted to know if I learned anything about Ellie Stuart."

De Groot grew concerned. "What did you learn?"

"Well, I'm right sure Ellie Stuart got herself another new DNA test today."

"She what?"

"Gen-Ident did one of them extree special DNA tests. Four tests in one. Turns out she's a chimera with two different DNAs in her body! Damned creepy you ask me."

"She has *two* DNAs?"

"Yep."

De Groot stood up, his heart pounding. "Did one of her DNAs match the DNA of Leland Radford?"

"Sure did!"

"*FUCK!* "How do you know it matched?"

"Well, see, my boss, Nancy, was there. She witnessed them test results. And I could tell by her face it matched. I kin read old Nancy like a book."

"That's your only proof?"

"Nope."

"What else?"

"Well, see when Nancy turned around to make a phone call, I peeked at the file on her desk. Saw the names *Radford/Stuart* right on top of her *MATCHED FILE* stack. Yes sir, Ellie's DNA matched the rich old fella's. And that's a fact!"

De Groot felt sick. "How accurate is this chimera test?"

"99.99999 percent certain. She's his daughter all right!"

De Groot hung up, then called Nikolai Pushkin. The big Russian had to handle her *now* . . . in hours . . . before tomorrow.

Pushkin didn't pick up.

He dialed again.

After five rings, Pushkin answered.

"Do it *now!*" De Groot shouted.

SIXTY SEVEN

Fletcher Falcone sat in his office, cursing as he counted the hundred thousand dollars he had to fork over to Tony Broutafachi's goon who would arrive any second. The money wasn't a problem. Handing it over before collecting his Radford probate money was the problem. But if he didn't hand it over, Broutafachi's hitman, a guy named Drago, would plant a bullet in his knee . . . or worse.

Falcone's phone rang and he picked up.

"Mr. Falcone?"

"Yes?"

"My name is Bob Darnell."

Falcone didn't recognize the name.

"I'm a Second Lieutenant in the U.S. Army. Our group advises the Iraqi military here in Baghdad."

Why's a lieutenant calling me from Baghdad? he wondered. "Did you know Rick Radford, Leland Radford's son?"

"Yes, sir. We were very good buddies."

"Rick was a wonderful young man, Lieutenant, and a terrific son. But perhaps we could talk tomorrow. You see, I'm very busy preparing for Rick's father's probate case right now."

"That's why I called, sir."

"The probate?"

"Yes."

Falcone wondered what he meant.

"I figured you should know that Rick married an Iraqi woman here."

Falcone's eyes went out of focus.

"What? Rick marr - ?"

" - yes, sir. Her name is Nafeesa Hakim. Rick was planning to tell his father about her, but the roadside bomb . . . killed him."

"Rick Radford *has* a *wife,* a widow*?*"

"Yes, sir. I just found out yesterday."

Falcone felt like he'd swallowed ice, as he realized the woman might have a claim to Leland Radford's fortune.

"Where is this Nas . . .?"

"Nafeesa Hakim. Actually, she flew out of Baghdad and will be landing at Louisville International Airport this evening. Then she's coming to show you her marriage certificate."

"Does she speak English?"

"Her English is quite good."

Falcone swallowed. "Does she have an attorney?"

"No, sir. She's alone and coming to your office."

SIXTY EIGHT

L ater that night, Fletcher Falcone was shocked. Nafeesa Hakim was not at all what he expected.

Not your basic Muslim woman. No head-to-toe black *chador*, no veil, no timid steps, no demure cast to her eyes. Nafeesa looked like a runway model as she walked into his office. Her long black hair framed dark luminous eyes, sculpted cheekbones and smooth tawny skin. Her black dress hugged long legs, a wasp-thin waist and full breasts.

Ms. Nafeesa Hakim was a stunning, twenty-four-year-old worthy of the *Sports Illustrated* Swimsuit cover. No wonder Rick Radford was smitten.

"Welcome Nafeesa, I'm Fletcher Falcone, executor of the Radford estate. It's nice to meet you."

"Very nice to meet you, Mr. Falcone." Warm, disarming smile.

Her English was almost accent free, the result Falcone had just learned, of her two years at the American University of Iraq.

Falcone led her over to a thin swarthy man with a thick black mustache and horn-rimmed glasses. The man stood and smiled.

"Nafeesa, please meet Dr. Yusuf Barzani, a fellow Iraqi, and a distinguished professor of Persian literature here at the University of Kentucky. I've asked Professor Barzani to verify your marriage certificate for me. You understand, of course."

"Yes, certainly."

Nafeesa shook hands and spoke briefly in Farsi with Professor Barzani. Then she sat in a chair facing Falcone's desk and crossed her legs, skin flashing in the slit. Flawless skin, Falcone noted.

"Do you have your marriage certificate?"

"Yes."

"The original?"

"It's right here." She opened her briefcase, took out the certificate and an English translation and placed them side-by-side on Falcone's desk.

Professor Barzani opened his briefcase, took out another Iraqi marriage certificate and placed it beside Nafeesa's.

Falcone thought both certificates looked identical.

Using a magnifying glass, Barzani scrutinized her entire certificate and seal. He rubbed each document between his fingers, comparing paper texture, then walked over to the window and held both certificates up to the sunlight, perhaps looking for an official imprint or watermark.

Moments later, he walked back, placed the certificate back on the desk, then looked at Nafessa and Falcone.

"In my judgment this marriage certificate is genuine."

Falcone nodded. "Good. Thank you Professor Barzani for your assistance. At this time, you understand, Nafeesa and I need to discuss the estate in private."

"Of course." Professor Barzani said goodbye and left.

"Would you care for something to drink, Nafeesa?"

"No, thank you."

"Perhaps some of your delicious Iraqi pistachios? I love them!" He tossed a handful in his mouth and gave her his best country lawyer smile.

She smiled back, but shook her head.

Falcone poured some Jim Beam, sipped some, then walked back and sat at his desk. He stared at her for several moments, impressed with what she'd accomplished. She seemed nervous. Most understandable, he thought.

"Nice try, Nafeesa."

"Pardon?"

"Nice try."

She frowned. "I'm sorry, I don't understand."

"Oh, I think you do."

She said nothing.

"The marriage," he said.

"What about it?"

"The certificate."

"As Professor Barzani said - my certificate is genuine."

"Except for one minor detail."

"What detail?"

"You never married Rick Radford."

She blinked. "But my certificate proves I married him."

Falcone smiled. "No, it proves you somehow persuaded a man named Khalid Al-Kareem, a director in Baghdad's Social Status Court, to give you this fraudulent marriage certificate."

Nafeesa looked shocked that he knew of Khalid Al-Kareem. She took worry beads from her purse and began fingering them.

"You see, when I was informed of your possible marriage to Rick, I had Professor Barzani hire an investigator in Baghdad. The investigator reported back to me an hour ago. He said that witnesses have signed sworn statements that Rick Radford was with them in Basra, three hundred miles south of Baghdad on the day you allegedly married him in Baghdad. They also swear you were not with him in Basra. Your family says you were in Baghdad that day and week. And they knew nothing of your wedding."

Nafeesa stared out the window.

"You may not realize it, Nafeesa, but using a counterfeit document to defraud our legal system for personal gain is a very serious crime in this country. And it's punishable by imprisonment or fines, or both."

She fingered her beads faster.

"Do you have anything to say, Ms. Hakim?"

He watched her confidence melt like hot wax.

"Ms. Hakim . . .?"

She closed her eyes and lowered her head. "Please allow me to explain."

"Of course."

She took a deep breath and eased it out. "The . . . war . . ." she said and took another breath. "The war destroyed my family, Mr. Falcone . . ." She dabbed her eyes. "On just one night, bombs killed my father, two brothers, younger sister and some cousins. It also destroyed our family business – and even the bank with our family savings! We lost everything, Mr. Falcone, do you understand? *Everything. Gone. Overnight!* We were penniless. Suddenly, I was searching for money to feed my family and pay for my mother's cancer treatments that her Doctor has stopped for non-payment. I struggle to find the money each week."

Falcone nodded, since his private investigator told him the same things.

"I'm sorry for your losses, Ms. Hakim. Truly I am."

Her eyes filled and she dabbed them with a Kleenex. "But I do not want legal trouble in the USA. So I will return home and try to care for my mother."

She stood to leave.

"Wait . . ."

"No, Mr. Falcone. Please understand - I do not want any legal problems in America. My family depends on me in Baghdad."

"Perhaps I can help." He gestured for her to sit back down.

"Help? How . . .?"

"With two hundred thousand dollars."

She sat down fast, her dark eyes locked on his. "I do not understand."

Falcone sipped more bourbon. "It's quite simple. We will proceed as though your marriage certificate represents a genuine marriage - that you were in fact married to Rick Radford."

She said nothing.

"Mr. Barzani will testify that your marriage certificate is authentic. Mr. Al-Kareem will testify that he issued it. The probate court will then accept their word, and your marriage."

She stared at him.

"Then the court will likely distribute the Radford estate between you and possibly a woman named Ellie Stuart who is attempting to prove that she's Leland Radford's biological daughter, even though several DNA tests, including her own test, have proven she's not."

Nafeesa's mouth opened, but nothing came out.

"So, instead of you getting a possible criminal conviction and jail time for attempted fraud, and no money from the Radford estate, you will receive two hundred thousand dollars through a special fund. Let's call it . . . *The Rick Radford Iraqi Relief Fund.* I'll say Leland set it up as a tribute to his son. But only you will have access to the money. And can use the money any way you wish."

Her worry beads slowed.

"And in return," Falcone continued, "*I* will retain de facto control of the remaining share of the estate assets in a special account accessible only by me."

She said nothing.

"And, after I sell off the estate assets, I will deposit an additional two hundred thousand dollars in your account. Again, only you can draw from it."

She stared back.

"In brief, Nafeesa, you get a total of four hundred thousand dollars."

Her worry beads stopped.

"But," he said, staring hard into her eyes, "if you ever try to claim money from my special account, I will know. And the court will immediately receive evidence proving your marriage is a fraud. And then a warrant will be issued for your arrest."

Nafeesa looked out the window for several moments, apparently absorbing everything he'd said, then turned back to him.

"You can do all this?"

"I can do all this."

He tossed more pistachios into his mouth.

"Well, Nafeesa . . .?"

She looked out the window again.

"When would I get this first two hundred thousand dollars?"

"A week after probate."

"But what about all my travel and hotel expenses here? I borrowed a lot of money to come here."

Falcone knew how Iraqis loved to negotiate. "I'll reimburse them."

She stared at him. "*Where* do I get the money?"

"Any Iraqi bank you want."

She paused. "I don't trust Iraqi banks."

"Me either. But I know a discreet Swiss bank."

She nodded.

SIXTY NINE

"I need to pick up my *Contracts* casebook," Quinn said, as he and Ellie hurried toward the back door of his apartment building.

Ellie scrutinized the people walking toward them. No obvious assassins. Just students, professors, a UPS driver, a Geek Squad guy. But why was his toolkit so long? she wondered. What's in it?

She'd become hyper-suspicious of everyone since the chimera test proved she was Leland Radford's biological daughter.

Quinn unlocked the back door and they stepped inside. He grabbed his mail, tossed the junk mail, kept two bills and a pizza coupon, then showed her a hand-addressed envelope.

Ellie noticed the return address: *Irene Whitten, The Pines*. She pointed to the postmark. "Look - Irene mailed this the day she was attacked in the garden."

Quinn nodded, then opened the envelope and took out the contents: a note was folded around a letter.

They read the note.

Dear Quinn,

Somebody been snooping around my room.
Probably looking for what Mr. Radford and
me signed up at the hospital. To be safe, I
put it here in this envelope. I reckon you
know best who to give it to. I'll see y'all at
the probate court.

Your friend,
Irene

Next, they read the enclosed statement written in shaky hand-
writing.

I, Leland T. Radford, being of sound mind,
as attested to by my physician, Dr. Thomas
A. Lyons III, learned moments ago from
Irene Whitten, my housekeeper, that I
fathered a child with Jacqueline Moreau
over twenty years ago. The news gives me
tremendous joy.

   I pray my child can be found and
brought to me very soon. But if I should pass
away first, please tell my child that I love
him and apologize for not knowing he exis-
ted until minutes ago.

   Finally, I hereby direct my attorney,
Fletcher Falcone, to revise my last will im-
mediately so that my surviving child is now
the sole heir of my estate, except for what I
have left for members of my staff.

Leland T. Radford
Witness: *Irene Whitten*

"Radford's last will!" Quinn said. "Signed, and witnessed by Irene."

"And the reason she was attacked," Ellie said.

"Yeah, and we need to give this to Fletcher Falcone. Then he has to give it to the probate judge fast."

Ellie nodded.

"We also have to give copies to your attorney, Henri Delacroix, before the probate hearing tomorrow."

"We have to do something else first!" she said.

"What?"

"Stay alive."

SEVENTY

Quinn's Uncle's Escalade hugged the hilly curves like it was on rails. They were driving through the Kentenia State Forest. Ellie loved how these green forests and rolling hills always seemed to embrace her like they were her "mountain mama," as John Denver sang.

A gray misty haze hunkered down over the hills today, as though concealing their pristine beauty from the greedy miners who wanted to strip them bare, the same strip-miners her father had fought off for decades.

On one hill, she saw a wispy rope of smoke curling up through the pine trees. Once, as a young kid, she walked to the source of a similar 'smoke rope' and found herself staring into the twin barrels of a moonshiner's shotgun. He shouted, "Git the hell out of here, youngun!" She ran home.

Stills were big business in these hills, especially after thousands of Kentucky coalmines closed and tossed miners on the street. To

feed their families, some ex-miners turned to the three Big-Ms –
Moonshine, Marijuana and Meth.

Quinn passed a slow Farmall tractor. They were driving toward
Professor Bossung's mountain cabin where they'd hide out until
tomorrow morning's probate hearing. Only Professor Bossung and
her attorney, Mr. Delacroix, knew they'd be at the cabin.

"Do I hear your brain working?" Quinn said.

"You do."

"Working on what?"

"What's behind my attacks. It's got to be the money."

"Yep. And behind the money would be – "

" - the Radford estate managers who might lose revenue if
I inherit."

"Or if you replace them. Or liquidate everything."

"Same with their boss, Fletcher Falcone, I assume."

"Absolutely," Quinn said. "He'll probably lose the most revenue. And frankly, I've had suspicions about jolly Mr. Falcone."

She looked at Quinn. "Why?"

"Little stuff that's been building up."

"Like . . .?"

"When I first interviewed him, I asked him if Leland Radford
had any other children. He said no, but it's *how* he said it. He sort
of blinked oddly, hesitated, then his eyes shifted right, which many
experts say can mean deception or flat-out lying."

"Anything else?"

"Yeah. When I asked him if I could talk to someone at *The Pines*,
he seemed uneasy, concerned. Now, I wonder if he was concerned
I'd learn about your mother . . . and ultimately you?"

"And you did."

He nodded. "And another thing. Falcone was Leland Radford's
attorney back when your mother worked at *The* Pines. Irene said
that Falcone met with Leland each week at *The Pines* and knew his
staff. It seems reasonable that Falcone must have met your mom

there over the years, or was introduced to her, or knew her name. Yet Falcone claimed he'd never even heard of Jacqueline Moreau until I mentioned her a few days ago."

Ellie nodded. "Irene would know if Falcone had met my mom. Is Irene still in a coma?"

"Yes."

Ellie said a quick prayer for her.

"But in Falcone's defense," Ellie said, "He kept saying I looked like Radford, remember?"

"Yeah."

"And he also looked shocked when the Southern Genetic Lab DNA tests proved I *wasn't* Radford's daughter."

"Lawyers can win Oscars."

"But he even *insisted* the lab conduct another test."

"Maybe because he knew -"

" - the retest would also prove I wasn't Radford's daughter!"

Quinn nodded.

"One thing that bothered me," she said, "is that Falcone is the one person who knew my address, and where we were driving, and when, and what vehicle you were driving."

"True," Quinn said, as he steered around a chunk of recapped truck tire.

"And speaking of driving," she said, "I just realized something. I saw a black Navigator with a red handicapped card on the mirror parked near Falcone's office. Red cards aren't that common."

"So . . .?"

"So the black Navigator that followed us from to the House of Grace in Barbourville also had a red handicapped card hanging on the rearview mirror."

"You sure?"

"Same size, same color."

Quinn looked surprised. "The law has an important term for all these converging circumstances."

"What term?"

"A shitload."

* * *

Nicolai Pushkin followed the beeping dot on his GPS tracking unit. Yesterday, after locating Quinn's uncle's Escalade, Pushkin attached a three-inch T-Trac GPS unit beneath its back bumper. Now, hanging back a couple of miles, he tracked the Escalade, enjoying every mile of these beautiful rolling hills and forests.

It's nice, he thought, *to have a rural assignment for a change.*

He breathed in the fresh country air and smiled.

* * *

Heinrich De Groot smelled over-fried meat and overripe hill-billies as he sipped his second Maker's Mark in the *Rendez-Booze Saloon.*

He looked around the saloon. The same beer-belly rednecks he saw yesterday. The angry humpback who knocked out the bully's glass eye looked happy today thanks to the blonde resting her hand on the hump in his crotch. Everyone cheered a Chevy Silverado crushing a Honda Civic on *Demolition Derby.*

Trailer trash, De Groot thought! *But at least they don't know who I am.*

Or the man who just strolled in wearing bib overalls, a fake beard and a John Deere hat. The man sat down opposite De Groot as a skinny waitress with green spiked-hair and flyswatter eyelashes appeared at the table.

"Jim Beam, four fingers," the man said.

Seconds later, she placed a full tumbler of bourbon in front of him. He gulped down half of it.

"So you got my message?" De Groot said. "Ellie Stuart's a chimera!"

The man nodded.

"And that her *chimera* test proves she is Radford's daughter."

Another nod. "But you're handling her."

"I'm trying." De Groot said.

"Very bad answer."

"The problem is, I called off Pushkin when we learned she *wasn't* Radford's daughter. Then when the new test says she *is* -"

" – you re-ordered him to handle her, right?" the man said.

"Right, but Pushkin's still looking for her."

"Another very bad answer," the man said.

De Groot said nothing.

"Millions of dollars are at stake, De Groot! Your people should have handled her days ago! If they hadn't fucked up, we wouldn't be sitting here now. Your people screwed up bad. *You* fix it! And fix it in the next few hours or - "

" – let's ask the judge for a delay."

"What do we say - your honor, we need more time to arrange an accident for Radford's daughter."

De Groot said nothing.

"Tell me when Ellie Stuart is *dead*!" said Fletcher Falcone.

Then he stood and walked out of the bar.

SEVENTY ONE

In the side mirror, Ellie saw the same white van trailing them. She considered it, like all vehicles, guilty until proven innocent. The van had maintained the same distance for miles. Two large men sat in front. She grew concerned.

As she started to tell Quinn, the van exited onto a dirt road. She breathed out and released her death grip on the armrest. *Face it,* she thought. *You've become a full-blown paranoid.*

Her phone rang: It was Henri Delacroix, her attorney. She wondered why he was calling, since they just met with him to discuss *tomorrow's probate hearing.*

She punched the speaker button. "Hi, Mr. Delacroix."

"Hey, Ellie. You and Quinn heading to the cabin?"

"Almost there."

"Good. But there's been an important last minute development."

"Oh . . ."

"Fletcher Falcone was visited by a young woman named Nafeesa Hakim. She has an Iraqi marriage certificate that states she married Rick Radford in Iraq."

Stunned, Ellie and Quinn stared at each other.

"They were married a few weeks before Rick was killed in action."

"The poor woman. How awful . . ." Ellie said.

"Yes, but Leland Radford and Fletcher Falcone never knew of the marriage."

"So now what?" Quinn said.

"So now the judge will have to determine the validity of her marriage. If valid, he'll decide, based on everything else, what claim, if any, she might be entitled to make on the estate."

"Does her marriage appear valid?" Quinn asked.

"Her marriage *certificate* does, according to an Iraqi professor. I'm going to talk to him and a Lieutenant in Iraq who phoned Falcone with this news. I'll let you know what I find out. And I'll see you both in court tomorrow."

"Okay."

They hung up.

Quinn shook his head. "This case never quiets down."

"But the probate ruling should quiet things, right?"

"Not necessarily. Appeals happen more than people think."

She pointed ahead at a huge boulder shaped like a bus.

"That's the boulder where Professor Bossung said we should turn off to get to his cabin."

Quinn slowed, turned into the forest and they bounced along on two dirt ruts under a canopy of tall oak trees. As they wove through shades of lime green and dark emerald, she realized this thick, serene Kentucky forest looked as primeval as when Daniel Boone hiked through in 1769. It was still a great place to hike . . . and unfortunately, a great place for an assassin to hide.

She pointed ahead to Professor Bossung's small cabin perched on a hill. Quinn crunched up the gravel drive and parked.

They stepped out and Ellie breathed in the sweet scent of the honeysuckle bushes beside her. She took one flower, slowly pulled out the long stamen and placed the clear drop of nectar on her tongue. She loved the honey taste.

She pulled out another stamen, placed the juicy drop of nectar on Quinn's tongue and smiled. "Tarzan like!"

Quinn unlocked the cabin door and they entered. It was charming. Knotty pine walls, redwood chairs and sofas, a fireplace, and bookshelves with law books, western novels and family pictures. She followed Quinn into the kitchen where she saw a small table and chairs and an antique butter churn.

"I'm starving," Quinn said.

"Me, too."

"But I just remembered Professor Bossung told me he removed all food from the cabin. A bear tried to break in."

"What? Assassins aren't enough?"

Quinn shrugged and opened the refrigerator. Empty.

"We gotta eat!" he said, rubbing his stomach. "Let's go back to that Mini Mart and gross out on junk food!"

"You go. I want to freshen up. And please get me some Moon Pies."

He smiled, but still hesitated to leave.

"Don't worry, Quinn. The Mini Mart's only two miles back. You'll be back in a few minutes. If the bear tries to break in, I'll barricade myself in the bathroom."

"I'm not worried about a bear."

"No one followed us here. I checked every few minutes."

He said nothing.

She handed him her cell phone. "Call that old farmer that Professor Bossung told we were coming. The farmer that watches this cabin for him."

"Luther."

"Yeah. I saw Luther's house just down the road. His light's on. Call and ask him to keep an eye on the cabin until you get back."

Quinn dialed Luther's number and waited.

"No answer."

"Leave a message."

"No voice mail."

"Just go ahead, Quinn. Don't worry. I'll be fine."

Quinn frowned, looked outside. "I'll be back in a few minutes. Promise you'll stay in the cabin. And keep the door locked to everyone except Luther."

"How will I know it's Luther?"

"He's eighty-four and limps."

"Oh . . ."

"But make him show you his birth certificate."

She pushed Quinn out the door. "Go get my damn Moon Pies!"

He hurried out to the Escalade.

She slid the metal bar across the door, walked to the window and watched Quinn drive off. He was seriously concerned about her safety. The last person seriously worried about her safety was Mark Miller – and the sad truth is - she should have been seriously worried about *Mark's* safety.

Because a roadside bomb took his life.

Fate.

Like fate had taken both sets of parents from her.

Would fate take Quinn away from her?

SEVENTY TWO

Nikolai Pushkin smiled as the big Escalade raced back down the hill toward the main road, leaving sweet young Ellie Stuart all for him. *Finally, I get a little udachi . . . luck!*

Pushkin walked toward the cabin. The dense forest and hilly terrain reminded him of the Urals and brought back pleasant memories of shooting wolves, pheasants, and some guys he didn't like. He'd come back here and hunt one day. But right now, his prey was just thirty yards away.

He watched Ellie's shadow move behind lace curtain.

He checked his syringe containing succinylcholine, a toxin that would kill her and disappear in her blood within minutes. The local medical examiner would assume she had a heart attack. But, when the autopsy found no heart disease and the tox report found no drugs, he would order more tests. His rural lab would not have the very sophisticated test that detected succinylcholine. Still, he might request the test. Which concerned Pushkin.

He would have preferred using the heroin he intended to inject them with at Quinn's uncle's mansion, but when the house alarm went off, he tossed it in the sewer.

Pushkin stepped closer to the cabin and something white caught his eye. A large propane tank. He saw the tank's badly corroded, rusty tubing where it entered the cabin. Corrosion and propane gas were a deadly combination when exposed to flames or sparks . . . like say the static sparks caused by bullets.

Propane explosions blew up trailers, homes, boats and their occupants each year.

But he had a problem – fat black clouds pushing in overhead looked ready to unleash a downpour any second - a downpour that could kill the fire before the fire killed the woman.

He grabbed a long thin shaft of wood and slipped it soundlessly through the door's outside handle and the door frame, locking her inside.

Thunder rumbled overhead like a gutter ball.

He rushed back to the side of the cabin, took out his Beretta, and tightened the suppressor. He moved behind two thick oak trees to shield himself from the explosion. He raised the weapon and aimed at the exact spot where the corroded tubing fed into the tank. He tightened his finger on the trigger.

Then he heard something . . .

. . . a sickening, familiar, deadly *click*.

Behind him.

He spun around and stared into the twin barrels of a Mossburg 12-gauge shotgun held by a scrawny old guy in bib overalls. His skin looked as withered as a Dead Sea scroll, but his blue eyes had locked on Pushkin like a stone-cold sniper.

Shit! Pushkin felt like he'd swallowed battery acid.

"Reckon you'll be droppin' yer gun, mister. Right slow!"

Pushkin realized he couldn't turn and fire before the old bastard blew him away.

"If'n you ain't droppin' it, I'll be droppin' you. Then I'll be draggin' your sorry ass inside the cabin, so's it's nice and legal lookin'!"

The old guy meant it. His hands were steady.

"You understand me good?"

"Yeah, yeah, I understand good." Pushkin placed his Beretta on the ground, wondering how to reach the Glock tucked in his back.

"You got one of them accents, ain't ya?"

"Yeah."

"Where ya from?"

"Sweden."

"What was you fixin' to shoot at, mister?"

Pushkin scrambled for an answer. "A big raccoon. Foaming at his mouth. Rabies maybe. Behind that big bush near the cabin. I'm with Harlan Exterminators. The owner says raccoons are getting into his cabin."

"Didn't mention no coons to me."

"Well, I saw a big sick one behind that bush." Pushkin pointed, as he inched his right hand closer to his Glock.

"You Harlan Exterminator fellas always work in fancy storebought suits?"

Pushkin thought quick. "Oh, that. I'm on my way to a big event over in Dillon."

"The Tractor Pull's *next* month."

"No. Tonight. A wedding."

"You Harlan Exterminator fellas must make good money to drive a big Mercedes."

Pushkin paused. "Heck no. I rented it for the wedding."

"You also rent that silencer fer yer gun?"

Who is this guy? Ex-cop? Pushkin searched for something to say. "Well, I didn't want to frighten the neighbors."

"You're lookin at the neighbor."

Pushkin's finger touched the handle of the Glock.

"Young fella . . ."

"Yeah?"

"I reckon you bes' brang' yer right hand 'round front, real slow and real empty. I'm old, but I ain't blind!"

Bastard sees everything. I gotta get closer, deflect his gun barrels.

"Okay. You win, mister." Pushkin took a step closer.

"Name's Luther."

"Okay, Luther."

Suddenly, a radio blasted from inside the cabin . . .

". . . AND A SEVERE STORM ALERT IS ISSUED FOR HARLAN COUNTY! HIGH WINDS ARE . . ."

The old man turned toward the loud voice . . .

Pushkin saw his chance - yanked out his Glock and swung it around -

- too late.

Luther's 12-gauge shells slammed into his neck and chest like mule kicks, knocking him off his feet and onto his back, staring up at thick black clouds. He felt warm blood gushing down his chest.

Kill shots, he knew.

Vot zasranec! I'm screwed . . .

SEVENTY THREE

MANCHESTER, PROBATE COURT

*T*he big day, Ellie thought.
And I'm still living!
But how?
Poor? Or rich?
That will be decided by the Right Honorable Emmett Vincent Shue any minute now.

Ellie sat between Quinn and her probate attorney, Henri Delacroix, in the distinguished Clay County Courthouse. The case had garnered local, national and even international media attention because of the unique DNA issues and the billion-dollar inheritance being litigated. Judge Shue had granted seats to those with vested interests, local folks, and reporters from the print, television and Internet media.

As Ellie looked around the packed courtroom, she feared another last-minute discovery would hit like an asteroid and blow the case wide open. Like yesterday's shocker that Nafeesa Hakim had married Lieutenant Rick Radford in Iraq.

She also feared Judge Shue would rule in favor of the vast majority of DNA evidence - the first four tests that concluded she *was not* Radford's biological daughter. He might not even admit the extremely rare *chimera*-DNA test that concluded she was. After all, the law had very little precedent with chimerism. And Judge Shue had never adjudicated a chimera case.

But he seemed ready to render a decision.

Now in his twenty-sixth year on the bench, Judge Shue had thick silver hair and large intelligent eyes that looked like they could spot a felon in a First Communion class. He also had the muscular shoulders of the University of Kentucky middle linebacker he'd once been. Henri Delacroix said shifty halfbacks couldn't slip past Shue back then, and shifty lawyers couldn't slip anything past him today. Emmett Vincent Shue was a no-nonsense, but fair judge who Ellie learned wrote award-winning poetry.

Judge Shue nodded toward Henri Delacroix and Fletcher Falcone.

"Mr. Delacroix, do you have any new information to share with the court this morning?"

"No, your Honor."

"Mr. Falcone, do you?"

"Well, your Honor, I would implore the court to accept the overwhelming preponderance of scientific evidence in this case, namely that four separate DNA tests from highly respected laboratories prove scientifically that Ms. Ellie Stuart can not possibly be the biological daughter of Mr. Leland Radford. I would also ask the court to exclude her new secret DNA test that purports to offer contradictory DNA findings. And I would further ask the court to exclude the alleged deathbed statement by Mr. Radford since it was signed by only one witness, and not two witnesses as required by Kentucky law, Section 394.020."

"And finally, my associate counsel, Mr. Earl T. Luxfooter, is representing Ms. Nafeesa Hakim and her marriage to the biological son of Mr. Leland Radford, namely, First Lieutenant Richard Daniel Radford – "

" - Mr. Falcone!" Judge Shue said, his blue-gray eyes peering over his horned-rimmed half-glasses.

"Yes, your honor?"

"I said *new* information. Your petitions already presented these arguments to the court with no small eloquence."

"Thank you, your honor, but if it would please the court –"

" - it would please the court if you sat down, counselor, so we can proceed."

Looking chastised, Falcone plopped his three hundred pounds down hard on his seat cushion, blasting air out like a blown Goodyear.

Judge Emmett Vincent Shue adjusted his glasses.

"First off, let me say that the probate of Mr. Leland T. Radford's estate has presented this court with a unique set of DNA issues. Ms. Ellie Stuart has petitioned the court claiming that she should be considered the biological daughter of Leland T. Radford, and the sole surviving member of his immediate family. And that, as such, under Kentucky law, she should be considered his rightful heir."

"In support of her claim, Ms. Stuart presented a special multi-specimen DNA test that she claims demonstrates she is a *chimera*, namely an individual born with *two* distinctly individual sets of DNA, and that the newly discovered set of her DNA matches Mr. Radford's DNA, thereby proving that she is his biological daughter."

The elderly bailiff started hiccupping. He gulped water and smiled.

Judge Shue continued, "Additionally, Ms. Stuart has presented the sworn testimony of Ms. Irene Whitten, who was Mr. Radford's housekeeper for thirty-one years. Ms. Whitten can't be with us today because she was recently attacked and sustained life threatening injuries. But fortunately, she has just regained consciousness and is now talking. Very good news indeed."

Ellie's eyes moistened at the wonderful news. Quinn placed his hand on hers.

"And, should we require Ms. Whitten's testimony, the court will allow her to testify via Skype. Ms. Whitten stated in a written document that on the night of March 29, just hours before Mr. Radford passed away in the hospital that she told him a secret she'd been forced to keep from him for twenty-one years. Namely, that he had fathered a child with a woman named Jacqueline Moreau, his household employee at the time. When Leland Radford learned of his child's existence, he became overjoyed with the news, despite his grave condition. Ms. Whitten wrote down Mr. Radford's statement at that time, which said in essence, "Irene, please try to locate my child. I want my child to inherit my estate, except for those items I've bequeathed to my household staff." Mr. Radford then signed his sworn statement. Ms. Whitten also signed it. A registered nurse also heard Mr. Radford make the statement, but before she could sign it, she was called to an emergency in the ER."

A cell phone rang out *Yankee Doodle.*

Judge Shue looked up. The phone went silent.

"Also in the room witnessing with Ms. Whitten and Mr. Radford at that time, was Ms. Judith Long, a registered nurse. Ms. Long has sworn that she too heard Mr. Radford make the aforementioned statement. but before she could sign it, she was called away to an emergency."

"Moreover, Mr. Radford's doctor, Dr. Thomas A. Lyons III, M.D., has signed a written document saying that he'd examined Mr. Radford ten minutes prior to Mr. Radford's aforementioned written statement and found him to be mentally competent."

"Furthermore, this court has established that Mr. Radford's housekeeper, Jacqueline Moreau, did in fact give birth to a baby girl nine months after she left *The Pines.* Ms. Whitten, and Ms. Loretta Mae Jefferson, a cook at the House of Grace where Jacqueline

Moreau resided during her pregnancy, have both signed affidavits stating that Jacqueline Moreau named her infant daughter - Alex - which as you may know is also a girl's name in French-speaking countries."

Whispers hissed through the courtroom.

"However, three months after giving birth to her baby Alex, Jacqueline Moreau unfortunately died in a car accident."

The courtroom hushed.

"Young baby Alex was then delivered in an undocumented, but *de facto* adoption to Harold and Joyce Stuart in Harlan, Kentucky. The Stuarts then gave baby Alex a new name. They named her . . . *Ellie*."

People gasped and began talking loudly.

Judge Shue pounded his gavel.

The room went graveyard quiet.

"For his part, Mr. Fletcher Falcone, executor of the Radford estate, has presented four separate DNA tests from respected laboratories that show Ms. Ellie Stuart's DNA does *not* match the DNA of Leland Radford, and therefore she can not possibly be his biological daughter. Mr. Falcone argues that this overwhelming preponderance of DNA evidence *proves* this."

"In a separate petition, Mr. Falcone's, associate counsel, Earl T. Luxfooter, representing Ms. Nafeesa Hakim, a citizen of Iraq, has presented this court with an authentic, official Iraqi state-issued certificate of marriage between her and First Lieutenant Richard Radford, the natural son of Mr. Leland Radford. Thus, Mrs. Nafeesa Radford, citing both Kentucky law and Iraqi law, claims she is entitled, as his widow, to participate in the inheritance of the estate of her deceased husband's father."

Ellie watched a chubby court clerk rush up and hand Judge Shue a note.

Judge Shue read the note, frowned, shook his head in obvious surprise, then stood up.

Ellie wondered what was wrong.

"The court will take a fifteen-minute recess."

"What's going on?" Ellie asked Henri Delacroix, fearing some new information would again change everything.

"I have no idea," Delacroix said.

Judge Shue looked concerned, maybe even alarmed as he signaled to two dark-suited men who'd just entered the courtroom.

The men followed Judge Shue into his chambers and shut the door.

SEVENTY FOUR

As Judge Shue's chamber door shut, someone tapped Ellie's shoulder. She turned and stared into the squinty little eyes of a very short man. They were eye to eye – even though she was sitting and he was standing. His shiny black Elvis pompadour swooped his height up an extra five inches. His lips looked like strips of veal. He reeked of lime cologne.

She'd seen him when he emerged from a stretch limousine with three large black animals. "Wolverines," Quinn said. The furry creatures remained with the chauffeur as the tiny man, surrounded by four briefcase-toting lawyer types, marched into the courthouse.

"Miss Stuart, allow me to introduce myself. My name is Mason V. Marweg. I was a very close friend of Leland Radford."

"Nice to meet you, Mr. Marweg."

His smile revealed perfect, snow-white teeth. He handed her a business card with gold embossed letters. His cufflinks sparkled like two-carat diamonds. "I'm chairman of the Marweg Mining Group.

My very good friend Leland Radford and I often chatted about my eventual acquisition of his 12,000-acre parcels here in southeastern Kentucky."

"But I'm told Mr. Radford did not want to sell his land."

Marweg smiled. "Well, yes, that was true a few years ago. But only because my former sales personnel were not sensitive to his valid environmental concerns. I, however, am quite sensitive to his concerns. Because they're *my* concerns. You know that technology today has made coal mining quiet clean."

Ellie said nothing.

"What if we could guarantee you that our new high-tech "green" mining would maintain the land's ecological integrity?

"Even with strip mining?"

Marweg fell back as though she'd tasered him.

"Strip mining is a most unfortunate term, Ms. Stuart. We call our unique process, *environmental surface enhancement.* We *enhance* our surfaces."

Ellie remembered a *Courier Journal* article condemning how Marweg Mining had left many *un*-enhanced ugly, naked surfaces behind.

"Mr. Marweg, this discussion is hypothetical, as you know. And *if* I am fortunate enough to inherit something, I would ask you to deal with Mr. Henri Delacroix on any real estate matters." Marweg looked up at Delacroix who towered over him and smiled. Marweg did not smile back. Instead, he scampered back to the security of his lawyers.

The courtroom door suddenly banged opened and Ellie saw Henri Delacroix's assistant hurry in and whisper something to him. Henri looked shocked, then leaned close to Ellie and Quinn.

"The police," he whispered, "have just arrested a man named Huntoon Harris for the murder of Mary Louise Breen, the elderly woman who knew your mother well at the House of Grace. Mary was suffocated in her sleep. This Huntoon Harris may have also been responsible for the recent attack on Irene Whitten at *The Pines*."

Ellie was speechless.

"Huntoon Harris wants to cut a deal. He's talking to the police. He's implicating one of the Radford estate managers, a man named Heinrich De Groot. That's De Groot next to the courtroom door, talking on his phone." Delacroix pointed him out.

Ellie turned and looked at the thin-faced man in a dark suit.

Delacroix leaned closer and whispered, "Huntoon Harris has also implicated someone else."

They waited.

"Mr. De Groot's boss."

Ellie looked at Fletcher Falcone.

Delacroix nodded. "Yeah, Falcone."

"Huntoon phoned Falcone's office often using CVS throwaway phones purchased with a Falcone & Partners credit card."

Ellie and Quinn nodded at each other, their suspicions of Falcone solidifying at warp speed.

The door to Judge's chamber clicked open. He walked out and headed toward the bench.

Judge Emmett Vincent Shue looked angry.

SEVENTY FIVE

"**P**lease excuse the interruption," Judge Emmett Shue said, settling back on the bench.

Ellie noticed his flushed face, hunched-up shoulders and white-knuckle grip on some documents. He looked beyond upset. He looked angry. Something happened in chambers.

He adjusted his glasses.

"First off, let me say that yesterday I spoke with an old friend, a General with the Army's Judge Advocate General's Corps in Washington. At my request, he spoke with a JAG major in charge of marriages between U.S. military personnel and Iraqis. The major said that First Lieutenant Richard Radford did in fact once talk to him about the possibility of marrying an Iraqi woman, but he did not mention the woman's name. A month later Lieutenant Radford was unfortunately killed in action."

Ellie saw Nafeesa Hakim begin fingering her worry beads.

"The major also spoke with three officers of the 34th Brigade Combat Team who were with Lieutenant Radford the entire day and night on the date of his alleged wedding. But *not* in Baghdad. They were with him in *Basra*, three hundred miles south that entire week."

Ellie heard whispers creep through the courtroom.

Nafeesa fingered her prayer beads faster.

"The major then visited the Iraqi Social Status director who issued the Radford-Hakim marriage certificate. The director swore that the date and wedding location on the certificate were absolutely accurate. He remembered Nafeesa Hakim in great detail. But for some reason couldn't recall whether Lieutenant Radford was white, black, short or tall, or aged twenty or fifty."

"The JAG major also learned that none of Lieutenant Radford's, or any of Ms. Hakim's friends, were aware of the alleged wedding. And that the priest and the only two witnesses at the alleged wedding, are unable to confirm the wedding, since they are all, sadly, deceased victims of the war."

The courtroom fell graveyard silent.

"In view of the US Army's proof that Mr. Radford was on patrol in Basra on the date of the alleged wedding in Baghdad, and all other surrounding circumstances, the court can find no basis on which to support the claim that Ms. Hakim was legally married to Lieutenant Radford. Therefore, this court has no alternative but to deny this petition."

"And, in view of the potentially fraudulent circumstances surrounding the marriage certificate itself, this court has requested that U.S. Immigration assist Ms. Hakim with her prompt return to Iraq."

Ellie noticed Nafeesa staring daggers at Falcone as though he'd promised her a far better outcome. But when Falcone refused to turn and look at her, she buried her face in her hands and wept.

The judge cleared his throat.

"Now, with regard to the petition of Ms. Ellie Stuart, let me say that this case presented the court with a major problem.

Contradictory DNA results. To resolve the contradiction, the court enlisted Dr. Robert Simon, a distinguished geneticist and Associate Dean of Medicine at the University of Louisville School of Medicine. His team conducted three multi-sample tests that came back with the same result. Namely, that Ellie Stuart she is a chimera with two individual sets of DNA, one of which matches the DNA of Mr. Leland Radford with a 99.9999% accuracy rating."

"In conclusion, based on irrefutable DNA proof and on all other corroborating evidence, this court finds that Ellie Stuart is the biological daughter of Jacqueline Moreau and Leland Radford . . ."

Quinn placed his hand on Ellie's.

". . . and based on the written and witnessed document, expressing Leland T. Radford's desire to leave his estate to his surviving child. . . ."

". . . and lastly, based on Kentucky law that states a surviving child shall inherit the estate of a deceased single parent, this court rules in favor of the petitioner, Ms. Ellie Stuart, finding that she is sole heir of Leland T. Radford's entire estate, with the exception of the generous allowances he bequeathed and devised to his household staff."

Tears spilled down Ellie's face as she buried her head in Quinn's shoulder.

SEVENTY SIX

"Congratulations, Ellie-Stuart-Radford!" Quinn whispered in her ear.

"Thank you, Quinn Parker." She melted into his warm embrace and the pleasant scent of his citrus aftershave and wanted to remain there for a week.

Then the stench of cigarettes ruined everything.

Turning, she realized the vile odor reeked from the obese body of Fletcher Falcone who'd snuck up behind her.

She stepped back and faced him.

How incredibly naïve she'd been. From the beginning, she'd assumed Falcone was the friendly country lawyer trying to help her. Now, she realized he'd most likely been behind everything – behind the sabotaged DNA tests, even behind the hit men sent to kill her – all because he'd known, perhaps from the beginning, that she was Leland Radford's daughter.

"Well, Ms. Stuart, congratulations to you," Falcone said, extending his chubby manicured fingers.

She fake-coughed so she didn't have to touch the bastard.

"This probate process has been at times hotly contested," he said, smiling, "but I must say you have played fair and square."

Unlike you! she thought.

"You understand, of course, that as executor for the estate, I was required to employ rather stern protective measures."

Like murder.

"You can also appreciate that the Radford estate is quite vast and complex and requires great experience in coordinating all its disciplines cost-effectively. My managerial team and I are really the only ones conversant with all its complexities . . . know where all the bodies are buried so to speak."

He grinned his eyes into puffy slits which made him look like a fat python.

"In brief, I would suggest that your interests can be best served if my highly experienced team continues managing your vast estate – but under *your* direction." Another grin.

She stared at him, speechless, amazed at his blind arrogance. Did he not see, or even *feel,* the incredible rage she felt toward him? Did the idiot actually think he could continue managing the estate?

Beside her, Quinn looked ready to punch out Falcone. She placed her hand on Quinn's to calm him, but it didn't help.

"Mr. Falcone . . ." Ellie said.

"Yes?"

"Let me be clear."

"Please do . . ."

"You are about as likely to continue handling this estate as angels are to fly out of your ass!"

Falcone fell backward as though she whacked him with a Louisville Slugger.

"Mr. Delacroix, if he wishes to, will manage the estate."

Delacroix smiled at Falcone.

"But – "

"Effective immediately!" she said, feeling her rage mushroom. She looked at Quinn and Delacroix who grinned back.

Falcone took another step back, looking shocked, like he couldn't possibly imagine what he'd done wrong.

Delacroix leaned over and said, "Mr. Falcone, I'll call you this afternoon to facilitate the transfer of all estate documents and files."

"I'll need a few days to – "

"We'll be at your office in one hour, Mr. Falcone. Our team will immediately assist your team in this transition . . . you know . . . to make sure nothing falls between the cracks."

"I'll help too," Quinn said, moving toward Falcone.

Ellie stepped in front of Quinn, surprised at his fury. She'd never seen him this angry.

Falcone backed up a few more steps, clearly stunned by the turn of events. Red-faced, he waddled back to his table where he stuffed papers into his briefcase, snapped it shut and huffed off toward the door.

"Mr. Falcone . . .!" Judge Shue said, putting down his cell phone.

"Yes . . .?"

"Please remain here."

"But your honor, I have very important business – "

"You have more important business right *here right now!*"

Ellie was surprised at the judge's stern tone.

"I'd like everyone in my chambers now, please."

SEVENTY SEVEN

Ellie, Henri Delacroix, Quinn, and Fletcher Falcone followed Judge Shue into his chambers. The judge still looked upset, angry even, and Ellie wondered why.

He settled in behind his polished oak desk stacked with long legal folders while everyone else sat in faded leather chairs, facing him. On the walls, Ellie saw his family pictures, a University of Kentucky football team photo, and pictures of the Judge with Colonel Sanders, George W. Bush, Barack Obama and Roy Rogers.

Judge Shue cleared his throat. "Minutes ago in this chamber, Mr. Roy Klume, a DNA scientist at Southern Genetics Laboratory, signed an affidavit stating that a man named Huntoon Leroy Harris, an ex-felon, threatened Mr. Klume's wife and daughters with grievous bodily harm unless Mr. Klume altered the DNA test of Ms. Ellie Stuart so that her DNA did not match Leland Radford's DNA. Acting under that threat, Mr. Klume altered that DNA test and subsequent tests in that way."

The judge picked up another paper.

"Huntoon Harris was also identified by a gardener at *The Pines* estate the same evening Ms. Irene Whitten was attacked and stabbed there. Mr. Harris was seen leaving in an plumbing van, even though no plumbing work was done there that day."

The judge sipped some water.

"Also the court learned that Mr. Harris's phone records indicate that he called you Mr. Falcone on a throwaway phone purchased by your firm, Falcone & Partners. He called several times during the days the DNA tests were falsified, immediately after he phoned your Radford financial manager, a Mr. Heinrich De Groot. However your secretary, Ms. Ramada Tomkins, said that neither Mr. De Groot, or you, or any of your offices has ever done any legal work for Huntoon Harris. This suggests that conversations between you and Mr. Harris were of a private nature, and in view of Mr. Harris's extensive criminal record, one might even surmise, of a less than legal nature, perhaps even a felonious nature."

"I can explain – "

" - explain later!"

Ellie noticed that the judge's neck was bright red and a vein puffed up at his temple. He squeezed a football-shaped glass paper-weight like he wanted to bounce it off Falcone's head, which, she noticed, was dotted with perspiration.

"Huntoon Harris also phoned Mr. De Groot several times during the DNA-falsifying time frame. Mr. De Groot then phoned your office, Mr. Falcone. One might conclude he was updating you."

"But your honor I –"

The Judge's phone rang. He took the call, listened a minute and hung up.

"Police are now questioning Mr. De Groot who is most eager to cooperate and talk with authorities about everything."

Falcone slumped down in his chair and stared at the floor, his face chalk white.

"And finally, Mr. Harris was arrested two hours ago. He also wants a plea deal. He affirms that you, Mr. Falcone, and only you, were behind all decisions with regard to Mr. Radford's estate. In brief, it seems that everyone's talking about you Mr. Falcone, except you."

Ellie thought Falcone looked ill, his face dripped with perspiration and he sopped it up with a handkerchief.

"Do you have anything to say, Mr. Falcone?"

"I want legal counsel."

"Wise decision in light of the prosecutor's decision to charge you now with conspiracy to falsify the DNA tests, and far more serious crimes based on Mr. Harris's and Mr. De Groot's new affidavits."

The judge pushed a button on his desk and a side door clicked open. Ellie recognized the county prosecutor and district attorney, and two detective types who walked over to Falcone.

Ellie listened with amazement as the tall gray-haired prosecutor read the long list of felony charges against Falcone, which seemed to include everything except parakeet abuse. A detective read Falcone his rights, cuffed his puffy wrists, and perp-walked him from the judge's chambers.

Judge Emmett Vincent Shue stood and then smiled.

"Ellie, I'm absolutely delighted that you've identified your biological father and mother. Your dad and I were good friends and fellow Kentucky Colonels. He was one of the most decent and kind men I've known. You would have been proud of him, Ellie. And I know he would be very proud of you. When you get time, please call, or visit and I'll give your some photos I have of him."

Ellie felt tears forming. "I'd love that very much, your Honor."

SEVENTY EIGHT

SIX MONTHS LATER
MARTINIQUE

Ellie felt like she was riding a bongo stick as she and Quinn bounced around in the back seat of the ancient Peugeot taxi. From the rearview mirror swung a purple voodoo doll. Beyond the voodoo doll, stood the 5,000-foot Mount Pelee volcano, steady as a rock, unlike 1902 when it shook and exploded, spewing burning lava down on the town of Saint-Pierre, killing 30,000 men, women and children.

Their taxi driver, Antoine, an elderly mulatto with an eye patch, raced along the narrow mountain road, hugging curves like a Grand Prix driver.

Their American Airlines flight landed at *Martinique Aimé Césaire International Airport* near the capital city, Fort-de-France. She'd read that Martinique was an integral part of France that had evolved over the centuries into a mixed salad of French, British, Asian, Indian, African and indigenous people, a charming blend of people . . .

. . . like my charming, beautiful mother, Jacqueline Moreau.

In minutes, I'll meet her parents, my grandparents and my extended family now. Ellie could barely contain her excitement and prayed they understood her rusty high school French.

They drove past colorful homes: yellow, pink, white, tan. Beautiful shades, like the islanders themselves. She smelled curry and wondered if someone was cooking *Colombo,* the island's famous chicken curry spiced with Indian masala. It smelled delicious.

Ellie's cell phone rang. She saw *Jessica Bishop* on Caller ID.

"Hey Jessie, what's up?"

"I just got back your father's genetic test results, the test to determine early-onset Alzheimer's."

Ellie felt her stomach clench.

"You want the results?"

"I'm not sure -"

" - it's good news, girlfriend!" Jessica said. "Your father did *not* have the Presinelin 1 or Presinelin 2 genes, nor did he have the APOE-4 gene, or the other genetic markers for early-onset Alzheimer's. So your memory should remain sharp!"

"That's great news . . . Bernice."

"Smart ass! Call me when you get back."

"I will, Jessie, and thanks."

They hung up. She told Quinn the wonderful news and he hugged her.

Antoine drove around a sharp turn as Quinn' phone rang. He answered, listened a few minutes, nodding some, looking serious, then pleased, then flat out amazed. Finally, he hung up and looked at her.

"That was your fantastic probate attorney."

"What'd Mr. Delacroix say?"

"That justice has triumphed!"

"How?"

"Fletcher Falcone, Huntoon Harris, and Heinrich de Groot have been convicted for the murder of Mary Louise Breen, the woman who knew your mother well at the House of Grace."

Ellie again felt sickened by Mary's death.

"De Groot and Falcone ordered Huntoon Harris to suffocate Mary in her sleep because she knew Leland Radford was your father and they feared she'd tell someone. Police lifted Huntoon's fingerprints from Mary's bed frame."

"Also, Falcone, Huntoon, and De Groot were convicted of the attempted murders of Irene Whitten and the U of L student whose name is spelled similarly to yours. By the way, both the student and Irene are fully recovered."

"That's wonderful news."

"Bottom line - Falcone, Huntoon, and De Groot were sentenced to life without the possibility of parole."

"Justice served."

"Yeah, but many jurors and Mary's relatives felt Huntoon and Falcone deserved the death penalty."

"Understandable."

"And prophetic."

"What?"

"Their wish was granted. As police led Falcone away from the courthouse, a sniper fired several bullets into his throat and chest. Falcone rolled down into a large drainage ditch face first and sank in three feet of oily sludge. Before they could hoist him out, he'd gagged and choked to death on the muddy gunk!"

"Jesus! Who shot him?"

Quinn shrugged. "The sniper escaped. But the police suspect it's a mob hit. Falcone had refused to pay his massive horseracing and gambling debts. Not smart. But it's also possible Fletcher's own cousin hired the sniper."

"His cousin?"

"Guy named BoDeene. Years ago Fletcher gave cousin Bodeene the money to start a methamphetamine lab beneath BoDeene's fertilizer store. When Bodeene found out that Uncle Fletcher had embezzled over four million dollars from him, cousin Bodeene swore revenge."

Ellie shook her head, amazed again at how badly she'd misread Falcone.

Antoine slowed the taxi to let some goats cross the road.

"Falcone also lied to the court about Nafeesa Hakim. He knew her marriage claim was fraudulent, but petitioned it as though legitimate. He promised her some money, while he would retain control of the estate money. She went along, because her family was starving."

Ellie nodded. "Where's Nafeesa now?"

"Back in Iraq."

"How's she doing?"

"Barely surviving. Henri Delacroix learned that she and Rick Radford had been very close. Rick supported her and her war-impoverished family. They were talking about marriage when he was killed."

"I feel sorry for Nafeesa."

"Me too. She's a victim of a crazy war."

"*Our* war," Ellie said. "A war that killed her family and destroyed her family's business and savings and then forced her onto the streets to feed her family."

"War is hell, Ellie."

"But she didn't start this one. And she obviously cared deeply for Rick, my half-brother, who obviously cared for her. I'd like to talk to her about Rick. Maybe get to know him through her. And I'd like to help her. You said her family business was ruined?"

"Totally ruined. Furniture store. Direct hit by a bomb aimed at an al Qaeda weapons garage one hundred feet away. The insurance company refused to pay."

"Why?"

"The Act of War exclusion. Left her family penniless."

Ellie couldn't begin to imagine the suffering and pain Nafeesa and her family had experienced.

"Let's rebuild her business. And set up a trust fund for her and her family. I'd like to get to know her."

Quinn nodded and placed his hand on hers.

"I'll ask Henri Delacroix to handle it."

SEVENTY NINE

" *Nous arrivons*. We arrive," Antoine the taxi driver said, honking and scattering the chickens off the gravel driveway.

Ellie opened the taxi window and breathed in the sweet scent of sandalwood and spice. Though the palm trees, she saw a small, older wood house nestled in the nook of a hill. The pastel yellow home had blue shutters and an orange tile roof that sloped down over a porch that wrapped around the entire home. She noticed a few missing roof tiles, some patched window screens and a garage with peeling paint.

Beyond the house, the sunny Caribbean glistened like spilled liquid cobalt.

On the porch, a tall, gray-haired man and woman got up from their rocking chairs and waved toward the taxi. Next to them stood some middle aged couples, teenagers, wide-eyed toddlers and two hounds sleeping in the sun.

She was looking at a very large family. *Her family!* The kind she'd always wanted to be part of.

———

"Your tribe awaits you." Quinn said.

"Yes, but I speak French like a three-year old. How's your French?"

He smiled. "Pre-natal."

Ellie gave Antoine a huge tip and he *merci beaucouped* several times as she and Quinn stepped from the taxi. They turned toward the elderly, smiling woman hurrying toward them in a flowery red dress. Ellie knew from emailed photos that this woman was her grandmother, Maudette Moreau, now in her seventies.

Ellie embraced her grandmother as her grandmother kissed Ellie's cheeks three times. Ellie's eyes filled with tears.

"*Ma chère, Ellie,* my . . . how you say . . . grand daughter."

"*Grandmère,* I'm so happy to finally meet you."

"Me too. *You look . . . tu ressembles à ta mère.*"

"I resemble my mother?"

"*Oui! Oui!* Like your mama. Your eyes! Your hair!"

Her tall Grandfather, Francois, embraced her and said, "Welcome, Ellie . . . to your Martinique family."

She was quickly surrounded by smiling relatives including her Aunt Claude and Uncle Samuel, cousins ZooZoo and Gaspard, and beautiful young Nina.

Ellie felt like the prodigal granddaughter returning home. She also felt an overwhelming sense of being welcomed into the family . . . being accepted by them . . . even belonging . . . and it all felt wonderful.

Thanks to Nina's excellent English, Ellie quickly learned how decades ago, her great-grandparents fell in love with the island so much they moved here from a village in Batilly-en-Puisaye, France.

Ellie also learned that her mother Jacqueline, at age twenty, had witnessed the rape and murder of a deaf girl. Jacqueline testified against the murderer despite death threats against her. The man was sentenced to life in prison, but his brother swore revenge on Jacqueline and on two occasions almost killed her. Fearing he'd succeed, Jacqueline's parents sent her to America.

In the beginning, she was homesick. But soon her letters explained how she was falling in love with *La Kentucky*. A year later, she was falling in love with *Le Kentuckian* – the man she worked for, a kind widower named Leland Radford.

"Monsieur Radford, he is your father, yes?"

"Yes."

"She love him *beaucoup*."

Ellie smiled. "And he loved her *beaucoup*."

That night everyone celebrated with a delicious feast of *Côtes de Veau au Fromage* and local delicacies. The next three days were a festival of delightful family stories, more mouth-watering French and Creole meals, all washed down with several bottles of *bon vins rouge de Martinique,* good red Martinique wines and local rum. Ellie offered to fly the entire family to Kentucky for *Le Grand American Thanksgiving.* Everyone said they'd try to come.

The next day, many of them accompanied Quinn and her to *Martinique Aimé Césaire International Airport.*

After tearful hugs, Ellie and Quinn got in line at the security check. She then turned around and nodded to the silver-haired attorney she'd met with yesterday.

The attorney nodded back, then walked over to her grandparents and handed them a document and some photographs. Her grandparents stared at the documents and photos, looking confused, then blinked a few times and looked at Ellie with puzzled expressions. Then they looked back at the attorney.

The lawyer explained it to them again.

With moist eyes, her grandparents looked at Ellie with shocked, incredulous, disbelieving, and finally grateful expressions, and then her grandmother mouthed, *"Merci, merci beaucoup,* Ellie. . . ."

Ellie smiled and waved goodbye, hoping they would enjoy their new villa with six bedrooms, lush gardens and a swimming pool overlooking the town of Sainte Anne and the Caribbean. Cousin Nina told Ellie that her grandparents had always loved the rambling estate and hoped one day to be lucky enough to see the inside.

Now they could *live* inside. They owned it.

EIGHTY

Minutes later, in the departure lounge, Ellie watched Quinn skillfully balancing two full cups of coffee as he sidestepped carry-on bags and a running two-year-old like he used to side-step defensive tacklers. Clearly he'd overcome his football knee injury . . . and his dependency on Vicodin.

He handed her a cup of coffee.

"Congratulations," she said.

"For what?"

"For not spilling coffee on my jeans again."

"Hey - good things happen when I do."

"Wrong! *Great* things happen!"

He smiled. "So it seems."

She remembered again how he'd tripped on the student center steps, spilled her coffee, and changed her life forever.

Thanks to him, she learned who she came from.

Thanks to her mother, she inherited a large, warm and loving family.

Thanks to her father, she inherited nearly one billion dollars, according to her attorney. So much money, she still couldn't quite comprehend it. But she could comprehend how the money could help people she really cared about. Like elderly Celeste and neighbor Sarah in Louisville, and her Martinique family, and Carrie and her mom in Harlan, and Nafeesa in Teheran, and Loretta Mae the cook at the House of Grace. But not Irene Whitten the housekeeper. Irene didn't need a dime – Leland Radford left her three million dollars.

And thanks to Quinn, Ellie'd received the most important thing of all. The courage to love someone again. Love them completely, despite her fear that fate might take them away from her.

She placed her hand on his arm and said, "It'll be good to get back home."

"We're not going home."

She stared at him.

"We're stopping off somewhere." He pulled their tickets from his sport coat, but hid the destination from her.

"Where?"

"Where do people have blue teeth?"

She wondered what he was talking about, then had a hunch . . . "As in cotton candy blue teeth?"

"Yep."

"No way!"

"Yep."

"*Disney World?*"

"Yep! Remember? I promised I'd take you."

"Yippee!" she shouted, drawing puzzled glances from passengers seated nearby.

Quinn smiled, but seemed to grow serious about something. "I've been thinking. . . ."

"About . . .?

"About that big Thanksgiving Day bash you're having for your whole Martinique family up at *The Pines.*"

"Yeah, almost everyone said they are coming. Should be great fun."

"It will be. But maybe everyone should stay a few extra days."

"That would be great . . . but why?" she asked.

"Maybe another party."

"What kind?"

He paused. "Maybe a wedding party . . ."

Know anyone who might enjoy reading

KENTUCKY WOMAN

If so, just phone AtlasBooks at 1800 2487 6553
Or go to AtlasBooks.com
and order Kentucky Woman

ISBN: 978-0-9846173–9-5

Visa, MasterCard, American Express accepted
Or order from mikebroganbooks.com

Also by Mike Brogan

G8

Donovan Rourke, a CIA Special Agent, discovers a man named Katill will assassinate the world's eight most powerful leaders at the G8 Summit in Brussels in three days. The President asks Donovan to handle the G8 security.

Donovan agrees…but reluctantly. His wife was murdered there, and he blames himself.

In Brussels, Donovan works with the European G8 Director, Monsieur de Waha, and a beautiful translator named Maccabee. They learn that Katill is the same man who murdered Donovan's wife.

They also learn that Katill has just penetrated the G8's billion-dollar wall of security.

Donovan sees the world leaders walking into Katill's deathtrap! He tries to warn them – but it's too late…and then his worst nightmare happens right before his eyes.

Also by Mike Brogan

MADISON'S AVENUE

First, she gets the frightening phone call from her father. Hours later, he'd dead. The police say it's suicide. But Madison McKean suspects murder – because her father, CEO of a large Manhattan ad agency, refused a takeover bid by a ruthless agency conglomerate. Madison inherits his agency – and his enemies. When she and her new friend Kevin zero in on the executive behind her father's death, they soon discover an ex-CIA hitman is zeroing in on them.

MADISON'S AVENUE takes you inside the boardrooms of today's cut-throat, billion dollar corporations – to the white sand beaches of the Caribbean – to the high hopes and low cleavage of the Cannes Ad Festival…a world where some people take the phrase 'bury the competition' literally.

Available at AtlasBooks.com
Or phone: 1 800 247 6553 ISBN: 978-0-692-00634-4
Visa, MasterCard, American Express accepted.
OR
order from MikeBroganBooks.com

Also by Mike Brogan

DEAD AIR

Dr. Hallie Mara, an attractive young MD, and her friend, Reed Kincaid, learn that someone has singled out many men, women and children to die in ten cities across the U.S. in just a few days.

But because Hallie has no hard proof, the police refuse to investigate.

When Hallie and Reed try to find proof, they unearth something far beyond their worst fears. And as they zero in on the man behind everything, the man zeros in on them. Barely escaping with their lives, they finally convince the police and Federal authorities that a horrific disaster is imminent. But by then there's a big problem: it may be too late.

Midwest Book Review calls DEAD AIR, "a Lord of the Rings of thrillers. One can't turn the pages fast enough."

Available at Amazon.com
ISBN 1-4137-4700-0

Also by Mike Brogan

BUSINESS TO KILL FOR

B usiness is war. And Luke Tanner is about to be its latest casualty. He's overheard men conspiring to gain control of a billion dollar business using a unique strategy – murder the two CEO's who control the business. The conspirators discover Luke has overheard them and kidnap his girlfriend. He tries to free her, but gets captured himself.

Finally they escape, only to discover that the $1 billion business is his company . . . and that it may be too late to save his mentor, the CEO. The story takes you from the backstabbing backrooms of a major ad agency to the life-threatening jungles of Mexico's Yucatan.

Writer's Digest gave BUSINESS TO KILL FOR a major award, calling it, "the equal of any thriller read in recent years . . ."

Available at Amazon.com
or MikeBroganBooks.com
ISBN 0-615-11570-5

ABOUT THE AUTHOR

MIKE BROGAN is the *Writers Digest* award-winning author of BUSINESS TO KILL FOR, a suspense thriller that *WD* called, "the equal of any thriller read in recent years." His DEAD AIR thriller also won national awards, as did MADISON's AVENUE.

His years in Kentucky, gave him a unique perspective in writing KENTUCKY WOMAN…as did the amazing, but true story that inspired him to write this new mystery thriller.

Brogan lives in Michigan where he's completing his next novel. To learn more, visit MikeBroganBooks.com